WORKING
TAINTED
Book Three
Roxy Rich

WORKING GIRL SERIES Tainted Book Three.

Legal Disclaimer.

This is a work of fiction. Unless otherwise indicated, all the names, characters, businesses, places, events and incidents in this book are either the product of the author's imagination or used in a fictitious manner. Any resemblance to actual persons, living or dead, or actual events are purely coincidental.

WARNING.

This book entails, human trafficking, child prostitution, prostitution, abuse, murder.

A Satanic Cult. Genetic experiments, kidnapping, organ trafficking, drink spiking, Along with scenes of torture. Please do not read if you have a delicate constitution.

Table of Contents

Dedications Page

Anne Crowe

20/09/1951
31/03/2024

For the mad Irish woman who brought me into this world.

Mum, you left us on Easter Sunday, 2024, when, fittingly, the Lord took you home.

Though we didn't always see eye to eye, I always loved you and held the utmost respect for you. You were fierce, funny, sometimes maddening, always loyal, and impossibly kind-hearted. This book, with its every page, is a small offering to you. I hope you love the character inspired by you, she's as wild, wise, and wonderful as you were in life.

Thank you for everything, Mum.

CHAPTER 1: TRAUMA & MEMORIES.

Jules lay beneath him, feeling every inch of his crushing weight drilling her into the mattress. He was a monstrous bulk, suffocating her not only with his body but also with the thick odour of sweat that flowed from him with every thrust. She tried to block out, his groans, the irritating friction of his skin against hers. She let her mind wander, let her vision fix on a crack in the ceiling, while her voice produced the required sounds, hoping that if she faked enough excitement, he'd finish sooner rather than later. The saltiness of his sweat trickled into her mouth despite her attempts to turn her head, the taste made her want to gag.

But she couldn't afford to. Not today, not ever. This was her life, her invisible prison, client after client, each with a story. Each with a reason, a justification, as to why they felt compelled to use her. Some blamed their wives, some their health, others blamed it on loneliness, as if she, of all people, would sympathize with that. They always felt the need to explain themselves, to confess, as if their guilt would make any of it better. But she never asked. She didn't care. She just wanted the money. The rest, she left at the door. Sometimes, one would just want to talk, to hold her in their arms like she was something precious.

But most of them were like this man, pigs, using her body to fill some void they didn't know how to escape. She hated them all. Every single one. They were the same kind of men she'd grown up with. Men who treated her like an object, something to be bought and traded.

The only difference now was that she made the rules. This was her life, her choice, or so she told herself. Jules had mastered the art of pretending. It was a skill she'd perfected from a young age, ever since her adoptive father had sold her innocence to the highest bidder. He'd passed her around like a toy, loaning her to his sadistic friends whenever they desired, each one more depraved than the last. And if she displeased them, her punishment was to spend even more time in their hands. She learned early on how to mask the pain, how to become invisible, a ghost in her own skin. It was easier to survive that way. She'd lost count of the injuries, the illnesses. Chlamydia had stolen her ability to conceive, another cruel joke.

As if the universe wanted to ensure that someone like her could never bring life into the world. Her father had one rule, they were never allowed to mark her face. She had to stay pretty, like a perfect doll, unmarred by the violence that ravaged the rest of her body and soul. The scars inside her, were so deep, that they still bled. The nightmares had never left her. No amount of time could erase the horrors she'd witnessed, the things she'd endured. Even after running away at seventeen, even after promising herself that she would never go back, never look back, the past still clung to her like a shadow. She was free, but she would never be whole. Now, all she had was survival. She sold her body, hour by hour, to keep a roof over her head, to buy things that made her feel like she had some semblance of control. But she hated it. She hated the men who came to her, with their groping hands and dead eyes. She hated the facade she had to wear, the smile, the fake pleasure. Every man who touched her took a piece of her soul, she often wondered how much of it was left. If she even had one anymore. The voice in her head was relentless, whispering that she was damaged beyond repair. That she was dirty, broken, and unworthy of love or happiness.

No matter how much she tried to drown it out, it was always there, reminding her that she didn't belong in the world of normal people. She was an outsider, a fraud pretending to live a normal life. The truth was, she didn't even know what normal was. Her past had taught her a hard lesson, people were users. They took what they wanted and left you with nothing. She was no different. She had learned to use them back, to get what she needed while she still had her looks. Men were vultures, feeding off her beauty while it lasted. She couldn't let them get too close. She didn't need friends. They were just competition. She kept her distance, always, even from the other girls at the parlour. They laughed together and bonded over shared experiences, but she stood apart. Alone. She didn't need anyone, at least, that's what she told herself. But sometimes, in the quiet moments when the mask slipped, she felt it. A deep, aching loneliness. A yearning for something more, for someone to see her, really see her, and love her despite the darkness that clung to her like a second skin.

But who could ever love someone like her? She was too broken, too stained by her past. The man above her grunted one last time, his body finally shuddering to a stop. It was over. For now. She waited until he rolled off her, then slowly got up, wiping the sweat from her skin. One day, she promised herself, she would leave this all behind. No more men, no more pretending, no more selling pieces of herself until there was nothing left. But that day seemed so far away, like a dream she wasn't sure she believed in anymore. Her adoptive father had been right about one thing, men were evil. Every single one who walked through the door was a liar, a cheater, a monster in disguise. They all wanted the same thing, and she gave it to them because she had no choice. She hated them, hated the way they looked at her, the way they touched her as if she were something they could own. But she was beautiful. That was the one thing she had, the one weapon in her arsenal. Her long blonde hair and her large liquid brown eyes captivated anyone who saw her. She knew how to use it, how to make them want her, how to make them pay. But beauty was fleeting. She could feel it slipping away, day by day, and with it, her hope. Outside, the sun was rising, its golden light spilling into the room. She looked out the window, tracing her reflection in the glass. She was still young, still beautiful, but inside she felt old, worn out, like a shadow of the girl she had once been. She longed for something more, something beyond this life of endless transactions. She wanted to escape, to see the world, to feel the wind in her hair and the sun on her skin. To be free. But freedom, for someone like her, was just another dream.

CHAPTER 2: SINS & DREAMS

At the tender age of twenty-four, Jules felt trapped. Her life, a grim shadow of what it could have been, stretched out before her like an endless maze. It was as if the world had placed invisible chains around her soul, forcing her to trudge through a routine she despised. Every day was the same. New clients, new justifications, but always the same hollow encounters. Yet, beneath the surface, there lingered a desperate yearning, a muted scream for something more. Jules thumbed through the magazine in her hands, its glossy pages full of lives she would never lead. Women in bikinis frolicked on golden sands, basking in the sun of distant shores. The bright turquoise waters of the Caribbean called to her, a promise of escape, a dream that teased her from beyond the bounds of her reality. But it was just that, a distant dream. She knew better than to think she could break free from the life she lived.

Fear had her firmly in its grip. The past clung to her like a suffocating blanket, reminding her that she wasn't made for those beaches. That life was for people who hadn't been tainted. "One day," she whispered to herself, staring out of the parlours window as another client walked in. A new face, but the same story. They always came with their excuses, their reasons for needing to use her body. Their wives were cold. Their girlfriends didn't understand them. They didn't feel like men anymore. Jules didn't care. She didn't want to know. But they kept talking, kept explaining as if her judgment mattered. As if her silence wasn't a deafening reminder that they were already damned. The weight of the morning bore down on her as she forced a smile, leading the man into the room she worked in. With each step, a piece of her crumbled. She lived for the brief moments of escape when her mind could wander, back to those beaches, back to those pristine waters, imagining herself floating away, disappearing from this life entirely. But those moments never lasted. Reality always pulled her back, dragging her down, deeper into the pit she had been thrown into long ago. Her childhood had been a series of horrors she could barely think about without shuddering. Her adoptive father had auctioned her off to his vile friends, a mere child sold to the highest bidder. Those men had taken her innocence, her ability to trust, and her future, leaving her with nothing but scars, both seen and unseen. They had broken her, piece by piece, until she barely recognized herself anymore. Even now, the memories haunted her in the quiet hours of the night, plaguing her with nightmares too real to shake off. Jules didn't know what love was. She had only known pain, deceit, and betrayal. And though she had managed to run away from that house of horrors at seventeen, she had never truly escaped.

The trauma still lived in her veins, a dark poison she could never rid herself of. Every touch, every client's grasp, reminded her of the life she couldn't leave behind, the life that had chained her soul long before she had the words to understand it. She hated this life. She hated the men who pawed at her body, who paid for her time as if she were nothing more than an object. But even more than that, she hated herself for letting it happen. Each encounter chipped away at her already fragile sense of self-worth, leaving her emptier than before. And yet, she continued. She didn't know how to stop. This was all she knew. Selling herself, hour by hour, to keep a roof over her head, to maintain some semblance of stability. She didn't know how to live any other way. And so, she waited. Another client, another night. The parlour was full of noise, men laughing, girls giggling in forced delight, the quiet rustle of money exchanging hands. But Jules had always felt like an outsider here, even among the other girls. She didn't have a family to support, and no drug habit to feed.

She wasn't here because she enjoyed it, or because she didn't know how to stop. She was here because she believed, deep down, that she wasn't worthy of anything better. She didn't belong in the world of 'normal' people. She had seen too much darkness and had been tainted by too many ugly truths. How could she ever fit in with those who hadn't seen the worst of humanity? Those who hadn't been touched by the kind of evil that shaped her life. She was broken, and she knew it. Her beauty, the thing that drew clients to her like moths to a flame, was just a mask. Beneath it, she was hollow, a shell of the girl she might have been. The last client of the day arrived as she was packing up. He was different from the others, tall, dark, and strikingly handsome. There was something about the way he carried himself, the wicked confidence in his smile, that unnerved her. He wasn't like the usual men who frequented the parlour. He didn't seem desperate or broken. He seemed... curious.

Their eyes met, and for a brief moment, Jules felt something stir inside her. It wasn't attraction, not exactly. It was more like recognition, a spark of something she couldn't quite place. He was watching her with those dark blue eyes, intense and unsettling, as if he saw right through her. She broke the silence first, turning to the receptionist and forcing a smile.

"House money, please." She said as the man handed over his money. He smiled back at her, that same unsettling grin, and took her hand as she led him to her room. The parlour was decorated to look luxurious, with rich velvet drapes, plush furniture, and dim lighting that was meant to be seductive. But to Jules, it was just another prison. The smell of sex and cheap cologne clung to the air, thick and suffocating. As she walked down the hallway, the sounds of other clients with other girls echoed around her, a reminder of the life she had chosen. Once they were in the room, she explained the rules.

"No bareback. No exceptions." She always made sure to lay down the boundaries. It was the one small way she kept control. But this man didn't seem to care. He wasn't here for that.

"I don't want anything strange." He said, his voice low and smooth. "I just... I don't know. I thought I wanted something, but now I'm not so sure."

His words hung in the air, heavy with unspoken meaning. Jules stared at him, trying to decipher what he was getting at. There was something about him that made her nervous. He wasn't like the others. He wasn't here just for her body.

"If you're not here for what we offer, you should probably go," she said, her voice cold and professional. She didn't want to get into whatever game he was playing. She didn't want to know him. She just wanted him gone, but he didn't leave. Instead, he smiled again, that same disarming grin that sent a shiver down her spine.

"I like you," he said. "You're too good for this place. Too good for this life." Jules felt a lump form in her throat. She had heard this before. Clients who thought they could save her, who wanted to take her away from all of this. But it was always a lie. No one could save her. Not from this life. Not from herself.

"I'm not interested." She said flatly, turning away from him.

But he didn't take the hint. "I'm not asking for anything. Just... dinner. That's all."

'Dinner. A normal thing, something people outside of this world did without thinking twice.' But to Jules, it was a foreign concept. She didn't do dinners. She didn't do normal. She hesitated, torn between the desire to keep her distance and the nagging curiosity that gnawed at her insides. There was something about him, something that made her want to know more. Against her better judgment, she found herself breaking her own rules. She scribbled her number on his palm, her hand shaking slightly as she did.

"I don't normally do this," she muttered, feeling foolish. But he smiled again as if he understood.

"I'll call you," he said, slipping a fifty-pound note into her hand before walking out the door. Just like that. No explanations, no expectations. He just... left.

Jules stood there, stunned. It didn't make sense. None of it did. Why had he paid her and left? Why had he asked for dinner instead of the usual? She didn't know what to think. But as she stared at the crumpled note in her hand, she realized something, she wanted him to call. For the first time in a long time, she found herself hoping. It was dangerous, she knew that. But the part of her that had been buried for so long, the part that still dreamed of those faraway beaches and crystal-clear waters, had been stirred awake. Maybe, just maybe, this was the beginning of something different. But deep down, she couldn't shake the feeling that it was all too good to be true. Men like him didn't fall for girls like her. They used them, just like everyone else. And yet, she couldn't help but wonder, what if this time it was different?

CHAPTER 3: RESPECT & DIGNITY.

The day had been ordinary, almost suffocating in its dullness, until *he* walked in. Jules couldn't shake Phillip from her thoughts as she made her way to the train station, the echo of his smooth voice and confident presence lingering in her mind like a dark spell. He was unlike any other client she'd encountered, and that unnerved her. Not because she wasn't used to men paying for her time, no, that was routine. But his approach was different, softer, calculated, and even disorienting in how quickly he'd slipped under her skin. She couldn't figure him out, and that mystery made her both curious and uneasy. She boarded the train, settling into a corner seat by the window, she let the rhythmic hum of the train carry her thoughts away. Outside, the world passed by in a blur. Fields of green, small villages nestled into the countryside like forgotten secrets. Everything looked so serene, a stark contrast to the chaos constantly bubbling beneath her surface. The quiet homes with their warm lights seemed worlds apart from the darkness that had shaped her life. She pressed her forehead against the cold glass, her breath misting up the window as she stared into the distance, wondering what it must be like to live a life untouched by darkness.

Her imagination wandered into those cosy homes, painting scenes of domestic bliss. Happy families gathered around dinner tables, laughing, living in a harmony she'd never known. But even her fantasies couldn't fully escape the darkness. There was always a lingering sense of dread, a whisper that not all those homes were filled with love. Not all families were like the ones in the movies. Jules knew better than to believe in fairy tales.

'Not all monsters live under the bed. Some sit at the dinner table,' she thought bitterly, a familiar chill creeping down her spine. Her mind, ever traitorous, drifted back to her childhood. A nightmare she never fully woke from. Her adoptive father, that vile excuse for a man, had sold her body to anyone willing to pay. To him, she was nothing more than a commodity, a tool to line his pockets. He had never cared for her as a daughter. She was just a means to an end, a prisoner in her own life, shackled by invisible chains made of trauma and betrayal. The men who had used her, who had violated her innocence, were people others trusted, doctors, lawyers, and police officers. Even the community doctor was part of the sick game, knowing full well what was happening and turning a blind eye, complicit in her suffering. They were supposed to protect, to heal, yet they were the very monsters that haunted her nights. When she was just eleven, she contracted her first venereal disease, chlamydia, from one of those men. She remembered the cold, clinical voice of the doctor explaining that the untreated infection had ruined her chance of ever having children.

As if that mattered. No one had cared about her, only that she was no longer 'profitable' for her father until she had been cleansed of the disease. Jules closed her eyes, trying to force the memories back into the dark corners of her mind where they belonged.

She didn't want to think about it, about him, about what had been taken from her, about how damaged she felt. But the darkness inside her was always lurking, ready to consume her if she let her guard down for even a second. She exhaled, focusing on the here and now. Phillip had distracted her from all of that, at least for a little while. There was something about him that intrigued her, something that made her feel like, just maybe, he could offer an escape from the hell she'd been trapped in for so long. But then, she had to remind herself, she couldn't trust men. Not ever. When her phone buzzed, her heart skipped a beat. She fumbled to answer, her hands still damp from the shower she had taken just before, the water dripping onto her bare skin.

"Hello?" she answered cautiously, her voice barely steady.

"Jules, it's Phillip," came the smooth, confident reply on the other end of the line. "We met earlier. I was wondering, would you let me take you to dinner tonight? I'll make it worth your while. Five hundred pounds just to start. What do you say?"

The proposition was cold and transactional, but somehow, hearing his voice again, she couldn't stop the flutter of excitement mixed with fear that rippled through her. She wasn't used to being asked out to dinner.

"Just dinner?" she repeated, more to herself than to him.

"Yes, and we can discuss... a proposition I have for you," Phillip said, his tone cryptic, sending a shiver down her spine. She hesitated, unsure of what exactly she was walking into, but something inside her pushed her forward. Maybe it was curiosity, maybe it was the money, maybe it was that tiny spark of hope that she could escape her reality, even if just for one night.

"Okay," she said finally. "Give me an hour to get ready."

"I'll send a car to pick you up," Phillip said, his voice smooth as velvet. "My driver will meet you at the corner of Winston Road. He'll be in a black Mercedes, wearing a black suit. You'll know him when you see him."

"Alright," Jules whispered, her mind racing. "I'll be ready."

As soon as the line went dead, Jules found herself standing in the middle of her tiny apartment, staring blankly at her phone. She wasn't sure what she had just agreed to.

'*What kind of man sends a car for a working girl?*'

This wasn't a movie, and she wasn't some Cinderella waiting to be whisked away to a happy ending. She knew better than to believe in fairy tales. Still, as she got dressed, sliding into a royal blue satin dress that hugged her curves in all the right places, she couldn't help but feel a rush of nervous excitement. She wasn't used to this, feeling special, feeling wanted. She wasn't used to being treated like anything other than a body to be used and discarded. And that made this dangerous. Extremely dangerous. She stared at herself in the mirror, applying her makeup with trembling hands. Her reflection looked back at her with eyes that were too tired, too haunted for someone her age. But there was a spark there too, a flicker of something that refused to be snuffed out, no matter how many times life had tried to crush it.

"Tonight," she whispered to her reflection, "you're not Jules. You're someone else. Someone strong, someone in control."

As the clock ticked closer to eight, she grabbed her small overnight bag, just in case and made her way out the door. The night air was cool against her skin, and as she stood waiting at the corner of Winston Road, she felt a familiar twinge of fear. When the black Mercedes finally pulled up, she hesitated for a moment, her heart pounding in her chest. The driver stepped out, tall and imposing in his black suit, and opened the door for her.

"Miss Jules," he said, his voice calm and professional. She nodded, forcing herself to smile as she stepped into the car, the door closing behind her with a quiet click. Inside, the leather seats were soft, the air perfumed with something expensive. As the car glided smoothly through the city streets, Jules felt the weight of her decision settle on her. She didn't know what Phillip's game was, but she had a feeling that tonight, everything would change. For better or for worse. The darkness inside her stirred, whispering warnings, but she silenced it, pushing it down. Tonight, she would play the part. Tonight, she would be whoever Phillip wanted her to be. Because, just maybe, this was her way out. Or maybe it was another trap. Either way, she had no choice but to see it through.

CHAPTER 4: THE PROPOSITION

Jules sank deeper into the luxurious leather seat of the black Maybach as it glided through the dimly lit streets of the city. The low hum of the engine drowned out the cacophony of her chaotic thoughts, but the silence was only a brief reprieve. She peered out the window, watching the world outside blur into a tapestry of neon lights and shadowy figures that seemed to meld into the night. She was on her way to meet Phillip, a man who had turned her mundane existence upside down with just a phone call. He was unlike anyone she had ever encountered, radiating confidence and an unsettling charm that made her stomach twist with anticipation and dread. She had agreed to meet him despite the gnawing feeling that clawed at her insides. Part of her wondered if this was a mistake, but the prospect of escape, of something more, was intoxicating. The driver, a tall figure in a crisp black suit, glanced at her through the rearview mirror, his face emotionless. The tension in the air was palpable. Jules couldn't shake the feeling that she was being watched, not just by the driver, but by unseen eyes lurking in the shadows of the city. Her heart raced as she pressed her palm against the cool window, hoping to find clarity in the passing lights.

'*What was she doing?*' She felt like a moth drawn to a flame, irresistibly attracted to the danger that Phillip represented. He had described himself as a wealthy businessman with a penchant for helping women escape their dark pasts, but it all sounded too good to be true. The car slowed, and Jules's heart leapt into her throat as they pulled up to the restaurant, a lavish establishment she'd only seen in magazines. The entrance was flanked by towering columns, and the red carpet rolled out like a sinister invitation. It felt like a trap, one she was willingly stepping into. She could feel the eyes of the valets and patrons drilling into her as if they sensed her vulnerability.

"Miss?" The driver's voice broke through her reverie, and she nodded mechanically as he opened the door for her. As she stepped out, a gust of cool air hit her, sending a shiver down her spine. Phillip stood just inside the entrance, a striking figure in a tailored suit, his dark hair slicked back. He had an aura of magnetism, drawing people to him like blind dogs to a meat market. When he spotted her, a smile spread across his face, a smile that didn't reach his eyes.

"Jules," he greeted, his voice smooth like silk as he took her hand, his grip firm but not harsh.

"You look stunning."

"Thank you," she replied, trying to match his enthusiasm. Even though she was feeling inferior beneath the weight of his gaze. He led her to a private booth tucked away in a corner of the dimly lit dining room, the soft flicker of candlelight casting shadows that danced like spectres on the walls. The intimate setting felt suffocating, an unspoken promise hanging heavy in the air. She felt the pressure of his presence like a noose tightening around her throat.

"I hope the grandeur of this place isn't too unsettling for you?" Phillip asked, his eyes glimmering with interest as he settled across from her.

"Not at all," she said, forcing a smile. Inside, her thoughts were a whirlwind of uncertainty. '*What was she doing here? Why had she agreed to meet him?*'

The waiter arrived with a bottle of the finest wine, pouring it into crystal glasses with a flourish. Phillip's smile never wavered, but there was something predatory about the way he leaned forward, resting his elbows on the table as he studied her.

"I know this is all a bit overwhelming," he said, his voice low and soothing, almost hypnotic.

"But I want you to feel comfortable with me."

"Comfortable," she echoed, the word tasting foreign on her tongue. There was a chill in the air, a sense of foreboding that lingered just beneath the surface. "I mean it," he continued, his gaze unwavering. "I understand what you're going through, Jules. I see the potential in you, I want to help you realise it."

Her heart raced at his words, but a flicker of doubt crept in. She had heard promises before, men who claimed they wanted to save her but only sought to control her. "What do you mean?" she asked, her voice shaking slightly despite her best efforts to remain composed.

"I know you're looking for a way out. This life... it can be a prison, can't it?" His voice was soft, almost tender, and she felt her defences crumbling beneath his gaze. Jules opened her mouth to respond, but the words caught in her throat.

'How could he know?' The nights spent trapped in dingy motels, the men who saw her as nothing more than a body to use and discard, it all swirled in her mind like a storm. Phillip leaned back, taking a sip of his wine, his eyes still locked onto hers.

"I grew up in a rough part of town. I've seen women like you before. Brave, resilient women caught in a cycle they didn't choose." Her breath hitched as he continued, his voice deep and resonant. "The first girl I ever loved ended up on the streets. I couldn't save her, but I've dedicated my life to helping others like her. Like you."

Jules swallowed hard, the weight of his words pressing down on her. She wanted to believe him. The idea of escaping her current life was intoxicating, but the nagging fear in the back of her mind wouldn't let go.

"What's the catch?" she managed to ask, her voice trembling.

He chuckled softly, shaking his head. "There's no catch, Jules. I want to provide you with a fresh start. No strings attached. Just the opportunity to live a life free of this burden."

"But why me?" she pressed, desperation creeping into her tone. "Why would you care?"

"Because I see you," he replied, his gaze unwavering, as if he could peel back the layers of her soul. "You're stronger than you realize. You deserve a chance to break free."

His sincerity disarmed her. She felt a flicker of hope igniting within her, but it was quickly extinguished by a wave of self-doubt. "I've never done anything like this before," she confessed, her voice barely above a whisper. Phillip leaned closer, his voice dropping to a conspiratorial tone.

"That's the beauty of it, Jules. You don't have to do it alone. I'll be with you every step of the way."

Her heart raced as she met his gaze, the intensity of it making her breath hitch. He was so confident, so sure of himself, and it was both thrilling and terrifying. The dark allure of his offer wrapped around her like a shroud.

'*What if this was her only chance?*' But as she sat there, trapped between desire and fear, something in her gut twisted. It felt too easy, too convenient. There had to be a catch, a dark side lurking beneath the surface of his charming exterior. "I don't know..." she began, but he silenced her with a raised hand.

"Trust me, Jules," he said, his tone almost pleading. "Just consider it. Think of what you could have, a life beyond these walls, beyond the darkness that surrounds you."

For a moment, she was swept away in his words, visions of a brighter future flashing before her eyes. A life without fear, without the constant dread of being used. But the hauntings of her reality loomed large, a relentless reminder of how easily things could go wrong.

"Why would you want to help me?" she asked again, needing to understand his motives.

"What do you gain from this?"

Phillip's smile faded slightly, his expression turning serious. "Because I can't stand the thought of another woman suffering like that. I want to make a difference, Jules. And I believe you can be a part of that difference."

His words resonated within her, stirring something deep inside. She could feel the desperation clawing at her, the yearning for a way out threatening to swallow her whole. But still, the shadows whispered warnings, taunting her with visions of betrayal and loss. "What if I say yes?" she asked, her voice barely a whisper.

"Then we begin your new life together," he replied, his eyes glinting with a predatory satisfaction that sent a chill down her spine. The tension in the air thickened, wrapping around her like a noose. Jules could feel her pulse quickening as she considered his offer. It was as if she was standing on the edge of a precipice, the dark abyss below calling to her. She could either leap into the unknown or retreat into the familiar darkness of her life.

"You can trust me," Phillip said, his voice smooth and seductive. "I'll be your guide. All I

need is your trust." Jules bit her lip, her mind racing. She wanted to believe him, to surrender to the seductive pull of his words. But her instincts screamed for her to run. Something was off, something sinister lurking just beneath the surface of his charm. As the minutes dragged on, Jules felt the walls closing in around her. The restaurant, once so glamorous, now felt stifling and claustrophobic. Phillip leaned back, watching her intently, the weight of his gaze was suffocating.

"I need time to think," she said finally, her voice trembling.

Phillip's expression darkened slightly, but he masked it quickly with that charming smile. "Of course. Take your time. But remember, opportunities like this don't come along often." The warning in his words hung heavy in the air, and Jules felt a wave of unease wash over her. She couldn't shake the feeling that she was stepping into something dark and twisted, a web of deceit that would ensnare her before she even realized what was happening. But as she looked into Phillip's eyes, something inside her yearned to believe. She had spent so long feeling trapped, so long drowning in the suffocating darkness of her existence. The thought of freedom, of a life where she could be more than just a shadow, was almost too tempting to resist.

"I'll think about it," she said again, her voice stronger this time.

"Good," he replied, his smile returning. "Just know that I'm here for you. I want to see you thrive." The dinner progressed, but Jules found it hard to focus. Phillip spoke with a charisma that was hard to ignore, weaving tales of his adventures and successes, and she found herself drawn into his world. But with every laugh, every smile, the nagging doubt in her gut grew louder, a relentless chorus warning her to tread carefully. As the evening wore on, Phillip's demeanour shifted slightly. He became more intense, more focused on her, Jules felt the air crackle with a tension that was both exciting and terrifying. It was as if he was gently pulling her into his orbit, she was powerless to resist. But just when she thought she might be falling for him, the shadows crept back in, whispering reminders of all the times she had been fooled before. She took a deep breath, forcing herself to remain grounded. The meal ended, and Phillip signalled for the bill.

"Shall we?" he asked, standing up and extending his hand. Jules hesitated, her heart racing as she looked at his outstretched hand. This was it, the moment where she could either take his hand and step into the unknown or turn and run. The fear was paralyzing, but the allure of his offer was almost overwhelming. She glanced at the door, wondering what lay beyond.

'*A life filled with uncertainty and fear. Or a chance at something more, something better?*'

With a shaky breath, she placed her hand in his, feeling the warmth of his grip engulf her. As he led her out of the restaurant and back into the night, Jules could almost hear the voices of her past screaming for her to stop, to run away, but it was too late. She was already ensnared in

Phillip's web, and the darkness was closing in around her, eager to pull her deeper into its embrace. Outside, the city loomed like a beast, its shadows stretching out toward her as she stepped onto the red carpet. Jules felt a thrill of exhilaration mixed with dread as she realized she was willingly walking into the unknown, lured by the seductive promise of freedom, a new life. As they approached the Maybach, Phillip turned to her, his gaze penetrating.

"You won't regret this, Jules," he said softly, the promise in his voice sending shivers down her spine. But as she climbed into the car, she couldn't shake the feeling that she was plunging into darkness, and there would be no turning back. The door closed with a soft click, sealing her fate as the driver pulled away from the curb, the shadows swallowing them whole. Jules stared out the window, the city lights blurring into streaks of colour, her heart pounding in her chest. She was stepping into a world where everything she had known would be shattered, a world that promised freedom but could just as easily lead to her undoing. The night was just beginning, and with Phillip beside her, she was about to plunge into a darkness she had never known.

CHAPTER 5: THE DECISION.

Jules sat by the window, staring into the darkened sky, the weight of Phillip's proposition pressing down on her like a storm cloud ready to burst. Her mind was a whirl of conflicting emotions, torn between the life she knew and the promise of something more. For as long as she could remember, her life had been a series of compromises, a battle for survival. Selling her body wasn't a choice she had relished, but it was the choice she had made, one that gave her control, autonomy, and above all, the means to survive. It was a life that offered no comfort but provided a twisted sense of safety, a sense of power, even if that power was an illusion. Now, Phillip was offering her a chance to leave it all behind. But the idea of stepping away from the only world she had ever known filled her with dread. What would she become if she wasn't a working girl? In this profession, she answered to no one.

No pimp, no boss, no lover had control over her. The thought of leaving that behind, leaving her independence behind, terrified her. What would she be without it? A failure? A fool? Lost in a world she didn't understand? Jules stood, her fingers trembling as she pressed them to the cold glass, her reflection a ghostly figure in the dim light. Her eyes, once sharp and hardened, now stared back at her, wide and full of uncertainty. The streets below were teeming with life, the lights of the city flickering like fireflies. She had fought her way up from the gutter, clawed her way out of the filth, and this life, as dark as it was, had saved her. It had given her a roof over her head, nice clothes, and the ability to pay her bills. It had allowed her to survive. Yet, as the days passed, Phillip's words echoed in her mind, stirring something deep within her, something she had long since buried. A different life.

A new beginning. It wasn't a promise he had made lightly, but it was a promise all the same, and Jules found herself yearning for it in ways she hadn't anticipated. For years, she had been content with the scraps of freedom her profession afforded her. She answered to no one. She made her own decisions, decided where her money went, who she saw, and when. But now, Phillip had shown her a door, a way out, and it scared her to death.

'*What if she walked through it and it slammed shut behind her? What if she couldn't go back?*' She had seen too many girls fall into traps. Girls who thought they had found a way out, only to be pulled into something far worse. Pretend boyfriends who were just pimps, friends who were only there for the money. She had heard the horror stories, the drugs, the beatings, the degradation. Jules had avoided all that. She didn't do drugs. She didn't have friends. She didn't want to be owned by anyone. Not ever again. As a child, she had been owned. Trapped in an adoptive home that felt more like a prison, where every breath she took, every step she made, was under someone else's control. When she finally ran away, she had sworn to herself that no one would ever have that power over her again. Yet here she was, considering Phillip's offer. The man with the dazzling smile and silver tongue, who had pulled her into his world so effortlessly. The man who was offering her more than she could have ever dreamed of a job at his ski resort, the chance to travel, to experience a life she had only ever seen in movies. But there was a price. There was always a price. She was to be his companion and attend events, galas, and dinners at his side for the next month.

A seemingly small price to pay for the promise of a new life. But Jules couldn't shake the feeling that there was more to it. That this was only the beginning of something she wouldn't be able to escape from once she was in too deep. Still, she couldn't deny the pull. She had never been abroad, never travelled beyond the grimy streets of the city that had raised her. The thought of seeing the Alps, of standing atop a snowy mountain with nothing but sky and earth around her, was almost too intoxicating to resist. Phillip had painted a picture of a world so foreign to her, so luxurious, that it felt like stepping into another dimension.

As they sat together in a quaint coffee shop, his voice smooth and calming, he spoke of his resort in the Alps. A place where he recruited staff for each season, where life was beautiful, serene, and everything she had ever wanted. Her heart ached with longing, a deep, primal desire for freedom that she had tried so hard to suppress.

"I can't promise it will be easy," Phillip had said, his voice low and sincere as he leaned in closer. "But I can promise I'll be there with you every step of the way."

Jules had stared into his eyes, searching for something, a lie, a trick, anything that would confirm her worst fears. But all she saw was warmth and kindness. It terrified her more than anything else. The opportunity of a lifetime, he had called it. And in that moment, she had believed him.

"I'll think about it," she had whispered, her voice trembling. But now, alone in the darkness of her small apartment, her heart raced with indecision. *'What if this was her only chance? What if she let it slip through her fingers, and she was left with nothing but regret?'* Phillip had shown her a world of possibility, a world where she could be something more than just a shadow. And yet, as she stared at her reflection, her pale face staring back at her like a ghost, she wondered if she was even capable of living that life.

'Normal. What did that even mean?'

She thought of the other girls. The ones who had gotten out, or at least tried to. Some had fallen into worse situations, dragged down by abusive boyfriends, by drugs, by pimps in disguise. Jules had been smart. She had avoided all of that. She had remained her own boss and answered to no one. She wasn't stupid. She knew the risks. But this was different.

Phillip was different. Or was he?

The next morning, she met him again, this time in the luxurious confines of a boutique, surrounded by silk, cashmere, and designer labels. The subtle tones of classical music filled the air, and the atmosphere was one of wealth and privilege. Jules felt like she had stepped into another world, a world where her old self didn't belong. Phillip stood beside her, calm and collected, his presence grounding her in this unfamiliar place. His grin was knowing, almost possessive as if he was pulling her deeper into his orbit with every passing moment. He led her through the store, showing her the racks of clothes, the expensive ski wear, the elegant evening gowns that shimmered under the boutique's soft lighting. Jules felt like she was in a dream, a surreal, intoxicating dream where every desire could be fulfilled with the swipe of a credit card.

"This is no less than you deserve, Jules," Phillip had said softly, his hand resting on her shoulder. "You're worth every penny."

His words gave her chills of excitement and for now, she believed him. She let herself be carried away by the moment, by the rush of adrenaline and excitement that surged through her as she tried on outfit after outfit. For the first time in her life, she felt beautiful. Powerful. But as they left the boutique, their arms laden with bags of designer clothes, a cold sense of unease settled in her chest. She was stepping into a world she didn't understand, a world that could consume her if she wasn't careful. Phillip was moulding her, shaping her into something new. He had arranged etiquette classes, and elocution lessons, even providing her with an apartment in a safe, upscale neighbourhood. He was giving her everything she had ever wanted, but at what cost? And then there was Vanessa. His wife. Jules's stomach twisted when Phillip casually mentioned her over dinner one evening.

"My wife, Vanessa, is looking forward to meeting you," he had said, his tone so nonchalant it took a moment for the words to sink in. Jules froze, her fork hovering in midair.

"Your wife?"

"Yes," Phillip said, smiling as if it was the most natural thing in the world. "She knows all about you. She's fine with it. We do this often, actually. Helping girls like you get back on their feet."

Jules's heart pounded in her chest, her mind racing. '*Vanessa knew? She was fine with it?' What kind of twisted game was this?*' She wanted to scream, to demand answers, but her throat tightened, and the words wouldn't come. Instead, she forced a smile, nodding as if everything was perfectly normal. But inside, her world was unravelling.

'*Who was Phillip, really? And what had she gotten herself into?*' As they left the restaurant, Phillip's hand resting lightly on her back, Jules couldn't shake the feeling that she was being drawn deeper into something dark and sinister. The life he had promised her was tantalizing, but the obvious red flags were impossible to ignore. She had stepped into the unknown, and there was no turning back. The city lights blurred into streaks of colour as they drove away, the darkness closing in around her. Jules stared out the window, her heart heavy with the weight of her choices. She had wanted freedom, but now she wondered if she had traded one cage for another. Phillip had offered her the world, but was he genuine?

CHAPTER 6: DANCE WITH THE DEVIL.

The city lights flickered against the window, casting a faint glow across Jules's face as the sleek, black car slid silently through the night. It had been a month since she stepped into Phillip's world, and each day felt like teetering on the edge of a precipice. His attention, his gifts, the opulence of the life he introduced her to, it all felt surreal. At first, she had been seduced by the grandeur, intoxicated by the idea that someone like her, a girl who'd clawed her way out of hell, could finally taste luxury. But now, tonight, something felt off. The car came to a halt outside yet another lavish venue, a sprawling estate bathed in gold light, as though it had been plucked from a dream. Jules should have felt like a queen in her gown, a masterpiece of silk and jewels, but instead, dread pooled in her stomach.

The past month had been filled with dizzying highs. Phillip took her shopping, draping her in designer dresses, parading her through exclusive galas and dinners like she was some prized possession. Yet, with each event, the knot in her gut grew tighter. Tonight, it was suffocating her. As she stepped out of the car, the chill of the night seeped through her, deeper than the cool air should have. She adjusted her dress, smoothing the fabric over her skin, but her hands trembled. A strange dissonance settled into her bones like the world around her was too bright, too flawless. She couldn't ignore the feeling that something was wrong.

Horribly, irrevocably wrong. Phillip appeared at her side, his hand slipping around her waist with practised ease. His touch, once a comfort, now felt like chains tightening around her. His smile, polished, charming, deadly, did nothing to soothe the growing fear gnawing at her insides.

"You look stunning, Jules. Every eye will be on you tonight," he whispered into her ear, his voice like velvet wrapping around her throat. She smiled, or at least tried to. But her body was rebelling. Her instincts screamed at her to run, to turn and flee from whatever lay behind the glittering façade of this world. Yet, she stayed. For a month, she had danced this dance, thinking she could survive it, that she could use it as her steppingstone to a better life.

But now... now she wasn't so sure. The night unfolded as it always did, men in tailored suits, women draped in gowns worth more than her entire life's earnings, the air thick with wealth and power. As she moved through the crowd, she could feel their eyes on her, hungry, calculating, cold. The elite, with their predatory smiles and glassy eyes, made her skin crawl. She was no stranger to being objectified, but this was different.

Here, she wasn't just a woman. She was something to be consumed, dissected, used. Phillip stayed by her side, a constant presence, guiding her through the sea of sharks. Yet even his presence felt more ominous tonight. There was a tension in him she hadn't noticed before, something coiled beneath his charming exterior. When he was called away for a meeting, leaving her alone among the wolves, the knot in her stomach twisted tighter. She drifted to the edges of the banquet hall, seeking the shadows, her heart pounding in her chest. The murmur of voices, the clink of glasses, it all faded into a dull roar as her thoughts spiralled. The air felt thick, suffocating, pressing down on her like a weight she couldn't shake off. And then, out of nowhere, the memories hit her like a tidal wave.

'The *laughter. The mocking voices. The hands.*' Her childhood flashed before her eyes in jagged fragments, the abuse, the helplessness, the nights spent trying to disappear. And here she was again, a pawn in someone else's game, being used, paraded, and devoured by people who saw her as nothing more than a pretty face, a body to dress up and show off. She closed her eyes, her breath coming in shallow gasps.

'*Get a grip, Jules. Don't fall apart. Not here. Not now.*' But it was too late. The walls were closing in on her, the memories mixing with the present until she couldn't tell where one ended and the other began. She needed to find Phillip. He always knew how to calm her down, how to make the world stop spinning, even if just for a moment. But as she searched the crowd, a growing sense of dread pooled in her chest. Tonight, everything felt different. Darker. She found him at the top of the grand staircase, descending slowly, his eyes locking onto hers with that same charming smile. But there was something behind it now, something she couldn't quite place.

"Where have you been?" she asked, her voice trembling with the effort to stay calm. "I had a quick meeting. Is everything alright, Jules?" he asked, his voice dripping with concern. "You look like you've seen a ghost."

Her pulse quickened. "I just…. something feels off tonight. I feel like…" She trailed off, not wanting to sound crazy, but the words stuck in her throat. She didn't trust anyone here, not even herself.

Phillip's expression softened. "It's just the nerves, sweetheart. These people, high-flyers, they're cutthroat. It's how the game is played." His hand found her waist again, pulling her close. "You're safe with me."

'*But was she?*' She wanted to believe him. After all, he had saved her. Pulled her out of the gutter and gave her a life she never could have dreamed of. But something about the way he spoke, the way he looked at her now, sent a chill crawling up her spine.

"I think I just need some air," she whispered.

"Shall I have the driver take you home?" His voice was warm, but something was lurking underneath it, something sharp.

"No. I'll be fine."

Phillip smiled, but it didn't reach his eyes. "Alright. Just don't wander too far."

As she turned away, his words echoed in her mind. '*Don't wander too far.*' It sounded less like a suggestion and more like a warning. The night pressed in on her, heavy with unseen danger. She didn't know what was waiting for her in the shadows, but she knew, deep in her bones that something was wrong. As much as she wanted to trust Phillip, the man who had brought her into this gilded world, she couldn't shake the feeling that the life he promised her was a lie. The next morning, as she packed her bags for the Alps, her mind was a storm of doubt and fear. Phillip had been her saviour, her confidant, her protector. But now, the idea of following him into the mountains, to a remote resort where she'd be surrounded by more strangers, more power players, filled her with dread she couldn't explain. She stood at the window, staring out into the city she had once ruled in her own way. Her reflection in the glass was a stranger. She wasn't that broken little girl anymore, but was she strong enough to survive this new game? In two days, she was supposed to leave everything behind and start a new life. But as the hours ticked by, all she could think was, '*What if this is just another cage?' What if this time, there is no way out.*'

CHAPTER 7: WILD & NEW

As the private jet pierced through the veil of clouds, Jules leaned closer to the window, her breath fogging the glass ever so slightly as she stared out into the abyss. The scene that unfolded before her wasn't just beautiful. It was haunting, overwhelming. The Alps rose like jagged teeth, tearing into the heavens, each peak an unforgiving monument to nature's raw power. The snow, glistening under the dying light of the sun, stretched as far as the eye could see. It wasn't the soft, delicate white of a postcard scene. No, it was sharp, blinding, suffocating in its purity. The mountains felt alive, almost sentient as if they were watching, waiting, daring anyone to step into their cold embrace. Jules felt a shiver that had nothing to do with the cold. There was something ancient about these mountains, something eternal, and as the jet descended lower, she couldn't shake the feeling that she was intruding upon a world not meant for people like her. It was both terrifying and intoxicating.

Phillip sat back in his seat, observing her with a calm, almost knowing smile. He had seen that look on her face before. He had seen it on many faces, those who came here seeking adventure, excitement, a temporary escape from their tortured lives. To him, these mountains were no longer awe-inspiring. They were a part of him, as familiar as his heartbeat, and just as relentless. He had lived through many winters here, surviving, adapting, and learning to respect the silent, brutal power of this place. As the jet landed on the snow-dusted runway, the excitement in Jules's chest twisted into something darker, an exhilaration tinged with fear. The hum of the engines faded, replaced by an eerie stillness.

She stepped onto the tarmac, the icy wind hitting her face like a slap. The cold was brutal, almost alive in its intensity. It wasn't just the chill of winter, it was a reminder that she was in a place that could crush her in an instant, a place where nature ruled, indifferent to the lives it swallowed whole. Jules drew in a sharp breath, the air burning her lungs with its freezing purity. The scent of pine and fir lingered in the air, but beneath that, there was something else, something ancient and primal, like the scent of stone and snow that had existed since time immemorial. The mountains loomed over her, their presence oppressive, casting long shadows that seemed to stretch out, reaching for her, as if they too sensed her intrusion.

The sound of her boots crunching in the snow was deafening in the stillness. All around her, there was a symphony of winter, the soft whoosh of the wind through the trees, the distant rumble of avalanches echoing like a warning, and the eerie silence that hung in the air, thick and suffocating. She felt small, insignificant, as though the mountains were waiting to swallow her whole. As they approached the chalet, her heart pounded, not from excitement, but from something deeper, more primal. The delicate snowflakes that drifted down seemed almost mocking in their beauty, tiny crystalline daggers falling from the sky, disappearing into the ground without a trace. The chalet itself was a picture of perfection, its eaves adorned with icicles that glittered like teeth, sharp and ready to strike. The fragile beauty of it all felt like a trap, a lure set by the mountains to draw in the unsuspecting adventurers.

Inside the chalet, the fire crackled softly, but its warmth felt hollow, a weak attempt to stave off the cold that lingered just beyond the windows. The flames danced and flickered, casting shadows across the room that seemed to move with a life of their own. Jules stood by the window, her breath fogging the glass as she stared out into the vast, unforgiving wilderness. There was no escape. The mountains were everywhere, their presence suffocating, their beauty a veneer hiding the deathly cold underneath. Her heart ached with a strange sense of belonging and fear. She had always longed for adventure, for something bigger than the quiet life she had left behind in Bristol, but now, standing here, wrapped in the cold embrace of the Alps, she wondered if she had bitten off more than she could chew. The vast expanse of snow and sky stretched out before her, a landscape so beautiful and yet so indifferent. She was nothing here, just another soul passing through. Phillip's voice broke through her reverie, pulling her back to reality. He was smiling at her, but his eyes held a glint of something darker. '*Or was she imagining it all?*'

This was his world, not hers. She was a guest here, a temporary fixture in the timeless dance between life and death that played out in these mountains. As the days passed, Jules found herself falling into a routine, though it felt more like a trance. The ski resort, with its picturesque chalets and bustling social scene, was a strange juxtaposition to the wild, untamed beauty that surrounded it. The main lodge, a grand structure of timber and stone, stood like a fortress at the centre of it all, a beacon of warmth and luxury amidst the cold, unforgiving landscape. Inside, the atmosphere was lively, but Jules couldn't shake the feeling that it was all a façade. The roaring fireplaces, the comfortable couches, the laughter, and the chatter, all felt so artificial, a fragile barrier against the relentless cold outside.

She watched as guests indulged in gourmet meals at the Michelin-starred restaurant, oblivious to the fact that just beyond the walls, the mountains waited, patient and unyielding. The ski slopes offered a temporary escape from the suffocating sense of dread that had settled over her, but even there, she couldn't outrun the feeling that something was wrong, deeply, fundamentally wrong. The adrenaline of skiing down the mountains, cutting through fresh powder, was exhilarating, but it was always tainted with a lingering fear, one wrong move, one moment of hesitation, and the mountains would claim her. The snow was soft, but beneath it was ice, rock, and death. Jules found herself surrounded by other young women, all eager, all excited to conquer the mountains. They laughed, they joked, they pushed themselves to the limits, but Jules could see the fear in their eyes, the same fear she felt. They were all pretending, trying to convince themselves that they were invincible, that the mountains were theirs to conquer. But the mountains didn't care. They had seen countless others like them come and go, their laughter fading into silence as the snow covered their tracks, their stories forgotten. The instructors guided them with practised ease, their voices calm and reassuring, but Jules sensed their mendacious tones. They knew the truth and had seen the mountains take their toll on those who dared to challenge them. Every fall was a reminder of how fragile they were, and how easily the mountains could crush them.

Jules learned to embrace the fear, to use it as fuel, but it never went away. It lingered as a constant companion, whispering in her ear, reminding her that she didn't belong here. In the evenings, after the long days at work, Jules retreated to the pub with the other staff members. The warmth of the fire, the camaraderie of shared drinks and laughter, provided a brief respite from the cold that seemed to seep into her very bones. But even here, in the heart of the resort, she couldn't escape the feeling that something strange was prevalent.

The conversations, the laughter, it all felt forced, like they were all trying too hard to forget where they were. The pub was a sanctuary of sorts, a place where the staff could escape the harsh reality of their surroundings, if only for a little while. But Jules could see the cracks in the pretence. The weariness in their eyes, the tension in their laughter, it was all there, just beneath the surface. They were all running from something, trying to lose themselves in the routine of work and play, but the mountains were always there, waiting. Jules threw herself into her work, whether it was serving in the restaurant or tending bar. She moved with a purpose, her hands steady even as her mind raced. The work was gruelling, the hours long, but it kept her grounded, kept her from thinking too much about the cold, about the mountains, about the gnawing fear that had taken root deep inside her.

As the days bled into weeks, Jules found herself changing. She wasn't the same person who had stepped off that jet weeks ago, full of excitement and wonder. The mountains had stripped her down, exposed her weaknesses, her fears. She had been humbled, and broken, and yet, somehow, she was stronger for it. But the mountains weren't done with her yet. They never were. They watched, and waited, biding their time. Jules knew, deep down, that the adventure was far from over. The real challenge was just beginning.

CHAPTER 8: THE SANDS OF TIME.

The days in the Alps blurred into weeks. Jules found herself sinking deeper into the rhythm of mountain life, wrapping the beauty of the towering peaks and the community of smiling faces around her like a comforting cloak. Each day began with the sharp bite of chilly air on her cheeks and the soft crunch of snow beneath her boots. But beneath the surface of that idyllic alpine paradise, something stirred, a presence she couldn't quite name, an unease that prickled at the edges of her awareness. She couldn't explain why, but the longer she stayed, the heavier the atmosphere became, despite the outward charm of the place.

The pristine snow-capped mountains were magnificent. The staff seemed warm, enthusiastic, and eager to please. But sometimes, when Jules stood alone outside, staring at the endless white expanse, a strange stillness pressed in around her. It was the kind of silence that made your heart race like you were being watched from a distance, observed from behind those great, unforgiving peaks. She remembered that first day vividly, the weight of her suitcase digging into her hand as the bus clambered up the winding roads, the curves revealing stunning vistas of snow and forest. It had seemed like a dream, a perfect escape from her life, from everything she had left behind. And yet, even then, something felt off.

A nagging whisper in the back of her mind had warned her that not everything was as it seemed. But Jules had pushed it away, blaming it on nerves. It was Phillip who had encouraged her to come, after all. He had been kind, almost too kind. He had spoken to her about transformation, about escaping her past, about starting anew in the mountains. His words had been persuasive, filled with promises of a new beginning, a chance to reinvent herself far away from the life that had drained her spirit.

"One girl at a time." He had said, his voice smooth, his smile reassuring. At the time, she hadn't thought much of it. Now, that phrase echoed in her head with a sinister undercurrent, like a warning she had failed to heed.

'One girl at a time. What did that mean?'

The resort had seemed beautiful, too beautiful, perhaps. The kind of beauty that felt false, like a painting masking something ugly underneath. The snow that had once enchanted her now felt cold, suffocating. The towering pines that lined the edges of the resort cast long shadows that crept over the lodge as the sun dipped behind the peaks like fingers reaching for something hidden in the dark. Jules threw herself into work, hoping that the distraction would ease her anxieties. She took skiing lessons alongside other young women, all of them eager, smiling, and laughing. But their joy felt forced as if they had been rehearsed. Something about their excitement unsettled her. They seemed too perfect, too eager to please. It was as if they were all under the same spell, like puppets performing in a play they didn't fully understand. One girl, Sarah, was different. Sarah had a nervous energy that set her apart from the others. A redhead with a bright smile that never quite reached her eyes, she had an incessant way of making conversation, her words always punctuated by a soft, nervous hiccup. At first, Jules had tried to keep her distance, but Sarah had persisted, her bubbly personality cracking through Jules's walls of isolation.

"You look like you need someone to talk to," Sarah had said one evening, her voice tinged with concern. Her hiccups had come more frequently that day, betraying her anxiety. Jules had been staring out of the window of the lodge, watching the snow fall in a hypnotic pattern, lost in thought. She hadn't wanted to talk, but there was something about Sarah's earnestness, the way her eyes searched Jules's face as if looking for answers to unspoken questions, that made her open up.

"I don't know what it is," Jules had said quietly, her voice trembling with the weight of her own uncertainty. "But something about this place... it feels wrong. Like I'm being pulled into something I don't understand."

Sarah's eyes had flickered with something, fear, recognition. She had leaned closer, her voice dropping to a whisper. "I know exactly what you mean."

There had been a pause, heavy with unspoken truths. Jules had felt a shiver crawl down her spine, and it wasn't from the cold.

"I was brought here by a man," Sarah had continued, her hiccups more erratic now. "Just like you, I thought it was a fresh start, a way out. He promised me freedom, safety, and a life without fear. But there's a price. There's always a price."

Jules's heart had begun to race, her mind spinning with questions.

"What do you mean? What price?"

Sarah had looked away, her gaze distant, as if she were remembering something painful.

"Have you heard about the competition nights?"

Jules's stomach had tightened. She had heard whispers, and rumours passed between the staff in hushed tones, but she had dismissed them as idle gossip.

"Competition nights?"

Sarah had nodded, her face pale. "The guests... they like to watch us. We're not just here to work, Jules. We're here to entertain." A chill had settled in Jules's chest, a sinking feeling of dread.

"What kind of entertainment?"

Sarah had hesitated, glancing around the room as if the very walls were listening.

"Skiing competitions. But it's not just about winning. It's about... surviving."

Jules had felt the blood drain from her face. "Surviving?"

"They watch us, Jules. They bet on us. If you lose... if you don't play along..."

The words hung in the air, heavy with implication. Jules had felt a wave of nausea wash over her. This couldn't be real. It sounded like something out of a nightmare, a twisted game where lives were at stake.

"I got a warning," Sarah said her voice barely a whisper. "The bartender in the village, she slipped me a note. She told me to lose, to make sure I don't stand out. I don't know what happens to the winners, but... they never come back."

Jules felt the walls closing in on her, the weight of the truth pressing down on her chest. The resort wasn't what it seemed. It was a trap, a gilded cage designed to lure young women in with promises of escape, only to turn them into pawns in some sick game.

"Why didn't you leave?" Jules asked, her voice shaky.

Sarah's eyes had filled with tears. "Because there's no way out. Once you're here, you're stuck. They watch everything and control everything. If you try to run, they'll find you. They always do." Jules felt a cold sweat break out on her skin. She had to get out of there. But how? The resort was isolated, surrounded by mountains and snow, miles from the nearest town. And if what Sarah said was true, they were being watched. Every move they made was being monitored. The skiing competitions were just days away, and the thought of being thrust into that twisted game filled Jules with terror. She had to figure out a way to escape before it was too late. But the resort was a maze of secrets, and every corner she turned seemed to lead her deeper into the darkness.

The next few days were a blur of anxiety and fear. Jules found herself glancing over her shoulder constantly, always feeling the eyes of the resort on her. The once-charming guests now seemed sinister, their smiles hiding something malevolent. Even the ski instructors, who had once appeared friendly and welcoming, now seemed to leer at her with cold, calculating eyes. As the day of the competition approached, the air grew thick with tension. The other women, who had once been so cheerful and enthusiastic, now seemed nervous, their laughter strained, their movements jittery. Jules could see the fear in their eyes, even as they tried to hide it. On the morning of the competition, Jules woke to the sound of footsteps outside her door. Her heart raced as she listened, her body frozen with fear. The footsteps paused for a moment, then moved on. She let out a shaky breath, her mind racing with thoughts of escape. But there was no escape. Not yet. Jules dressed in silence, her hands trembling as she pulled on her ski gear. She had to stay calm, had to blend in. If she stood out, if she caught anyone's attention, she knew she wouldn't make it out of the Alps. She'd vanish without a trace if what Sarah said was the truth. As she made her way to the starting line, the chilly air biting at her skin, Jules felt all the eyes on her. She could feel the tension in the air, and the anticipation of the guests as they watched the women line up, ready to race for their lives. The whistle blew, and the competition began.

CHAPTER 9: RED FLAGS.

On the first competition day, the atmosphere at the resort crackled with an undercurrent of excitement that masked something far more sinister. The crisp mountain air hummed with anticipation as the sun's rays glinted off the snow-covered peaks, casting brilliant light across the slopes. For many, it was just another day of winter festivities, but for the staff, the young female workers, the stakes felt unnervingly high. The competition was not just a harmless show of skill. The female employees, all of them strikingly similar in age and appearance, were more than nervous. There was an unspoken fear that gripped their hearts. They wanted to impress, yes, but more than that, they wanted to avoid the icy disapproval of Phillip and Vanessa, the enigmatic leaders of the resort. Both had a presence that commanded attention, an authority that demanded obedience without explanation. From the moment the first rays of dawn kissed the Alps, the resort was buzzing. Guests, in their designer ski gear, were already zipping up the lifts, faces flushed with excitement and the thrill of competition.

But for the female staff, identifiable by their perfectly fitted uniforms, there was something more at stake than mere victory.

Sarah, the small redhead who had struck up a friendship with Jules, was among them. She was the kind of girl who radiated energy and excitement, but today, beneath the surface, Jules noticed a thin sheen of anxiety clinging to her like the snowflakes that dotted her fiery hair. The competition itself was a dazzling display of skill and speed. Guests and staff alike hurtled down the slopes with reckless abandon, weaving between the flags and executing jumps that would make even the most seasoned skier flinch. The digital scoreboard at the base of the mountain kept a cold, mechanical tally of times, its red numbers flashing under the winter sky. Each time a staff member completed a run, they would cast a furtive glance towards Phillip and Vanessa, who stood by the finish line, their eyes hidden behind reflective sunglasses. Jules could feel it, every single staff member was desperate to win.

'But was it truly for the prize? Or was it for something far more intangible, far more vital, like survival?' Sarah, for her part, was a force to be reckoned with. Her small frame was carved through the snow with unmatched precision. Each turn was executed flawlessly, each jump a testament to her raw talent. The crowd watched in awe, murmurs of approval following her like an echo. By the time she crossed the finish line for the final time, it was clear to everyone that Sarah had outshone them all. But to Jules, something was off. It gnawed at her, a silent whisper at the back of her mind. Sarah had confided in her just days before, speaking in hushed tones about a note she had received, a warning.

"Don't win," it had said, cryptic but clear. "Lose every skiing competition." Yet, here she was, standing at the top of the leaderboard. The prize ceremony was held at the base of the mountain, the crowd gathered beneath the looming peaks, their excitement palpable. Phillip and Vanessa stepped onto the makeshift stage, their presence commanding an eerie reverence from the assembled workers and guests. Vanessa, with her immaculate hair and polished smile, spoke first, her voice smooth as silk as she congratulated everyone on their participation. But it was a rehearsed warmth, a mask that never quite reached her eyes.

"And now," Vanessa said, her voice slicing through the chilly air like a blade, "we've come to the moment we've all been waiting for. The winner of today's competition, who has demonstrated exceptional skill and sportsmanship, is... Sarah!"

The crowd erupted, but Jules couldn't shake the gnawing unease in her gut. Sarah's face lit up, but there was something unnatural about her smile. Her eyes, darting between the stage and the crowd, betrayed a flicker of something darker, fear? Or perhaps realization? As Sarah ascended the steps to claim her trophy, her legs seemed unsteady, as though each step took more effort than the last. She accepted the prize, her smile still wide but strained, and for a moment, she basked in the applause. But then, Phillip approached her. His hand rested on her shoulder, fingers curling slightly as he leaned in close, his lips moving in a whisper too soft for anyone else to hear. Whatever he said caused a visible reaction in Sarah, her smile faltered, and her eyes widened for just a second before she regained control of her expression. Jules's heart clenched as she watched the scene unfold. Vanessa joined them, her demeanour unreadable, and together, they led Sarah off the stage and through a side exit, vanishing from sight. The crowd, lost in their own revelry, seemed to barely notice, but Jules did. It sent a spike of dread straight through her. Something was wrong.

'*Why had Sarah won?*' Jules's mind raced, the pieces of the puzzle tumbling over one another. '*Hadn't Sarah said she was warned to lose? So, why had she suddenly defied that warning? Or... was she forced to win?*'

The rest of the evening passed in a blur of festivities. Music played, laughter echoed across the slopes, and yet Sarah was nowhere to be found. As the hours stretched on and the guests slowly retreated to their lodgings, Jules's unease only grew. She had asked several other staff members if they had seen Sarah, but they merely shrugged, too engrossed in the celebration to care. But Jules cared. She cared too much. The fire pit outside the main lodge crackled and spat embers into the cold night as Jules sat there, her mind spiralling into dark corners. The flames flickered across her face, casting long, dancing shadows that mocked her thoughts. She couldn't ignore it anymore, the feeling that something was deeply, terribly wrong at this resort.

'*Why had Sarah been whisked away so suddenly? Why had Phillip and Vanessa acted so strangely?*' Then there were the rumours. The whispers from the locals in the village who had warned the girls to leave, the strange warnings Sarah had shared about not making enemies with the guests. Jules's mind reeled as she recalled Sarah's story about the man who had brought her to the resort, showering her with gifts and promises. It had sounded too good to be true back then, and now it felt like the first crack in a carefully constructed agenda. *'Was this the same for all the girls here? Were they all lured by promises of a better life, only to become trapped in something far darker?'*

Jules couldn't wait any longer. She had to find out what had happened to Sarah.

The lodge was eerily quiet as Jules slipped inside. The remnants of the evening's festivities littered the communal area, with empty glasses, crumpled napkins, and a faint smell of wine lingering in the air. She moved quickly, her footsteps soft on the thick carpet, as she made her way toward the staff quarters. When she reached Sarah's room, she knocked softly at first. No answer. Louder this time. Still nothing. Her heart pounded as she pushed the door open, only to find the room empty. The bed was neatly made, the lamp by the bedside still on, casting a soft glow over the untouched room. Sarah was gone. Panic bubbled up in Jules's chest, but she forced herself to stay calm. There was one place left to check, the administrative offices. The office was dimly lit, save for a single bulb glowing above Vanessa's desk. Jules approached it cautiously, her breath shallow as she scanned the room for anything that might provide a clue. She hesitated for a moment, her hand hovering over the papers scattered on Vanessa's desk, before rifling through them.

There was nothing at first, just invoices, guest lists, and other mundane documents. But then her hand brushed against the edge of a locked drawer. Her pulse quickened as she spotted a set of keys hanging on the wall. She grabbed them, her hands trembling as she tried each one in the lock until *click*. The drawer slid open, revealing a stack of files, each one labelled with a name. Jules's breath hitched as she flipped through the folders, recognizing the names of several female staff members. Her fingers stilled on one of Sarah's. She pulled it out, her hands shaking as she opened it. Inside were notes, detailed, invasive notes about Sarah's life. Her upbringing, her arrival at the resort, and her personal details made Jules's heart sink. It was like someone had been watching Sarah, documenting her every move. Before she could read further, the sound of footsteps echoed from the hallway. Jules's heart raced as she hurried to shove the file back into the drawer, locking it just as the door swung open. Phillip stood in the doorway, his eyes cold and calculating.

"What are you doing here?" His voice was ice.

Jules forced a smile, her mind scrambling for an excuse.

"I was looking for Sarah. I was worried when she disappeared after the ceremony."

Phillip's gaze bore into her, but after a moment, he relaxed. "Sarah's fine. She needed some time to rest. You should go to bed. It's been a long day."

Jules nodded, not trusting herself to say more. She slipped past him, her mind racing with the weight of what she had uncovered. Whatever was happening at this resort, it was far more dangerous than she had imagined. She wasn't going to stop until she uncovered the truth.

CHAPTER 10: SACRIFICIAL LAMBS.

The moment Sarah opened her eyes, she was engulfed in a nightmare. Cold, metallic restraints bound her wrists and ankles, locking her in place. The room spun as she fought through the lingering fog of a drug-induced haze. Her vision blurred, flickering between flashes of gold and deep red. Slowly, her surroundings came into focus, and the sight that met her eyes plunged her into terror. Standing in a circle around her were figures, their faces obscured by featureless gold masks. They wore long, blood-red robes that flowed like dark rivers beneath the dim light. Sarah's heartbeat thundered in her chest, every beat louder than the muffled chanting that filled the room. Her mouth was taped shut, stifling her scream.

'*This can't be real*,' she thought. '*It's a nightmare. I'll wake up soon.*'

But no matter how much she struggled, the cold, unyielding metal of her shackles dug deeper into her skin. It wasn't a dream. This was really happening. Panic surged through her veins, her breath coming in shallow gasps as the cloaked figures continued their eerie chant in an unfamiliar, guttural language. The words twisted in the air like ancient incantations from a world long forgotten. Sarah's eyes darted around the room. The walls were covered in dark tapestries, symbols she couldn't recognize, their intricate patterns almost hypnotic in the dim glow of flickering candles. At the centre of the room stood an altar, where she was restrained. Fear gripped her like icy hands around her throat. She struggled harder, twisting her body to free herself, but the chains only clinked and tightened. Suddenly, her attention snapped to the front of the circle, where one of the figures stepped forward.

In his hands, he held a gleaming, jewelled knife with a serrated edge. The sight of the blade, glinting in the candlelight, made Sarah's blood run cold. She watched in horror as the man in the mask approached a small goat tethered to a stone block at the side of the altar. With a swift, practised motion, he sliced the animal's throat. Warm, crimson blood spilt onto the floor, pooling around the stone and sending thick, metallic fumes into the air. The chanting rose in volume, a discordant, primal sound that set Sarah's nerves on fire. Her stomach churned. She closed her eyes, trying to shut it all out, but the horrific scene was burned into her mind. When she opened her eyes again, she saw the cloaked figures passing around a chalice, drinking from it in turn. They raised the cup to their lips, the contents swirling inside, dark, thick, and glistening in the low light. It was blood. She recoiled in revulsion, but her body remained locked in place. A figure stepped toward her, holding the knife. Sarah tried to scream, but only a faint, muffled sound escaped her taped mouth. The figure tore her white gown, a flimsy piece of cloth barely covering her, ripping it from her chest to her ankles. The chilly air hit her exposed skin, and the reality of her vulnerability struck like a thunderbolt. She was nothing but an offering, laid bare on the altar for whatever dark purpose they had in store. The chanting continued, louder now, almost deafening. The figure holding the knife handed it to another, this one smaller, the robe a deeper shade of red. A woman, Sarah assumed, though she couldn't be sure. The woman raised the knife above her head, the tip pointed directly at Sarah's heart. Tears streamed down Sarah's face as the blade hovered in the air. Her eyes widened in pure terror as she anticipated the final, fatal blow. But before it could strike, darkness swallowed her, and the world went black.

Jules awoke in an unfamiliar bed, her heart pounding as if she had just surfaced from a drowning dream. She blinked, disoriented. The room was dim, the curtains drawn tight against the morning light. Her head throbbed with a dull ache. '*Where was she?*'

The last thing she remembered was standing by the fire pit outside the lodge, trying to escape the suffocating atmosphere of the celebration. '*How had she ended up here?*' Her hand brushed against something warm. Slowly, she turned her head and saw him, a man she didn't recognize, lying beside her, the sheets tangled around his naked body. Panic surged through her veins. She shot out of bed, scrambling to gather her clothes from the floor. The man stirred, stretching like a lazy cat before turning his head to her. He was muscular, his skin tanned and glistening in the low light, his blue eyes watching her with a lazy smile.

"Leaving so soon?" His voice was smooth, too smooth. Jules' hands shook as she pulled on her pants.

"I... I must go. I'm late for work," she stammered, her voice barely hiding the panic rising in her throat.

The man chuckled softly. "You don't remember last night, do you?"

Jules froze, a cold pit forming in her stomach. "What happened last night?" she demanded, her voice shaking with a mix of confusion and anger. He raised an eyebrow, his grin widening.

"It was a special night. The resort's secret recipe. They put something extra in the drinks for the competition. Makes things... interesting." Jules' mind raced. She didn't remember drinking much, but now it all made sense. The haze, the disorientation, waking up next to a stranger she'd never seen before. Fury coursed through her.

"What the hell did they put in those drinks?!" she hissed, her voice rising in anger. The man shrugged nonchalantly, running a hand through his tousled hair.

"It's part of the tradition. You'll get used to it."

"Like hell, I will," Jules snapped, grabbing the rest of her things and storming toward the door. Before she left, she turned back for one last look at the man. He was handsome, yes, but there was something dark behind his smile. Something predatory.

"Don't worry," he called after her, "you'll see me again."

Jules slammed the door behind her, heart racing. She didn't care who he was or what had happened last night. All she could think about was finding Sarah. She needed to know if her friend was safe. The hallways of the resort were eerily quiet as Jules made her way toward the staff quarters. Her footsteps echoed in the silence, and she couldn't shake the feeling that something was terribly wrong. As she passed by other staff members, she noticed the same haunted look in their eyes. The same walk of shame. They avoided her gaze, their heads down, their movements stiff and mechanical. It was as if the resort had drained the life out of them, leaving only empty shells behind. Jules's heart pounded in her chest.

'*What the hell was going on here?*'

She knocked on Sarah's door, her fist hitting the wood harder with each passing second of silence. No answer. She tried the handle. It turned easily in her hand, and the door creaked open. The room was empty. Completely and utterly empty. No clothes, no personal items, not even a single sheet left on the bed. It was as if Sarah had never been there. Jules's stomach twisted in knots. Her hands shook as she stepped inside, her eyes scanning the barren room for any sign of her friend. But there was nothing. The room had been wiped clean, erasing all traces of Sarah's existence. Panic surged through her.

'*What had they done to her? Where was she?*' Jules backed out of the room, her mind racing with a thousand dark possibilities. She needed answers. She needed to know what had happened to Sarah, to all the girls who had vanished without a trace. By the time Jules arrived at the morning staff meeting, her mind was a blur of fear and suspicion. She scanned the room, counting the faces. Forty-seven. There should have been fifty. Three girls were missing. Sarah was gone. Carla was gone. And another girl she didn't know well, had vanished too. Christina, a fellow staff member, sidled up beside her, her face pale, and eyes wide with fear.

"Have you seen Carla? Her room was completely empty this morning. It's like she just disappeared."

Jules swallowed hard, her mouth dry. "Sarah's gone too," she whispered back. "Her room...

There's nothing left. No trace of her."

Christina's face paled even further. "What's happening to us?"

Before Jules could answer, Phillip and Vanessa entered the room, their expressions cold and unreadable as they handed out the daily duty lists. Jules watched them closely, her stomach churning with unease. Phillip had once made her promise to act like she didn't know him in front of the other girls, but now she wondered what other secrets he was hiding. Whatever was going on in this place, it was dark. Sinister.

CHAPTER 11: BRIBERY.

The door to Phillip and Vanessa's office creaked ominously as Jules stepped through it. Her heart pounded with a mix of unease and confusion as Vanessa led her inside. The stares of the other workers, their eyes piercing her like needles, clung to her back. The tension in the air was palpable, and though Jules held her head high, she couldn't shake the feeling that something was terribly wrong. It wasn't just the mysterious disappearance of Sarah and the others, no, something far darker was going on here, at this opulent resort.

The office was dimly lit, despite the ornate chandelier hanging overhead. The room reeked of wealth and power, from the towering bookshelves that stretched to the ceiling, crammed with ancient tomes and dusty volumes, to the imposing oak desk that dominated the centre of the space. The desk gleamed under the weak light, its surface almost too perfect, like it had been scrubbed clean of secrets too dark to reveal. Jules's eyes flickered toward the burgundy leather armchairs positioned in front of the desk. They beckoned like the jaws of a trap, waiting to snap shut. Phillip stood behind the desk, his smile thin and insincere. There was something cold, predatory even, in his gaze as he gestured for Jules to sit. Vanessa hovered nearby, her sharp eyes glittering with an unreadable emotion.

"Jules, we've been watching you," Vanessa began, her voice as smooth and cold as the

Alpine wind outside. "You've impressed us. Phillip and I think you could be... useful." Jules's stomach twisted. She forced a polite smile, though her instincts screamed at her to run. She took a seat, her fingers gripping the arms of the chair as Vanessa continued. "As you know, running a resort like this requires more than just managing guests," Vanessa said, her voice low and deliberate. "It requires control. Understanding. And loyalty." The words hung in the air, thick and heavy. Jules could feel the weight of it pressing down on her. She shifted uncomfortably but didn't break eye contact with Vanessa, even as Phillip circled behind her like a vulture eyeing its next meal.

"You see," Vanessa continued, "there are... rumours. Lies spread by the local villagers meant to scare away our workers. That's what happened to Sarah and the others. They were weak. They left because they were influenced by those outside forces. But we're offering you something different. A chance to stay. To thrive."

Jules's mind raced. She knew, deep down, that this was a lie. Sarah hadn't left. She had vanished. Like a ghost, wiped clean from existence. And it wasn't just her, Carla and Jennifer were gone too. Jules had heard the whispers and seen the fear in the eyes of the other workers. This place was wrong. Yet, here she was, being offered a promotion of sorts. "What exactly do you want from me?" Jules asked, her voice steady, though her heart thundered in her chest. Phillip stepped forward; his breath hot against her neck as he spoke.

"We need someone to keep an eye on things. To make sure the staff... behave. That they remain loyal. That they don't fall prey to the...rumour mill."

Jules clenched her jaw, trying to suppress the growing dread gnawing at her insides. She could feel the trap closing around her, but she couldn't quite see the teeth yet.

"And in return?" she asked, her voice barely above a whisper.

Phillip smiled, but it didn't reach his eyes.

"In return, you get benefits. A salary increase. Access to the private library. And... Zander Hall." Jules stiffened at the mention of his name. Zander. The man she'd woken up next to after the competition night, her mind a blank slate. She had no memory of what had happened, only the unsettling sense that something had been taken from her, something she couldn't quite grasp.

"Zander has taken a liking to you," Phillip continued. "He's important to us. We need him to feel... welcome. Comfortable. And you, my dear, are key to that." Jules felt sick. The implication was clear. She was being offered up like some kind of prize to keep Zander satisfied. The thought made her skin crawl, but she kept her face neutral, unwilling to let them see the revulsion bubbling inside her. Vanessa leaned forward, her smile sharp and cruel.

"It's a small price to pay, don't you think? For everything we're offering you."

Jules didn't answer. Her mind raced, trying to piece together the twisted puzzle in front of her. '*What was this place? What had happened to Sarah? And why were Phillip and Vanessa so eager to keep Zander happy? There was something else at play here, something far darker than she had ever imagined.*'

"Think it over," Vanessa said, rising to her feet. "But don't take too long. Time is... fleeting." Jules stood on shaky legs, her head spinning as she made her way out of the office. As soon as the door clicked shut behind her, she exhaled sharply, her body trembling with a mix of fear and anger. She felt like she had just been in the presence of something truly malevolent, something ancient and evil that had wrapped itself in the guise of wealth and luxury. She needed to get to the bottom of this. She needed to find out what had really happened to Sarah. But first, she had to survive the night with Zander. The following days passed in a blur. Jules found herself caught between the endless tasks assigned to her and the creeping sense of dread that permeated every corner of the resort. She kept her distance from Phillip and Vanessa, but their presence loomed over her like a dark shadow, always watching, always waiting. The new girls, Tara, Lola, and Tracey, arrived at the resort with wide-eyed excitement, oblivious to the darkness, the lies, and the hidden agendas. Jules watched them with a mix of pity and dread, knowing that their innocence would soon be shattered.

They didn't know what they were walking into. None of them did. Jules tried to focus on her work, but her mind kept drifting back to the missing girls. She had scoured every inch of the resort and asked subtle questions, but no one knew anything. It was as if Sarah, Carla, and Jennifer had never existed. Their rooms were empty, their belongings gone, wiped clean like they had been erased from reality. One evening, as Jules was cleaning up after the bar had closed, she felt a presence behind her. She turned to find Zander standing in the doorway, his eyes gleaming with a predatory hunger.

"Jules," he said, his voice smooth and unsettling. "I've been looking for you."

Jules swallowed hard, her heart pounding in her chest. She didn't trust Zander. There was something off about him, something dangerous. But she couldn't afford to anger him, not when Phillip and Vanessa were so eager to keep him happy.

"I've been... busy," she replied, forcing a smile.

Zander stepped closer, his gaze never leaving hers. "I'm sure you have. But I've missed our time together. I was hoping we could... reconnect. Before the next competition."

Jules's stomach churned. She knew what he wanted. She could see it in his eyes, the way he looked at her like she was something to be consumed. But she wasn't going to let him win.

'Not this time.'

"I'm sorry, Zander," she said, her voice firm. "But I'm not interested."

For a moment, Zander's smile faltered, and a flicker of anger crossed his face. But then it was gone, replaced by the same cold, calculating gaze.

"That's a shame," he said softly. "I thought we could have... fun."

Jules took a step back, her heart racing. She needed to get out of here, away from him, away from this place. But as she turned to leave, Zander grabbed her wrist, his grip tight and unyielding. "You don't get to say no," he whispered, his breath hot against her skin. "Not here." Jules yanked her arm free, her eyes blazing with anger.

"Let go of me. I was told to keep you company on competition nights, only."

Zander smiled a cruel, twisted smile. "You'll regret this, Jules. Phillip and Vanessa won't be happy."

CHAPTER 12: PREY.

When the morning sun clawed its way over the jagged peaks on the day of the tournament, the air was thick with an uneasy tension. Excitement simmered beneath the surface, but it felt tarnished like something dark lurked just out of sight. Jules, surrounded by the new recruits, tried to hide her growing anxiety as she briefed them on their tasks for the day. Her voice was steady, but her mind was a tempest. The competition was meant to be a day of celebration, a grand event where the elite mingled with the common folk. They would race down the slopes together, the rich and powerful side by side with the staff, but everyone knew it wasn't that simple. The guests wore their smiles like masks, hiding something far more sinister beneath. A small voice in the back of Jules' mind kept whispering warnings, the kind you couldn't shake no matter how hard you tried. Something was wrong. Something terrible was going to happen. Her skin prickled with a sense of impending doom as she watched the skiers, the wealthy guests laughing as they glided down the snow-covered mountains. There was a predatory gleam in their eyes, an air of malevolence as they eyed the workers who dared to outshine them on the slopes. It was as if they were on a hunt, and the workers were their prey. Jules shuddered. Their disdain was palpable, their resentment growing with every worker who skied better or faster than them.

The hatred in their eyes sent a chill through her soul. This wasn't just a competition. The thrill of the race was a façade, a distraction from the darker game being played behind the scenes. Tracey, one of the newest members of the team, was oblivious to the undercurrents of danger. As she laced up her ski boots, her stomach churned with anticipation. She had heard the whispers about the tournament, the unspoken rivalry between the guests and the staff, but she was determined to prove herself. She would show these entitled aristocrats that she was just as good as any of them. She had been one of them once, after all. Before her life had crumbled into ash, Tracey had lived in a world of wealth and privilege.

She had grown up in the lap of luxury, skiing every winter with her parents in the finest resorts, the chilly air biting at her cheeks as she raced down the slopes. But that life had vanished in an instant, ripped away from her the day her parent's helicopter crashed into the side of a mountain, leaving her orphaned and alone. Her inheritance should have secured her future, but it was stolen from her by Aunt Miranda, a woman who saw Tracey as nothing more than a ticket to her dead sister's fortune. The life of opulence Tracey had known was replaced by a prison of cruelty. Locked in a damp, dark basement, she had become little more than a ghost, forgotten, and discarded. Meals were sparse, her company nothing more than the skittering of a door mouse in the shadows. But Tracey had not allowed herself to break. Every night, she dreamed of escape, of reclaiming her freedom and the life she had lost. And one night, she did. She slipped away into the night, leaving Aunt Miranda and the hell she had endured behind. But freedom came with a price. Alone, destitute, and with no one to turn to, she wandered the streets, clinging to the memory of her parents and the warmth they had once provided. That's when she met Markus. He had saved her from that bleak existence, offering her a place in his world, a world that was still cruel, but at least she had a chance to fight back. And now, here she was, standing among these pampered, shallow people, the same kind who had destroyed her life.

The guests, draped in their designer ski gear, mingled with the workers, their laughter echoing across the slopes. But behind their smiles, Tracey could see the disdain, the way they looked down their noses at the staff, daring them to step out of line. This race wasn't just for fun. It was about power. Dominance. Tracey could feel it in the air, thick as the cold mountain fog. She had to beat them. They were all like her Aunt Miranda, arrogant, entitled, thinking they could control everything and everyone. But not her. Not anymore. She would win this race, no matter what. It wasn't just about skiing. It was about reclaiming her pride, her dignity. It was about showing them that they couldn't break her. The competitors lined up at the starting gate, their breath fogging in the chilly air. Tracey's heart hammered in her chest, as she stood her ground, locking eyes with the guests who smirked at her with that same smug confidence. Let them underestimate her. She'd show them.

The whistle blew, and she launched herself down the slope. The wind howled in her ears as she raced forward, her skis cutting through the snow with deadly precision. Around her, the other competitors pushed themselves to the limit, but Tracey was relentless. She weaved through the trees, her muscles burning, her lungs screaming for air, but she didn't falter. She couldn't. At the finish line, she crossed first, her heart leaping with triumph as she glanced back at the others. Their faces were twisted with rage, and their arrogance shattered.

Tracey had done it. She had beaten them at their own game. But as she stood there, victorious, a shadow passed over her victory. The air was thick with a sense of foreboding, she knew this was far from over. As the winners were called to the podium to receive their trophies, Tracey basked in the applause of her colleagues, but there was something hollow about it. She could feel their eyes on her, the guests watching her with a kind of hungry hatred. This wasn't about a trophy.

This was about control, and they had just lost a battle they hadn't expected to lose. Tracey's victory had painted a target on her back. The ceremony ended, and Tracey, along with the other winners, were quietly led away from the celebration. The night swallowed them whole, and she disappeared, never to be seen again. Jules had intended to follow them, her curiosity gnawing at her, but before she could move, a hand gripped her wrist, sending a jolt of icy electricity through her body. She spun around, face to face with Zander, his smile sharp and predatory.

"I think you're mine tonight," he whispered, his voice a low growl. Jules's face flushed. She had been trying to avoid him all evening. He was persistent, and she knew there was no escaping him now. Reluctantly, she nodded, though her mind screamed at her to run. Zander led her away from the crowd, deeper into the night.

"Where are we going?" she asked, her voice barely above a whisper, her nerves fraying with each step.

"You'll see," he replied, his grin widening.

The night had taken a turn, a sharp descent into something much darker than Jules had expected. The festivities had started innocently enough, but now, as Zander led her further from the cheerful chaos of the after-party, a dense fog of unease clouded her thoughts. Her heart thudded painfully in her chest, its erratic rhythm betraying the terror she was desperately trying to suppress. Zander's cryptic words echoed in her mind.

"You'll see." He did not explain, only a devious smile that sent a shiver racing down her spine. With every step they took away from the bright lights and the jubilant laughter, Jules felt herself falling deeper into some unseen pit, a world governed by rules she didn't understand and barely dared to question.

'Why was he taking her away from the others? Where was he leading her?' The restaurant he brought her to was popular, but tonight it felt different, darker. The owner greeted them with too much warmth, as if they were guests of honour in a macabre event they had yet to fully comprehend. Jules's skin prickled with discomfort as they were guided to a secluded corner, far from the other patrons' prying eyes. A pit formed in her stomach as she settled into her chair, her movements hesitant, her mind racing. Zander ordered their food with a confidence that only heightened her unease. His composure was unsettling, a mask

she couldn't decipher. The flickering candlelight threw shadows across his face, giving him a sinister air that was impossible to ignore.

"Why am I here?" she demanded, her voice barely masking the sharp edge of anger that laced it. Her patience was wearing thin, and she couldn't take the mystery any longer.

"Why not?" Zander's reply was nonchalant, dismissive, as though her fear was an amusement, a curiosity to him. Her eyes narrowed, her pulse quickening.

"What are you trying to accomplish? There are plenty of other girls you could have chosen."

Her words hung in the air, a blend of accusation and confusion.

His smile widened, a glint of something dark flickering behind his eyes.

"Rest assured, you are safe with me," he said with a mocking sincerity. "I promise there is no ulterior motive, no special drink to worry about."

Jules leaned forward, her voice dropping to a near hiss.

"If you think I'm going to sleep with you again, you're in for a rude awakening."

Zander ran a hand through his hair, the first sign of frustration breaking through his polished demeanour.

"Jules, we didn't have sex," he said, his voice clipped. "I prefer my women to be fully compos mentis. When I make love to a woman, I expect her to reciprocate." His smile was cold and predatory, it left her stunned, reeling from his words.

"But... you told me I was amazing," she muttered, confusion swirling in her thoughts.

"Can we not dwell on this?" Zander interrupted, his tone shifting back to something softer, more insidious. "I brought you here because I want to know you, the real you. My intentions are pure, I assure you."

Jules teetered on the edge of disbelief, her heart still pounding with apprehension. A part of her wanted to bolt, to escape his gaze, but another part of her, the part that craved understanding in this chaotic, twisted world, stayed.

"Well, you didn't take advantage of me last time, so I guess I owe you one," she said, her voice tinged with bitter humour as she took a sip of wine, her mind whirling. A sense of dread had anchored itself in her chest, yet she couldn't tear herself away from the unfolding scene. Zander raised his glass, his smile curling in a way that suggested more than he was willing to say out loud.

"A toast then. To strangers meeting for the first time."

His charm was intoxicating, but the sinister undertones never faded. They talked for what felt like hours, their conversation drifting through various topics. Jules found herself begrudgingly drawn in, the layers of Zander's personality revealing themselves bit by bit. But the unease never left. It gnawed at her from the inside, a constant reminder of how wrong everything felt. As the night wore on and the plates were cleared, Zander leaned back in his chair and fixed her with a look that sent another wave of anxiety crashing over her.

"You'll have to stay in my room again tonight," he said, his voice casual, as though it were the most normal thing in the world. Jules's blood ran cold. She couldn't hide the suspicion that darkened her expression.

"Why?" she asked, her voice barely above a whisper, as if she was afraid of the answer.

"It's for your own protection," Zander replied, his tone betraying no emotion, only a strange undercurrent of concern. "You're vulnerable at the party. If you're alone, someone might try to take advantage of you."

Jules stared at him, her mind a tangled mess of confusion and disbelief. *'Why was he suddenly so concerned for her well-being? This didn't feel right. None of this did.'*

"Why are you looking out for me?" she pressed, unwilling to let the conversation die.

Zander's gaze softened, his voice dropping into something close to sincerity.

"Because, from the moment I saw you, I felt this overwhelming urge to protect you. You're...

different from anyone I've ever met."

Her mind screamed at her not to believe him, that this was all part of some elaborate game. But a twisted part of her, the part that had been broken and rebuilt by years of manipulation, wanted to trust him. Against her better judgment, she agreed. As they made their way back to his room, Jules couldn't shake the sensation of something watching her, something lurking just beyond her field of vision. The mountain resort, once so alluring and glamorous, now felt suffocating. The air itself seemed thick with unseen threats, and every shadow seemed to shift with sinister intent. When they arrived, Zander gestured toward the bed with a sweeping motion.

"You take the bed, I'll take the couch," he said, his voice strangely tender. Jules hesitated at the door, her hand gripping the frame as she warred with herself.

'*Could she really trust him?*' She barely knew him, and this sudden shift in his demeanour only amplified her suspicions. But her body ached with exhaustion, and her mind was clouded with conflicting emotions. As she slipped into the bed, she felt the weight of dread pressing down on her. Every inch of her skin tingled with unease, her senses screaming that something was off. The luxurious sheets felt like a cage, wrapping her in a false sense of security. '*He doesn't want you. No one will ever want you,*' the intrusive voice in her mind whispered, taunting her, cutting through her defences. She squeezed her eyes shut, trying to block out the voice, but it was relentless. Sleep evaded her. For an hour, she tossed and turned, her mind too busy, too alert, to succumb to the comfort of unconsciousness. Every creak of the floorboards, every sigh of the wind outside the window, felt like a threat.

Finally, Zander's voice cut through the oppressive silence.

"Can't sleep?" he asked, his voice filled with an eerie calm.

Jules turned to face him, her nerves on edge. "No," she admitted quietly. "My mind... it's preoccupied. Competition days are always like this. It feels like we're on display like we are trophies for the guests to admire."

Zander shifted in his seat, his gaze fixated on her with an intensity that made her skin prickle with electricity.

"Why do you feel like that?" he asked, his voice probing, searching for something deeper. Jules hesitated, then sighed.

"It's not just me. All the girls feel it. We're just... animals in a zoo to them. They watch us, judge us as if we're nothing more than entertainment." Her voice quivered with the weight of her confession. "I often wonder if that's why Sarah left. She couldn't take it anymore."

Zander's expression darkened, his eyes flashing with something she couldn't quite place.

"Jules, you're letting your imagination get the better of you," he said, his voice low and

dangerous. "These people, they're different. They live by their own rules. They're powerful and wealthy. Who knows what they've done to get there? My advice? Keep your head down, follow the rules, and don't make waves. You don't want to make enemies of people like them." Jules shivered at the cold truth of his words. She had always known, deep down, that the world she was entangled in was far more sinister than it appeared on the surface. But hearing it spoken aloud, so bluntly, made it even more real. Zander stretched and yawned, breaking the tension that had settled between them.

"Now," he said, "let's get some sleep. You'll need your strength for what comes next." Jules stared up at the ceiling, her mind churning with unanswered questions.

'*What was this place? What had she gotten herself into?*'

CHAPTER 13: GONE GIRLS.

As the weight of the situation settled over Zander, a subtle but unmistakable shift darkened his expression. He sat in the chair across the room, his body rigid, his eyes flickering in the dim light like a predator lurking in the shadows. He knew far too much about the resort, its high-profile clientele, its twisted desires, and the grim consequences that befell anyone who dared to interfere. He understood the game that was being played, but there was no room for weakness. Not yet. He couldn't let Jules in on the truth. Not until he knew for certain where her loyalties lay. There was too much at risk. So, instead of speaking, he leaned back into the chair and feigned sleep, listening to the tense silence of the room. Jules was restless, her mind racing as she lay in bed, tossing and turning in the oppressive quiet. She berated herself internally, realizing she had let too much slip in their conversation. She had revealed her suspicions and cracked open a door that was meant to remain closed.

'Had she put herself in danger by voicing her thoughts aloud?'

She glanced toward Zander, his figure unmoving in the chair, and wondered if he could be trusted. *'Could he be involved in whatever dark secrets the resort held?'*

Her heart hammered in her chest as she silently prayed for his steady breathing to indicate he had fallen into a deep sleep. But despite her best efforts to stay alert, exhaustion eventually overtook her, and she drifted off into a fitful slumber. Morning came like a cold slap, the unsettling tension still hanging thick in the air. Jules stirred; her mind clouded with anxiety as memories from the night before flooded back.

Zander was already gone from the chair, leaving only the lingering unease that seemed to cling to the walls like a shadow.

'*Had she revealed too much? Could Zander be part of whatever agenda lay hidden at the resort?*' Jules retreated to her quarters, desperate to gather her thoughts. She needed time to think, to figure out her next move, but instead found herself drawn to the comfort of a book. She had always used reading as an escape, and today was no different. She immersed herself in *Michelle Remembers*, allowing the provocative narrative to momentarily pull her away from the gnawing dread that coiled within her. But even the pages of the book couldn't keep the darkness at bay for long. Her thoughts were haunted by the conversation with Zander, his words laced with vague insinuations. She couldn't shake the feeling that danger was closing in around her, suffocating her. The hot shower that followed offered no reprieve. As the water cascaded down her body, Jules's mind spiralled into a chaotic tangle of fears and suspicions. The voice, dark and taunting, slithered back into her consciousness, whispering insidiously in her ear.

'*You couldn't even stay awake last night. Those girls are dead because of you. You were supposed to help them, and you failed.*'

She clenched her jaw, trying to block out the words. But no matter how hard she fought, the thoughts clung to her like a persistent nightmare.

'*What if they're right? What if the girls really are dead?*'

Her mind replayed the previous night's conversation, Zander's cryptic nods, and his careful, measured responses. He hadn't said much, but what little he had shared now felt loaded with ominous meaning. Panic surged through her veins. '*Am I next?*' she wondered. '*Did I put myself in danger by saying too much?*'

The silence that followed was deafening, broken only by the soft creaking of the floorboards and the faint rustle of leaves outside her window. Every noise amplified the dread that gnawed at her, filling her imagination with grim possibilities.

'*I'm spiralling,*' she thought, trying to calm herself. '*I need to stop thinking like this.*' She stepped out of the shower and dressed quickly, the dread still clinging to her like a second skin. The workday was no easier. Standing among her colleagues, Jules couldn't shake the nagging feeling that twisted in her gut. A headcount revealed the chilling truth, five staff members were missing. Tracey, the newest girl who had triumphed in the previous night's ski competition, was one of them. The hollow absence of these young women gnawed at her. '*Where were they? Where was Tracey?*'

Jules scanned the faces of her coworkers, searching for some sign of shared concern. The atmosphere was thick with tension, but no one spoke about the missing girls. Tara and Lola exchanged nervous glances, fidgeting anxiously, their discomfort palpable. It was clear they had attended the notorious afterparty the night before, likely succumbing to its potent drinks and waking up in an unfamiliar place with one of the resort's elite guests. Christina, however, seemed more shaken than the others. Her eyes were puffy as if she had been crying, and when her gaze locked with Jules's, a wave of unspoken fear passed between them. Jules's stomach twisted as her suspicions deepened.

'*What had happened during the afterparty?*
What horrors were hiding behind the resort's luxurious facade?'

The days dragged on, and the missing girls remained unaccounted for. More rumours circulated among the staff, whispering tales of disappearances and strange events that no one dared to speak of openly. Each new girl that arrived seemed to carry with her an unshakable sense of dread as if they had already resigned themselves to the inevitable. Zander remained a puzzle in Jules's mind. He was kind, too kind perhaps. He always seemed to be looking out for her, keeping her away from the wild afterparties, but his attentiveness only made her more suspicious. '*Was he truly trying to protect her, or was he hiding something?*'

The way he skirted around the truth left her frustrated, her trust in him hanging by a thread. One morning, Jules approached a small group of employees who huddled in the hallway, their faces drawn with tension. She lowered her voice, barely audible over the faint hum of the building's heating system.

"What's going on?" Christina, standing off to the side, flinched visibly at the question. Her face was still streaked with the remnants of tears, twisted into a mask of fear. After a moment's hesitation, she stepped forward, her hands trembling as she held out a crumpled piece of paper. Jules took the note, her heart pounding in her chest as she unfolded it. The handwriting was rushed, and frantic, the words hastily scrawled across the page:

If you're reading this, I'm already dead, I never got the chance to go home

Her breath caught in her throat. She looked up at Christina, her voice barely a whisper.

"How do you know Tracey wrote this?"

Christina's eyes were wide with fear, her voice shaking as she replied,

"I know her handwriting. We worked together in the restaurant. We... we were seeing each other." She hesitated, her voice breaking slightly. "We would leave notes for each other, hidden under the mattresses so no one would find them. That's where I found this."

Jules felt the ground shift beneath her. The note was real. Tracey had written it. And if the message was true, Tracey wasn't missing, she was dead.

An icy chill crawled down her spine as she folded the note, her thoughts racing.

'*What was happening here?*' The disappearances weren't just rumours. Girls were vanishing, and the resort was covering it up. She had to do something. She had to find out the truth, even if it meant putting herself in danger.

'*But who could she trust? Zander? Vanessa and Phillip, the resort's overseers, who had a vested interest in keeping an eye on the staff?*' Jules had no allies here, only enemies. That Saturday, she made her decision. She would stay awake, watching from the shadows as the night unfolded. She had to find out where the girls were being taken. The risk was enormous, but she couldn't live with herself if she did nothing. These girls, Tracey, and her other friends, deserved justice. Jules was determined to uncover the truth, no matter the cost. As night fell, the dread settled in her chest like a lead weight. The voice returned, whispering once more, its dark tone wrapping around her thoughts like a noose.

CHAPTER 14: BLINDLY FALLING

"Listen to me. I don't know what's really happening here, but I'm desperate to get my hands on that letter," Jules's voice was a rasped whisper, betraying her growing paranoia. The moonlight outside the cabin flickered through the window like a slivered blade, casting eerie shadows on the walls. She eyed Christina, her gaze wild, almost frantic. "Do you still have it? It's evidence." Christina's trembling hand reached into her jacket pocket, the crumpled paper barely visible in the dim light. She hesitated before passing it to Jules, her eyes wide with fear.

"You need to be careful. Whatever's going on, it's bigger than we thought." Her voice cracked, barely audible, as if she feared the very walls could hear her. Jules took the letter with a quick, sharp motion. She wasn't sure if it was fear or adrenaline coursing through her veins. She could feel the weight of it, the terror that clung to this place, to this cursed ski resort. Something ancient, something evil, lurked beneath the pristine snow. It wasn't just about the skiing competition anymore. It wasn't even about winning. It was about the missing girls, the ones who vanished without a trace once the awards were handed out, their names never mentioned again.

"I'll stay awake this Saturday. I'll stay up all night if I have to," Jules said, her voice now steadier, her resolve hardening. "I need to find out what's happening to them. Just, promise me, Christina. You won't try to win. Make sure your skiing is below average. Whatever you do, *don't win*."

Christina nodded solemnly, her face pale, her eyes dull with fear. "I promise."

The letter felt heavy in Jules's hand as she folded it and stuffed it into her jacket. She glanced at Christina one last time, her eyes filled with unspoken warnings, and then turned, disappearing into the night, her heart pounding with an unfamiliar intensity. That Saturday, the air was crisp, biting at Jules's exposed skin as she arrived at the competition. The festive atmosphere at the resort seemed almost mocking, the cheerful banners and bright lights standing in stark contrast to the dread that coiled deep within her. She couldn't shake the feeling that something terrible was about to happen. Zander was there, of course.

He was always there, lurking like a shadow on the edge of her vision. Jules had only ever seen him on competition days, a tall, imposing figure in his black coat, his eyes sharp and unreadable. He always was watching her, and she had begun to wonder if he was more than just a bystander. Maybe he was the key to it all, the orchestrator behind the disappearances. She couldn't shake the feeling that Zander knew more than he was letting on. But what was his role in all of this? Was he protecting something, or was he the one pulling the strings? The slopes loomed ahead, cold, and treacherous, their beauty hiding a dark secret. Jules forced herself to focus, but the voice in her head wouldn't stop.

'*Don't win. Winning is dangerous. But what if I have to win? What if winning is the only way to know what happens next?*'

She skied down the icy slope, her movements fluid but mechanical. Her mind was a storm, the questions swirling around in a frenzy. And then, as she neared the final bend, it happened.

The sun hit her eyes, no, not the sun. Something else. A blinding flash of light reflected off the snow, burning into her retinas like a knife. She stumbled, her balance faltering as the world around her spun in disorienting spirals. Her skis slid out from under her, and she tumbled, crashing hard into the snow, the cold seeping into her bones. When she looked up, dazed, and confused, she saw him. Zander. He stood at the edge of the crowd, his eyes locked on hers, a strange look of satisfaction on his face. In his hand, a small mirror gleamed, catching the light just so, sending it right into her path. He had done this. He had blinded her on purpose. Jules's fury ignited, but she held it in, her mind racing. He didn't want her to win. He couldn't let her get that far. But why? As the medics rushed toward her, fussing over her injuries, Jules tried to wave them off. Phillip, one of the resort managers, insisted she needed medical attention. But she didn't care. All she could think about was Zander's gaze, piercing, intense, full of something that sent a chill down her spine.

'*He was toying with her, but why? What was his endgame?*'

After the doctors cleared her, Jules stormed toward Zander, her eyes burning with fury. "What the hell are you playing at?" she spat, her voice low and venomous. She wanted to tear into him, to make him pay for what he had done. But Zander merely looked at her, his face unreadable.

"I recommend you take the night off," he said, his voice cool and detached. "You've had a nasty fall. I'll talk to Phillip. We'll get you some rest." With that, he turned on his heel and walked away, disappearing into the crowd before she could even process his words. She stood there, seething, her fists clenched at her sides. He had caused the accident. He had deliberately sabotaged her, and now he was acting like he was doing her a favour. When she returned to her room, still fuming, she found an unexpected surprise. A brand-new pair of skis sat by the door, elegantly tied with a pink silk bow. Jules stared at them, her anger boiling over. On the ground beside them, a note lay in neat careful handwriting.

"*I'm glad to see you bounce well. You left me no choice. I hope this small offering makes up for my earlier behaviour. With all my adoration, Z.*"

Jules's hands trembled as she read the words. She wanted to scream, to tear the skis apart, to throw them out the window.

'*How dare he?*'

How dare he play with her like this, as if her life was just a game? But she couldn't afford to replace the skis. She was trapped, forced to accept his twisted gift.

'*What does he want from me? Why is he doing this?*'

The questions screamed in her mind, but there were no answers. Only the cold, sickening realization that Zander had her right where he wanted her. The skis stood like a grotesque monument to her helplessness, their polished surface reflecting the flickering light of the lamp. Jules felt a knot form in her stomach.

'*What kind of message was this? A gift? A threat? Or something worse, something she couldn't yet comprehend?*'

She collapsed onto her bed, her fists pounding into the pillow, her screams muffled by the fabric. Rage consumed her, mixed with frustration and fear. Zander was playing with her, and she had no idea how to stop him. Through the haze of her anger, a dark thought crept into her mind. Maybe she couldn't stop him. Maybe she was too late. But one thing was certain, she wasn't going to let him take any more girls. Not while she still had a breath in her body. As the night stretched on, Jules lay there, staring at the ceiling, the sinister presence of the skis looming in the corner of her vision. The resort was not what it seemed. The slopes were soaked in blood, and the snow carried whispers of the missing. But Jules wouldn't be next. She would uncover the truth, no matter what it took. Even if it meant going into the heart of the darkness, alone. Even if it meant confronting Zander head-on. She would stop him. Because if she didn't, the resort would claim her, just like it had claimed the others.

CHAPTER 15: SATANIC PANIC

The night clung to Jules like a second skin, wrapping her in its sinister embrace. Alone in her dimly lit room, she couldn't shake the chilling unease that gnawed at her. The cold blue glow of her laptop illuminated her pale face as she scoured through every available source of information. Her fingers flew over the keys, eyes darting from one suspicious article to the next, every detail adding to the horrific puzzle she was piecing together. She could feel the dread twisting tighter around her chest with each passing minute. Zander, that name tasted bitter on her tongue. He was everywhere, always in the background, always watching.

The more she researched, the deeper she fell into a vortex of terror, convinced that this was bigger, darker, and more terrifying than anything she had ever imagined. There was no doubt in her mind now, that Zander was orchestrating something unspeakable. Something that made girls disappear without a trace. The lodge had gone quiet. The raucous after-party had fizzled into the darkness, leaving the resort in eerie silence.

'*Now*!! *It had to be now.*'

The air was thick with the weight of unspoken horrors, and Jules's heart pounded against her ribs as if trying to escape the inevitable. She grabbed her coat, her throat tight with tension, and slipped out of her room, her body moving through the hallway like a shadow. No one could know she was out. The basement. That forbidden place. No one went there. No one was allowed to. Jules's thoughts raced as she descended the stone stairs, the cold walls whispering secrets from long ago. Each step echoed in the silence, louder in her mind than they really were, adding to the panic that clawed at her insides. Flickering torchlights cast eerie, distorted shadows along the walls, and Jules felt as though she was being swallowed by the darkness itself. The air grew colder, thick with dread. Her breath turned shallow as the faint sound of chanting drifted up the staircase like an ancient curse. The closer she got, the more she could hear them, those voices. They weren't human. They couldn't be.

Finally, she reached the bottom, her hand trembling as she grasped the door handle. She pushed it open just enough to peek inside. What she saw made her blood run cold. The dimly lit room was filled with hooded figures, their faces hidden behind grotesque gold masks, their robes blood-red and flowing like liquid around their feet. They stood in a tight circle, chanting in a language Jules didn't understand, their voices rising and falling in a haunting melody that filled the air with suffocating terror. In the centre of the room was an altar, an ancient, stone monstrosity. A woman lay naked atop it, her face obscured by an ornate mask, her body writhing in some obscene ritual. Jules felt her stomach churn, bile rising in her throat. The woman was touching herself, and the figures around her watched in ritualistic reverence, their chants growing louder with each passing moment.

Above the altar, suspended upside-down, was a young girl. One of the workers from the lodge. Jules recognized her, and her heart seized in horror. The girl's face was slack, her eyes glazed over, as though she had already left her body. Then, from the shadows, a figure stepped forward, handing the masked woman a jewelled dagger. Jules's mind screamed at her to move, to run, but she was frozen, locked in place by the macabre spectacle unfolding before her. The woman on the altar lifted the dagger high, and with one swift motion, she sliced through the throat of the hanging girl. Blood poured from the wound, cascading over the stone altar, and splashing onto the naked woman's body. The woman arched her back, moaning in ecstasy as the crimson fluid bathed her skin. She smeared it across her body, her movements frenzied, as if the blood was feeding her, giving her life. The chanting reached a fever pitch, a chaotic, unholy symphony that reverberated through Jules's bones. Jules clamped a hand over her mouth, suppressing the scream that threatened to tear from her throat. She couldn't believe what she was seeing.

This was no dream, no hallucination, this was real. All of it. Suddenly, a hand clamped down on her shoulder, pulling her back into the darkness. She didn't even have time to scream before everything went black. When she awoke, daylight was breaking through the blinds in her room. Her entire body ached as though she had been hit by a truck. For a moment, she thought maybe it had all been a nightmare, a twisted figment of her imagination. But then she touched her neck and felt it. The puncture wound. Her breath caught in her throat, fingers trembling as she traced the small, needle-like mark just beneath her skin.

'*They drugged me.*'

Panic surged through her. She scrambled out of bed, her limbs weak, her head spinning with disorientation. She stumbled to the mirror and pulled up her shirt, revealing a tapestry of purple bruises across her torso. Her body bore the marks of the fall on the slopes, but there was something else. Something darker. The memories of the basement flooded back. The chanting. The blood. The girl hanging upside down, her throat slit, the way her life had been snuffed out like a candle. Jules staggered back, bile rising again in her throat. She had seen too much. And Zander. Zander had to be behind this. It was the only explanation. He had been orchestrating it all from the shadows, pulling strings, setting traps. She couldn't prove it, not yet, but the pieces were falling into place. A knock at the door startled her, and she tensed, every muscle in her body on high alert. Phillip stepped in, his face etched with concern.

"You've been through a lot. You should take some time off," he said gently, but his words barely registered. Her mind was spinning, and all she could see was the blood. The girl. The altar. Phillip left, leaving Jules alone in the suffocating silence of her room. She sank onto the bed, her hands gripping the covers so tightly that her knuckles turned white. Her mind was a storm of fear and fury, her heart pounding in her chest like a war drum. The voice inside her head that had once been her tormentor was now something else. It whispered to her, telling her what she needed to hear.

'They're watching you. They'll come for you.'

But it also told her something else, something she didn't want to believe.

'You're strong enough to fight back.'

She closed her eyes, fighting the rising tide of nausea that came with the memory of the night before. She had to stop this. She had to bring them down. No one else could. If she didn't act, more girls would vanish, their lives extinguished like the one she had seen sacrificed in that basement. She knew she was in over her head, but it didn't matter. The voice urged her forward, promising that together, they could dismantle this web of horror and lies.

With renewed determination, Jules rose from the bed, her eyes burning with the intensity of someone who had nothing left to lose. She wouldn't rest. She wouldn't stop until every last one of them was brought to justice. Zander, Phillip, and whoever else was involved, they would all pay. As she stood before the mirror one last time, she whispered to her reflection,

"Together, we will stop them."

Her reflection seemed to nod in agreement.

CHAPTER 16: DOUBLE AGENT

The halls of the resort seemed to pulse with an unbearable sense of doom as Jules walked them, each step echoing against the cold walls, pulling her further into the heart of a nightmare she could no longer escape. The image of the girl from that night, her body suspended, then gutted in front of a masked congregation, had rooted itself deep in Jules's mind, a grotesque spectre that haunted her every thought. The memory of the blood, the knife, the chanting... it was more than she could handle, and yet she couldn't erase it. That night had been real. She was sure of it now. There had been a sacrifice. A human sacrifice.

Jules shuddered, goosebumps prickling her skin as she grappled with the horror of what she'd witnessed. The twisted reality she had stumbled upon was far more dangerous than she'd ever imagined. She needed to talk to someone. She needed Christina. Someone she could trust, someone who would believe her. Two heads, she told herself, were better than one.

'*Three*,' the voice inside her head sneered. '*Don't forget about me.*'

The voice had been growing louder, more persistent since that night. It had shifted from its usual taunting to something almost... guiding. But Jules wasn't ready to trust it, not fully.

Yet every time she found herself alone, it was there, lurking at the edges of her thoughts, whispering insidious truths. As she approached Christina's door, her steps slowed, doubt creeping in.

'*What would she even say? How could she explain something so unbelievable?*'

Even if Christina trusted her, would she be able to handle the gravity of it all? What if talking to her made things worse, and exposed her to more danger? Jules hesitated, her hand hovering just inches from knocking. The note from Tracey burned a hole in her pocket, its presence a constant reminder that time was slipping away. She hadn't given it to Phillip or Vanessa yet, and if one of the other girls mentioned it before she did...

She swallowed hard, forcing herself to stay calm. But her thoughts spiralled, and her heart pounded against her chest. Every option seemed laced with peril. Before she could knock, a sound drew her attention. The door next to Christina's creaked open, and Taylor, one of the newer girls, stood there. Her eyes were wide, filled with something that made Jules's stomach tighten, a mixture of fear and urgency.

"She's gone," Taylor whispered, gesturing for Jules to step inside. Her voice was barely audible, but its weight sent Jules's heart plummeting.

"Gone?" Jules repeated, stepping into the dimly lit room. She felt a cold sweat forming at the nape of her neck. "What do you mean gone?"

Taylor shut the door softly behind her before turning to face Jules. Her face was pale, her hands trembling slightly.

"Christina... and five other girls. They all disappeared last night." Jules froze, her mind struggling to process the words.

"Gone? How is that possible? Where did they go?"

Taylor shook her head, her lips trembling as she spoke.

"I don't know. They won their events last night, got their awards, and then... they were just gone. No goodbyes, no explanations. Just... gone." She wiped a tear from her cheek, her voice cracking. "I don't think they went home, Jules. Something's wrong. Christina loved it here."

Jules felt a wave of nausea wash over her. The night's horrors, the altar, the blood, the chanting, flooded back into her mind.

'Could it be connected? Of course, it was. How could it not be?'

The winners. The girls who had been praised and paraded around... they were the ones who vanished. The voice in her head piped up again, cold and mocking.

'They didn't 'disappear.' They were taken. Sacrificed.'

Jules's stomach twisted, bile rising in her throat. No. She refused to believe it. But deep down, she knew it was true. Taylor's voice interrupted her thoughts, thick with desperation. "Christina was my friend, Jules. She wouldn't just leave. Something's happened to her. Something... bad." Jules nodded slowly, feeling a lump form in her throat.

"We have to do something," she whispered, her voice trembling. "I can't just stand by and watch more girls disappear. We owe it to Christina."

Taylor looked at her with wide, frightened eyes.

"What can we do? We're just... we're just two girls in a place we don't understand. We don't know who to trust."

Jules's jaw tightened.

"I don't care. We need to find out what's going on. We need to figure out who's behind this." She took a deep breath, steadying herself. "I need you to help me, Taylor. Talk to the other girls. Find out how they got here, and how they were recruited. See if any of them have family back home waiting for them. We need to know if we're all here for the same reason."

Taylor nodded, her fear palpable, but she met Jules's gaze with determination.

"I'll try. But we must be careful. They're watching us."

The air in the room seemed to thicken with tension as if the walls themselves were closing in on them. Jules could feel it, the weight of unseen eyes, the oppressive sense that they were never truly alone. Taylor was right. They had to be careful. Just then, the sound of footsteps echoed in the hallway outside. Both girls froze, their hearts pounding in their chests. Vanessa's sharp voice floated down the corridor, her morning routine in full swing.

Taylor shot Jules a panicked glance, but Jules motioned for her to stay calm. They quickly shifted the conversation, pretending to discuss the competition as Vanessa's footsteps grew closer. The tension was unbearable, but Vanessa passed by without even glancing at the door.

When the footsteps faded, Taylor let out a shaky breath.

"Do you think she knows?" she whispered, her voice barely audible. Jules didn't hesitate.

"I don't trust her. She's cold and calculating. If anyone's involved, it's Vanessa."

They sat in silence for a moment, the gravity of their situation sinking in. Then, Jules leaned closer, her voice low and urgent.

"Taylor, whatever you do, don't win your race. Don't stand out. The winners are the ones who disappear."

Taylor's eyes widened in shock. "What do you mean?"

Jules's voice trembled with the weight of her revelation.

"It's the winners, Taylor. The girls who win... they're the ones being taken. That's what they all have in common." Taylor stared at her, the realization slowly dawning.

"But... Phillip told us to do our best. He said it was important to impress the guests."

Jules's face darkened, her expression hardening.

"The guests aren't here to be impressed. They're here to watch. They're part of whatever this is. I've seen the way they look at us. Like we're not people. Like we're something to be... consumed." Taylor swallowed hard, her fear evident.

"What can we do?" Jules stood, her resolve strengthening.

"We keep our heads down. We stay quiet. And we figure out who's behind this before it's too late." As she moved toward the door, she turned back to Taylor, her voice filled with urgency. "Talk to the girls.

Find out what you can. But be careful. If you hear anything, come to me. We can't afford to make any mistakes."

Taylor nodded, her face pale but determined. "I'll be careful."

With that, Jules slipped out of the room, her mind racing. The pieces were slowly falling into place, but the picture they formed was terrifying. She couldn't do this alone. But she had no choice. The voice in her head returned, cold and calculating.

'*You're not alone. You have me.*'

Jules shivered, but she knew the voice was right. She couldn't trust anyone, except herself.

And the voice.

CHAPTER 17: TRUST

The room was suffocating, the air thick with unspoken malice as Jules pushed the door open. Vanessa was waiting, her sudden presence sent a jolt of ice down Jules's spine, her heart skipping a beat. How long had she been lurking in the shadows? Watching. Listening. Vanessa's lips curved into a dangerous smile, one that held promises of deception.

"Would you mind joining me for a chat in the office Jules?" Vanessa's voice dripped with false warmth, but beneath it was something far more sinister. Jules tried to keep her voice steady, concealing the rising dread that gnawed at her insides.

"Of course, Vanessa. I was just on my way to see you and Phillip." The lie felt flimsy, brittle, even to her own ears. Vanessa's gaze sharpened a predator-sensing weakness.

"Really? Somehow, I'm not so sure I believe you." Her voice was saccharine but with an edge so sharp it could draw blood. The subtle threat was clear. Jules slid her hands into her pockets, feeling the crumpled note still tucked safely there. The note. Her only weapon, perhaps even, her death sentence. Vanessa led the way, her steps precise, as though each was part of a well-rehearsed dance of control. When they reached the office, the door closed with a finality that made Jules jump out of her skin. Phillip was already inside, seated behind his polished desk, his expression unreadable. Yet there was something darker in his eyes today, a simmering threat beneath his calm exterior.

"Jules," Phillip's voice was like velvet stretched over a blade, "we've noticed... certain behaviours that give us cause for concern." Jules's heart was a drumbeat in her ears, her pulse frantic, but outwardly she maintained a veneer of calm.

"I don't know what you mean, Phillip. I've done exactly as you asked. I've been gathering information."

"Is that so?" Vanessa interjected, circling Jules like a vulture awaiting its meal.

"Then explain the note." Her tone was so cold, that Jules could almost see the frost forming on the words.

'The note. They knew.'

Her mind raced, searching for the right lie, the right deflection, but nothing felt strong enough to shield her from their relentless gaze.

"I... I was coming to show you the note," Jules stammered, her voice faltering despite her best efforts. "I was just trying to gauge what the others thought before I brought it to you."

Vanessa moved closer, her presence oppressive, a hunter closing in on wounded prey. "You've been very secretive, Jules. Untrustworthy."

Phillip leaned forward, the air around him seeming to darken.

"Enough with the games," he said, his voice now carrying a dangerous weight.

"There is more at stake here than you realize. Do you think you can play both sides? We *own* you, Jules." Jules felt the room close in around her, the walls creeping ever closer. Her pulse quickened, the weight of their scrutiny threatening to crush her. But even as fear constricted her, a spark of defiance flickered within. She straightened in her chair, forcing her voice to be steady. "What do you want from me?"

Vanessa's lips twisted into a malicious grin, her eyes gleaming with a wicked delight.

"Oh, my dear, we have such... *expectations* for you. But first, hand over the note."

For a moment, Jules hesitated, her hand hovering over her pocket. Giving it to them felt like handing over her last piece of leverage, but refusing would undoubtedly make matters worse. With a small, bitter sigh, she pulled the note from her pocket and passed it to Vanessa.

Vanessa took it with a look of smug satisfaction before sliding it across the desk to Phillip. He didn't bother to look at it, his gaze locked on Jules, his smile a knife slowly turning in her gut.

"Good. Now, listen carefully," Phillip said, his tone icy. "You will follow our instructions without question. Any sign of resistance, any hint of betrayal, and we will make sure your father knows exactly where to find you. You remember him, don't you?"

Jules's blood ran cold at the mention of her father. It was like a switch had been flipped in her mind, plunging her into a nightmare she thought she had escaped years ago. She could still hear his voice, smell the stale alcohol on his breath, and feel the cold terror of being under his control. Her voice was barely a whisper as she said,

"You can't... you can't bring him into this."

Vanessa's laugh was cold and hollow, like the echo of something long dead.

"Oh, we most certainly can. And we will unless you prove your loyalty to us."

Phillip leaned back, his eyes gleaming with malicious intent.

"You understand now, don't you? We control your fate. You belong to us."

Jules felt the world tilt beneath her feet, the weight of their control crushing her spirit. But she couldn't break, not now. She couldn't let them see how deeply their words had cut. Drawing a shaky breath, she forced herself to look Phillip in the eye.

"What do you want me to do?"

A slow, cruel smile spread across Phillip's face.

"It's simple. We want you to report back on Zander."

Zander. The name hit her like a punch to the gut. Phillip's suspicions about him had been lurking in the background, but now they had come into sharp focus.

'*Did Zander pose a threat to their operation? Or was this just another twisted game?*'

"I want you to keep an eye on him," Phillip continued, his voice a quiet menace. "We don't trust him. And we need to know if he can be... persuaded to join us, or if he's going to be a problem." Jules's mind reeled. Zander had always been a mystery, an enigma wrapped in charm and shadows. But now, the very people she feared most were demanding that she betray him or face her worst nightmare.

"I... I understand," she muttered, her voice barely audible. Vanessa's laugh rang through the room again, sending another shiver down Jules's spine.

"Good girl. Do as we say, and we'll make sure your father stays far, far away. But cross us... and he'll be here before you can even scream."

As they laid out their next set of demands, Jules barely heard them. Her mind was spinning, tangled in a web of fear and confusion. She felt like she was drowning, each breath harder to take than the last.

'*How had it come to this? How had she let herself fall so deep into their trap?*'

When the meeting finally ended, Jules walked out of the office with a forced smile plastered on her face. She knew they were watching, scrutinizing her every move. She couldn't let them see her break. Back in her room, the silence pressed in around her. She sat on the edge of her bed, her hands shaking as she tried to come up with a plan. But the fear was too thick, choking her thoughts, clouding her judgment. She couldn't think straight.

And then, a knock at the door. Her heart leapt into her throat as she cautiously opened it. Zander stood there, his expression grim, his voice low as he said,

"We need to talk. I know what's going on.'

Jules's mind raced.

'*Could she trust him? Or was this all part of Vanessa and Phillip's twisted game?*'

Her heart wanted to believe him, but her mind screamed caution.

"I don't know if I can trust you, Zander," she whispered, her voice betraying the turmoil within her. Zander stepped closer, his eyes intense.

"You can trust me. I want to help you."

But trust was a fragile thing, and in this world of shadows and deceit, Jules didn't know who the saviour was, or who was the monster. As the night crept on, the only certainty was that time was running out.

CHAPTER 18: TORMENT

The wind howled through the darkened woods, carrying with it the scent of damp earth and pine. Jules's heart raced as she made her way toward the secluded meeting spot. Every step felt heavier than the last, her anxiety wrapping around her like a cloak of lead. She scanned her surroundings, half-expecting the shadows to stir, for Vanessa or Phillip to step out from the dark with their eyes gleaming, hungry for blood. Her breath came in sharp, quick bursts, as the reality of the situation settled in her bones. She had gotten herself into something far more dangerous than she could ever have imagined. As the first glimmers of dawn pierced the sky, Zander emerged from the thicket, his face hard, almost feral. His sharp jawline was taut with tension, his eyes dark and unreadable. With no words of comfort or preamble, he dove into the nightmare waiting to consume them both.

"Jules, we don't have much time," he said in a tone that was more of an order than a statement. "Vanessa and Phillip are involved in something much darker than I initially thought." He glanced around as if the trees themselves were eavesdropping. "I've used my tech company to infiltrate their operation, but what I've uncovered..." His voice faltered for a moment. "It's worse than you could imagine."

Zander's words hung in the air, thick and suffocating, leaving Jules struggling to breathe. "What do you mean?" she asked, though deep down, she already knew. The grim atmosphere around the resort, the whispers in the dead of night, it was all building to something terrible.

"They're part of a satanic cult. They run human trafficking operations. The bodies we find in the mountains... they're sacrifices, Jules." Zander's eyes bored into her. "And your father, he's not just tangled in their web. He's at the centre of it. He's one of the directors in their company, helping to facilitate every sick and twisted thing they do."

Jules's world tilted. Her breath hitched, a cold knot forming in her chest. She had always known something was off about her father, his coldness, his distance, but this? This was beyond anything she could have fathomed. A grotesque picture of his true nature painted itself in her mind, bloodied and dripping with malice. Zander stepped closer, his voice dropping to a near whisper.

"There's more." His tone was grave. "My sister... She was one of their victims. I think they killed her, Jules. Years ago. After she got clean, she worked at a bar not far from here. Then she vanished. No trace, no leads. I've spent the last four years tracking her last steps, and they led me straight to Vanessa and Phillip." A sharp pang of guilt hit Jules. All this time, she had been working for monsters, unknowingly complicit in their atrocities. Her father's dark secrets were crashing down on her, threatening to bury her alive.

"I didn't know... I had no idea,' she whispered, her voice trembling, barely audible over the wind.

"You weren't supposed to know," Zander said quietly, his eyes softening for a moment. "But now that you do, you're in this. We both are. We need to expose them and take them down. This is the closest I've come in years to bringing them to justice. But I can't do it alone. I need your help." Jules stared at him, her mind reeling. Every fibre of her being screamed for her to run, to disappear into the shadows and leave this horror behind. But the rage inside her was boiling, bubbling to the surface, consuming her fear. They had used her, manipulated her, and her father... her own flesh and blood had been a part of this hell. There was no turning back now.

"I'll help you," she said, her voice laced with fierce determination. "But we need to be smart about this. One wrong move, and we're both dead." Zander nodded solemnly.

"We stay under the radar. No mistakes. Vanessa and Phillip can't know we're onto them."

As he spoke, a question gnawed at the back of Jules's mind. Her father.

'What had pushed him into this vile world? Was it greed? Power? Or something darker still?' She had to know.

"My father," she said, her voice tightening. "Why? Why would he be involved in something like this? I mean I knew he was a bad man, but this. This is another level."

Zander's gaze darkened. "We've never talked about him, have we?"

"No!" Jules said coldly, her fingers digging into the fabric of her coat.

"We've never talked about anything real. We barely know each other." Zander's lips twisted into a grim smile.

"I know more about you than you think, Jules. I know what they did to you, what he did to you. I chose you for a reason."

A chill ran down her spine. "What do you mean?"

"You weren't just another victim, Jules. I thought at first you had Stockholm syndrome, that you were too far gone, too wrapped up in their lies. But you're not. You're stronger than that. You're a survivor, and I need someone like you on my side. You need this, just like I do."

The words struck her like a blow. The memories, long buried, rose to the surface. Her father's cold eyes watching her from the shadows, the faint scent of blood on his clothes when she was a child, the whispers of strange rituals that she had forced herself to forget. She remembered it all now, his sacrifices, the muffled cries, the horrifying moments of her childhood that she had locked away in the deepest, darkest corners of her mind. Her body shook with the force of the revelation. Had he groomed her for this world, preparing her to take his place in the cult? She had always thought she was his only victim. But now...

"I need you, Jules. We need each other," Zander said, his tone laced with urgency.

"We gather evidence, find their weaknesses, and then we strike. But we need to act fast."

Jules nodded slowly, her jaw clenched. Her father wasn't just a monster, he was the architect of her nightmares, the one who had shaped her torment from the shadows.

"I'll help you take them down," she whispered, the words heavy with her growing thirst for vengeance. "When the time comes, I'll make sure my father pays for what he's done."

The next few weeks passed in a haze of lies and covert operations. Jules moved through her daily routines with a practised calm, her mask of submission firmly in place. Vanessa and Phillip continued to treat her as a pawn, unaware that she was working to dismantle their empire from within. Every interaction with them was a dance on the razor's edge, every moment a delicate balance between deceit and discovery. Under Zander's guidance, she began to gather evidence, conversations overheard, documents stolen in the dead of night, the faintest glimmers of their cruel operations. Her laptop became her fortress, a vault of secrets locked away behind layers of encryption. Zander's tech skills were unmatched, his ability to erase their digital footprints the only thing keeping them alive. Each night, she combed through her findings, piecing together the puzzle of her father's sins, cataloguing every name, every face, every date that could bring them down. She was meticulous, calculating, and driven by a singular, burning desire. Revenge. But the more she uncovered, the darker the picture became. This wasn't about the satanic cult or the trafficking operation.

There was something far more ancient, far more sinister at play, something older than all of them. Rituals that transcended death, sacrifices that went beyond mere bloodshed. And at the centre of it all was her father, his face a mask of pure, malevolent intent. Jules's nightmares grew worse. Every time she closed her eyes, she saw his face, smiling as he led the victims to their deaths. She could smell the blood in the air and feel the cold stone beneath her feet as she watched in horror. The rituals weren't about power, they were about control, about bending the very fabric of reality to their will. Zander's words echoed in her mind.

"*You need this as much as I do.*" He was right. She did. Because this wasn't just about justice. It was about reclaiming her life, taking back what had been stolen from her piece by piece. When the time came, she would make sure her father paid the ultimate price. A storm was coming, and with it, Jules was ready to unleash hell.

CHAPTER 19: LOVE & WAR.

Every night, Jules plunged into the shadowy abyss of her investigation, losing herself in the grotesque world of cults, human trafficking, and the sickening power games played by Vanessa and Phillip. The light from her computer screen felt cold, casting ghostly shadows across her face as she meticulously sifted through the darkness of their operations. Names, faces, dates, all etched into her mind as though branded, there with fire. The missing girls haunted her, their photographs staring back at her like the condemned souls they were.

Her obsession grew sharper with each passing day. She combed through every report, every hidden corner of the internet, for the tiniest crack in Vanessa and Phillip's armour. They were predators, but Jules knew that even the most dangerous animals had weaknesses.

She just had to find them before time ran out. Every Saturday, new girls vanished into the cult's grasp, and every Sunday, fresh victims appeared at the resort, drugged, confused, and oblivious to their fate. Jules could feel their terror, taste the fear they must have swallowed as their lives were torn from them. Zander was by her side through it all. At first, it had been just business, two people united by a common goal. But something had shifted. Zander, with his quiet strength and burning resolve, had become more than just a partner. His presence was grounding, even when the weight of the mission threatened to crush them both.

He had a way of keeping her from falling into the abyss of her mind, where guilt and memories of her father lurked, waiting to devour her sanity. Zander, too, had his demons. His sister, one of the many girls who had disappeared, haunted him as much as the victims haunted

Jules. He hadn't spoken much about her, but Jules saw it in his eyes, in the way his voice would harden when they talked about the cult. His desire for justice was personal, it fuelled his every move. They were bound together now, not just by their mission but by something deeper. Something more dangerous. The long nights they spent together, pouring over files, and brainstorming strategies, became more than just work. Their silences were no longer awkward but filled with tension that was thick enough to choke on.

It terrified Jules how much she had come to rely on him. Zander was more than just her partner, he was the one thing keeping her from unravelling completely. Zander, on the other hand, had fallen for her in a way that scared him. He didn't let on, not at first, but Jules had gotten under his skin. She was tough, intelligent, and resilient. She made him feel alive in ways he hadn't felt since losing his sister. But the closer they got; the more complicated things became. They spent nights strategizing in Zander's chalet, their conversations stretching well into the early hours of the morning. Zander was the voice of reason, always urging patience, reminding Jules not to rush headlong into action.

"We have to make sure every single one of them is captured," Zander had said one night, his voice as dark and heavy as the shadows in the room. "If we move too fast, they'll scatter. It'll all be for nothing."

Jules hated waiting. Each Saturday felt like another nail in her heart. She could feel the weight of the girls' blood on her hands, her guilt seeping into her bones. It was suffocating. But Zander was right, acting too soon would only give Vanessa and Phillip the upper hand. They needed an airtight case. They needed patience. But time was running out.

Zander, sensing Jules's emotional turmoil, took it upon himself to investigate her father. He believed there might be more to her past than she was letting on. Perhaps her father's connections tied her to Vanessa and Phillip in ways she hadn't even realized.

The deeper Zander dug, the more he uncovered, the more determined he became to protect Jules, not just from Vanessa and Phillip, but from her past. As time went on, the walls began to close in on them. Their every move felt watched, every interaction with Vanessa and Phillip a dangerous dance. Jules noticed the subtle shifts in their behaviour, Vanessa's eyes lingering on her a little too long, Phillip's casual remarks tinged with suspicion. They knew something was up. Jules could feel it, the tension tightening like a noose around her neck.

The pressure was building, not just from their mission, but from the unspoken feelings simmering between her and Zander. Jules found herself drawn to him in ways that she didn't want to admit. Every time they were alone together, the tension between them became almost unbearable.

'*He is gorgeous,*' the voice in her head would tease her, every time she was with him. '*If you don't kiss him, I will. You would be a fool to let this one slip between your fingers. You want him, don't you?*'

She hated that voice, hated how it made her feel vulnerable. This wasn't the time to get lost in emotions. They had a mission to complete. Yet, she couldn't deny the way her heart would race whenever Zander was near, the way her skin tingled at the slightest touch.

One evening, as they worked together in Zander's chalet, Zander made a discovery that shifted everything. He had been digging through old newspaper articles, poring over political connections and hidden dealings. And then he found it, an article that tied Vanessa and Phillip to a high-ranking local politician. Jules's heart skipped a beat as she read over Zander's shoulder. This was it. The connection they had been searching for. Vanessa and Phillip weren't just local criminals, they had powerful allies in the political system. The implications were terrifying. This wasn't just about a small, isolated cult. It was bigger than they had ever imagined.

"We can't act yet," Zander muttered, his jaw clenched. "We need more evidence. We need to bring down the entire system, not just Vanessa and Phillip."

Jules nodded, but inside, she was screaming. '*How many more girls would vanish before they had enough evidence? How many more lives would be lost to the darkness?*'

As the hours wore on, the tension between Jules and Zander became unbearable. They were sitting close, too close, Jules could feel the heat radiating off his body. She could smell him, his scent intoxicating, making her mind spin.

'*Just kiss him already,*' the voice in her head taunted her again, refusing to leave her in peace. Jules clenched her fists, trying to focus on the documents in front of her, but the tension was too thick. Then it happened. Zander moved closer, his breath warm against her neck, sending a shiver down her spine. She froze, feeling the weight of his presence behind her. The moment was charged, electrified.

"You alright?" His voice was low, filled with concern.

Jules swallowed hard, her mouth suddenly dry. "Yeah, I'm fine," she muttered, but her voice betrayed her. She wasn't fine. She was anything but fine. Zander's lips quirked into a small smile as he stepped even closer, the space between them now almost non-existent. She turned to face him, her heart pounding so loudly she was sure he could hear it. Their faces were inches apart, and for a fleeting moment, the world around them ceased to exist. It was just him and her, locked in this unbearable tension. Then Zander, with that mischievous twinkle in his eye, broke the silence.

"That was close," he said, his voice a teasing whisper. "I thought you were going to kiss me then."

Jules blinked, caught off guard. "A kiss?"

He chuckled, his grin widening. "A Scottish one," he added, his voice playful.

For a moment, Jules was lost. Her heart fluttered, and she almost laughed at the absurdity of the situation. Here they were, knee-deep in a world of horror and darkness, and yet Zander could still find a way to make her smile, to tease her. But the moment was dangerous, too much was at stake, and her feelings were a distraction she couldn't afford.

She quickly stepped back, shaking her head as if trying to clear it of the fog clouding her judgment.

"Let's just get back to work," she said, her voice sharper than she intended.

Zander's smile faded slightly, and for a moment, his eyes reflected a flicker of hurt. But he nodded, turning back to his laptop, the unspoken tension still lingering in the air like smoke.

Jules watched him for a moment longer, her heart still racing. She wanted to say something, anything, to break the tension, but the words wouldn't come. She couldn't let herself get distracted by him, no matter how much she wanted to. They had a job to do, and the stakes were too high. But even as they returned to their work, the darkness around them seemed to thicken, and the electricity seemed to radiate. They were running out of time, Jules could feel it. Vanessa and Phillip were onto them. And now, with the discovery of the political connection, the danger had only multiplied. The chess pieces were moving, and it was only a matter of time before the noose tightened around their necks.

CHAPTER 20: CHAINS

For Jules, each decision felt like a high-stakes game of chess, every move heavy with consequence as she and Zander navigated the treacherous terrain of their mission. One fateful evening, while sifting through encrypted data on her laptop, she stumbled upon a revelation so shocking it felt like a blade sliding between her ribs. This exposé had the power to dismantle Vanessa and Phillip's sordid operation while implicating her father, a prominent politician, and even the head of the local police force. They had hit gold, an explosive trove of secrets hidden in the office computer that had been hacked, laying bare a conspiracy woven with the darkest threads of greed and betrayal. The chilling details poured forth. Payments were made for sacrifices, hush money exchanged under the table, and the rich and elite named in the files detailing their gruesome appetites for murder and torture.

This was what they had been searching for, the grotesque underbelly of their world, a network ensnared in a global human trafficking organization. The enormity of the situation sent her heart racing, a potent blend of terror and determination coursing through her veins. Zander's instincts had been spot-on from the beginning, they had uncovered a monstrous truth. Driven by an overwhelming sense of impending doom, Jules and Zander became consumed by their mission, tirelessly amassing evidence before it was too late. The tension coiled tightly around them like a snake ready to strike, each moment a reminder of the dangerous game they played. With another competition night looming on the horizon, the air thickened with anxiety. Eleven more girls had vanished after the last event, their absence serving as a grim reminder of the stakes at play.

Jules seethed with anger, anger at Zander, anger at herself.

"We can't keep allowing this to happen, Zander. I don't think I can wait much longer. Surely, we have enough evidence now?"

His eyes, dark and hooded, betrayed the turmoil boiling beneath his calm exterior.

"You're right. This Saturday, we must put an end to this madness, or at the very least, rescue who we can."

Jules nodded, gratitude mingling with the dread that swirled in her gut. Zander had utilized his extensive knowledge of online security to assemble a team back in the United States, gathering information on the lodge's visitors and revealing a shadowy realm of exploitation and trafficking. Reluctant to disclose the full scope of his covert mission to her, Zander's resolve to rescue the abducted girls compelled him to finally share the truth. Their tragedy was the driving force behind a relentless quest for justice. Under the leadership of his trusted ally Andy, a former special forces operative, they prepared for an audacious rescue mission, readying themselves to document the horrors lurking within the lodge's confines. The dark shadow of sacrifice loomed over them, but a glimmer of hope flickered in their hearts as they sought to save the thirteen girls whose fates now hung by a thread.

Amid danger and deceit, Jules and Zander remained steadfast, their connection deepening with each passing moment. Yet, lurking beneath the surface of their partnership, a gnawing suspicion plagued Jules, did Zander's unwavering commitment conceal a more sinister motive? The insidious voice returned, whispering insecurity and doubt, insisting she should trust no one, not even Zander. He was a good guy. It was stupid to think otherwise. Yet, throughout her life, she had learned not to place her trust fully in anyone, and the little voice warned her,

'*Always think the worst of people, that way, you will never be disappointed.*'

Jules shook her head in a frenzy as if trying to ward off invisible demons. But in truth, the real demon resided within her. As the evening of the competition descended, the atmosphere turned ominous, shrouded in a veil of apprehension. Jules and Zander meticulously prepared to execute their carefully devised plan. Every detail had been scrutinized, every action meticulously calculated to protect the endangered girls. Despite the heavy weight on Jules's heart, the main hall buzzed with electric energy as guests and staff mingled, blissfully unaware of the darkness they would face. Vanessa and Phillip prowled through the crowd like predators, their smiles concealing a malignant intent, that simply creeped Jules out. Every laugh and every gesture were tainted with hidden motives, obscuring the truth of the atrocities veiled behind the resort's glamorous facade. The resort masked a sinister reality, where unspeakable horrors unfolded behind closed doors. Tonight was their opportunity, Jules, and Zander's chance to expose the nightmares lurking in plain sight.

Next to her, Zander radiated a grim determination, his gaze locked onto the challenge ahead. They exchanged a silent nod, a wordless understanding of the perilous path they were about to tread. Outside, Andy stood vigilant, poised to spring into action at the faintest signal from Zander. As the first girl stepped onto the stage, Jules's heart raced, anticipation and dread intertwining. She fought to maintain a calm demeanour, the secretive exchanges carried out in the encrypted confines of Zander's room igniting a storm of conflicting emotions within her. She should be out there, helping save the girls she had vowed to protect. Anger flared within her, at Zander for insisting she remain hidden, at herself for not being braver. But duty prevailed, and Andy had been entrusted with the critical task of tracking the girls' movements with his team of trained mercenaries and ex-veterans. Zander had explained to Jules how they had saved countless victims from human trafficking operations worldwide.

They understood the dangers, accustomed to placing their lives on the line. Jules had no training, Zander insisted she would only

who thrived on chaos. Zander trusted him with his life. Now and then, the roar of an avalanche echoed through the mountains, a haunting reminder of how unforgiving these peaks could be. It was as if nature itself was conspiring against them, determined to make their task even more perilous. Yet, there was an eerie beauty to it all. The headlights illuminated the snow-laden trees, the snowflakes catching the light and shimmering like tiny diamonds in the darkness. The peaks, towering and ancient, stood silent and cold, watching over them like ancient sentinels. For a fleeting moment, Zander could almost forget the horrors that lay ahead, but the thought of the girls brought him crashing back to the grim reality.

Their target, the lorry ahead, contained precious cargo, and innocent lives. Girls, are stolen and trafficked by the monstrous network known as the 'House of Asmodeus.' For months, Zander and his team had been chasing this elusive shadow, trying to crack open the vile world that thrived beneath the surface of wealth and privilege. They had come close before, but this was their first real break. The girls in that truck were more than just victims, they were a chance to take down a piece of the network and expose the rotten core of human trafficking that extended across continents. The van shuddered as they hit a patch of rough terrain, pulling Zander from his thoughts. He glanced back at the rest of his team, huddled in the back. Tek, their tech expert, was hunched over a laptop, tracking the truck's every move with a GPS beacon they had managed to plant earlier. Noah, the muscle of the group, was methodically checking his weapon, his face a mask of calm in the face of what they were about to do. The others were similarly focused, silently preparing for the confrontation to come. Each man here had a personal stake in this fight. For Andy, it was his sister, one of the countless lives destroyed by Asmodeus.

"We're getting close," Andy muttered, his voice barely audible over the engine's growl.

"The city limits should be just over that ridge."

Zander nodded, his body tensing in anticipation. The twisting, ice-riddled path gave way to smoother roads as they descended from the mountains, the skyline of Geneva twinkling in the distance, like a false promise of safety. The city, with its bustling streets and glittering lake-front, harboured secrets as dark as the forests they had just passed. Somewhere down there, in the shadows cast by the lights of wealth and power, was a warehouse, a place where the auction would take place. The very thought of it churned Zander's stomach.

Tek called from the back, his voice urgent.

"They've stopped. GPS says they're at a storage facility on the shore of Lake Geneva."

Andy's knuckles whitened as he gripped the steering wheel tighter.

"Right," he grunted. "We've got a small window. Let's not waste it."

The van roared down the final stretch of road, its occupants bracing themselves for what was to come. The sprawling city around them began to thin out as they neared the lake, the streets darker, and quieter. The industrial district loomed ahead, a far cry from the idyllic lakeside villas and chic cafes of Geneva's city centre. Here, in the forgotten corners, was where monsters thrived. As they neared the storage facility, the team went silent. Zander's pulse quickened. He glanced at Andy, who nodded, his expression hardening into a mask of pure focus.

This was it.

"We stop here," Zander ordered, his voice cutting through the tension. "We go in quiet, we get those girls, and we end this."

The van rolled to a halt about nine hundred yards from the warehouse, tucked behind an abandoned building. Andy killed the engine, and the team silently piled out. The cold hit them like a wall, but none of them flinched. They were trained for this. Balaclavas pulled down, weapons ready, they moved as one down the narrow alley that ran alongside the warehouse. Snow crunched beneath their boots, but otherwise, they were ghosts in the night.

Tek moved ahead, his fingers flying across a handheld device as he hacked into the warehouse's surveillance system.

"Cameras are down," he whispered, his breath misting in the freezing air. "We're good to go." The team moved swiftly, following Tek's lead as he guided them through a side entrance to the neighbouring warehouse. Inside, the warehouse was dark and cold, the silence almost oppressive. Zander's eyes swept the space, his mind racing as he processed the layout. The 'House of Asmodeus' had been a ghost until now, but Zander had learned enough to know their operations were always meticulously planned. Their auctions weren't just about selling human lives, they were about showmanship. Blood. Fear. From the adjacent third floor, they could look down into the heart of the operation. The buyers, wealthy and powerful, sat in isolated booths along the corridors, their identities hidden behind masks of civility. Below, on a stage bathed in harsh fluorescent light, the merchandise was paraded, young women, terrified and hollow-eyed, waiting to be sold to the highest bidder. Behind the stage were the holding cells, small, dark cages where the girls were kept like animals before being led to the slaughter.

"There," Tek whispered, pointing at the thermal images on his screen. "Security is tight, thirty guards, eight staff. But we know the layout. We've seen this before."

Zander nodded, his gaze dark and cold. He turned to the others.

"You know what to do. We get in, we take them out, and we save those girls. No mercy."

CHAPTER 22: RESCUE

The night had a sinister chill, an oppressive quiet that clung to the team as they slid from one rooftop to the next, advancing towards the grotesque auction house below. Every breath they took was shallow and deliberate, their bodies synchronized with the eerie silence that blanketed the city like a thick fog. High above, the stars glimmered coldly, as if indifferent to the horrors playing out beneath them. The world held its breath, anticipating something terrible yet inevitable. The air was thick with dread. On the final rooftop, the tech expert moved with precision, his fingers ghosting over the keypad that would grant them entry into the building. He tapped into his state-of-the-art equipment, overriding the lock with a soft click. The door creaked open, revealing a narrow staircase that spiralled into darkness below. The faint, suffocating scent of mildew and damp stone wafted from within, hinting at the dark secrets that lay hidden underneath. One by one, the team descended the stairs, their boots making the faintest sound against the concrete, their movements as fluid and silent as shadows. Zander, the team leader, took the lead, his mind racing.

This was it, the moment they had been preparing for. There was no room for error. The basement below housed the depraved spectacle they had vowed to destroy. They had no idea what horrors awaited them, but they were certain of one thing, they were walking into a pit of vipers. The tech expert, Tek, remained glued to his laptop, his eyes flicking between the live feed and his hacking tools, ensuring the auction hadn't yet started. The clock was ticking. The tension among them was palpable. Wealthy men from all over the world were already being escorted by the house's security team into their private cubicles, where they would witness the sick parade of human flesh sold to the highest bidder.

Zander felt the weight of their mission pressing down on him. Each second that passed brought them closer to a point of no return. Their targets were powerful, untouchable by the usual legal channels, and Zander's team had been tasked with a grim duty, one that might very well cost them their lives. Every member of Zander's team had a score to settle, each of them driven by the ghosts of their pasts, there was no turning back. Zander and Andy took point, moving swiftly down a dimly lit corridor, their steps carefully measured as they approached the basement doors. The air grew colder, the faint hum of machinery vibrating beneath the surface. Without hesitation, they dispatched two guards with lethal efficiency, their bodies slumping to the ground in silence. The only sound was the soft hiss of air leaving their lungs as they collapsed. The corridor ahead was lined with thick, dark red doors, each marked with a number, silent monuments to the grotesque business conducted within.

Faint flickers of light danced along the walls from the guard's torches as they patrolled, their presence a looming threat in the oppressive silence. Zander motioned for the team to split up, his finger drawing a circle in the air. Each of them had a role, each had a target, and there was no room for hesitation. Noah, a giant of a man with ebony skin and a menacing presence, moved like a ghost. His towering frame belied the silence with which he approached his first target. Zander and Andy continued down the corridor, disappearing into the dark while Mick and Scooby headed towards the opposite end. Noah's path took him toward the private cubicles where the buyers sat. Men who traded in human lives as easily as they would in stocks or real estate. The buyers were spread out in cubicles, hidden behind soundproof glass, each eager to claim a piece of human misery for sale. Noah could hear their voices as he pressed his ear to the first door, muffled conversations in a mix of languages. His tranquilliser gun was primed, his massive hand steady as he prepared to eliminate the bidders without causing too much noise. He entered the first cubicle, unseen and unheard, and in one fluid motion, he fired. The dart hit its mark, sinking into the soft flesh of the buyer's neck.

The man gasped, his glass of whiskey slipping from his hand and shattering on the floor, but his cry of surprise was muffled by the privacy glass. In the next cubicle, the buyer, dressed in a blue velvet dinner jacket, saw Noah too late. He tried to scream, but the sound died in his throat as Noah overpowered him, the tranquilliser gun hissing as the dart buried itself in the man's flesh. His body slumped forward, collapsing into unconsciousness.

Noah worked swiftly, and methodically, taking down each buyer with brutal efficiency. Their wealth, their power, it meant nothing in this moment. They were no more than prey to Noah, caught in a web of their own depravity. Meanwhile, Zander and Andy found themselves edging closer to the heart of the operation. The further they went, the more unsettling the atmosphere became. The corridor seemed to stretch into eternity, the faint hum of generators and the distant sound of chains clinking together echoing off the walls. Zander's stomach churned. Somewhere ahead, in the belly of this monstrous place, the girls were waiting. Their lives hung in the balance, and it was up to Zander's team to deliver them from the nightmare that had consumed them. Suddenly, the silence shattered as the sound of gunfire erupted ahead. Zander's heart leapt into his throat. He motioned to Andy, and the two of them bolted forward, their weapons drawn, ready for whatever hell awaited them.

The air grew thick with the stench of sweat and blood. They rounded the corner, and there, in the dim light, stood a group of security guards, rifles in hand. Without missing a beat, Andy hurled a tear gas grenade into the fray. The corridor filled with choking, acrid smoke as the guards fumbled with their masks, momentarily blinded. Zander and Andy seized the opportunity, springing into action with the practised ease of seasoned soldiers. The muffled crack of gunfire filled the air, the guards falling one by one, their bodies crumpling to the ground in lifeless heaps. Blood sprayed the walls, the crimson streaks stark against the cold concrete, turning the corridor into a nightmarish slaughterhouse. Zander felt the warmth of it splattered across his face, mixing with the sweat pouring down his brow. The world seemed to narrow down to the rhythm of the fight, the chaos of battle overtaking every thought. There was no room for mercy. These men were complicit in horrors beyond comprehension, and their deaths were the only justice the team could offer. Amid the carnage, a voice crackled through Zander's earpiece. It was Noah.

"The buyers are down. Proceeding to extraction," he said, his voice a low rumble. Zander nodded, though Noah couldn't see him. He wiped the blood from his face and pressed forward, his heart pounding in his chest. They were close, so close to the girls now. He could feel it, the weight of the moment pressing down on him like a vice.

At the far end of the corridor, they reached the holding cells. The sight that greeted them turned Zander's stomach. The metal bars that lined the walls stood as a stark reminder of the brutality these girls had faced. Inside the cells, the girls huddled together, their eyes wide with terror, their bodies trembling from both cold and fear. They were gaunt, their cheeks hollow, their skin marred with bruises and cuts. Some were no more than children, barely in their teens, their faces etched with the kind of hopelessness that only comes from witnessing the darkest side of humanity. Zander's breath hitched in his throat as he unlocked the first cell, his hands shaking.

"We're here to get you out," he whispered, his voice thick with emotion.

The girls stared at him, their expressions a mixture of disbelief and fear. They had been promised salvation before, only to be betrayed, and sold into even worse fates. But this time was different. Zander's team wasn't here to negotiate. They were here to save or die trying.

Noah arrived, his massive form filling the doorway. He moved quickly, his presence calming the girls as he lifted one of them into his arms, her frail body barely a weight to him.

Zander did the same, his mind racing as he counted the seconds, every heartbeat a reminder that they were running out of time. As they moved through the corridors, the sound of approaching sirens began to echo in the distance. The law was coming, but Zander knew better than to trust it. There was always a chance that the buyers, those powerful, untouchable men, had the police in their pockets. They couldn't afford to linger. The team hustled the girls into the waiting van, their bodies shivering in the cold night air. Zander took one last glance at the auction house, a grotesque monument to human suffering. They had won this battle, but the war was far from over. As the van sped away, Zander's thoughts turned to his sister. Somewhere, she was out there, a victim of this same vile network. He vowed, silently, that he would burn every last one of these operations to the ground if it meant finding her.

But for now, there was only the sound of the engine and the soft, muffled sobs of the rescued girls, their lives forever scarred by the darkness they had just escaped.

CHAPTER 23: HAUNTED.

The night air was thick with the victims' cries and whimpers. Zander's team drove in grim silence as the city lights faded into the rearview, the darkened landscape stretching endlessly ahead. The getaway van cut through the desolation, carrying the broken, trembling survivors toward the only sanctuary they could offer, a meeting with Sage on the outskirts of the city.

Sage. Zander's mind drifted to her. She had become an essential part of their operations, a lifeline for the victims they saved. There was something unbreakable about Sage, though her cracks were deep and jagged. They all had their demons. Hers ran dark and ancient, but she channelled them into a relentless drive to save those trapped in the suffocating grip of human trafficking. She had learned the hard way, just like they all had. Her transformation from an idealistic crusader to a battle-hardened fighter was a story carved out of betrayal, loss, and corruption. As the van drew closer to the meeting point, the landscape began to shift. The industrial sprawl gave way to a desolate expanse of wilderness on the city's outskirts, a place where the shadows seemed to grow longer and darker. Scooby, sitting in the passenger seat, glanced out at the moonless night. His jaw clenched; muscles tensed as memories bubbled to the surface. It was always like this when he worked closely with Sage, an unspoken understanding between them, one born from shared tragedies.

They had met years ago, when Scooby had just started on his long, gruelling journey to find his sister's missing daughter, Emily. She had been abducted while on a trip to Thailand, a vacation that was supposed to be a celebration of her graduation. She never returned.

The search had led Scooby into the underbelly of human trafficking, where he quickly learned just how deep the rot went. The system was broken, fractured and corrupt, beyond saving. He had been ready to give up, consumed by the helplessness of it all, when he met Sage. Sage had been part of the American Human Trafficking Task Force then, full of fire and fury, determined to bring down the traffickers one by one. She had seen Scooby's file on Emily, read his story, and something had struck her. Maybe it was his desperation, his relentless pursuit of justice, or perhaps it was simply that Sage knew what it felt like to have the system fail you when it mattered most. They had been thrown together on a job, a joint task force raid to bust a trafficking ring in South America, and from there, an unlikely partnership had formed. Scooby had opened her eyes to the depth of the corruption within the very system she was trying to fight for. She had been so determined to believe that the good guys could win, that justice was a clean, sharp blade. But it wasn't. The system bled like a wound infected from the inside, and Scooby had shown her where the disease festered. He wasn't supposed to be on that raid, but he had his own contacts, his own ways of slipping into places he didn't belong. He had helped her find what her superiors had insisted wasn't there. A mole. Someone within the task force had tipped off the traffickers, and by the time they arrived, the girls they were supposed to rescue were gone. All except one.

Sage had found the girl huddled in a corner, her tiny body shaking with fear, her wide eyes pleading for help. The look in that girl's eyes still haunted Sage. She had saved her, held her, and promised her safety. But just days later, in the supposed security of a safe house, that girl had died. Someone had leaked the location, and a sniper had found her before she could testify, or she could name the monsters who had done this to her. The shot had been clean, quick, right through the heart. Sage had been holding her when she felt the girl's body go limp, the life snuffed out in an instant. That was the moment Sage knew she was done.

Done with the lies, the corruption, the endless cycle of betrayal. She had handed in her badge the next day, walked away from the task force, and never looked back. But she didn't stop fighting. She couldn't. The fire still burned inside her, darker now, more dangerous, but it fuelled her in a way that the rules and regulations of the task force never could. That was when Zander found her, broken but not yet shattered, and offered her a new path, a place where the rules didn't apply, where justice wasn't a clean-cut thing. It was bloody and brutal and necessary. As the van approached the meeting point, Zander glanced over at Scooby.

The man was silent, his usually sharp eyes distant, lost in memories of his own.

Scooby had never found his niece. Emily had vanished without a trace, swallowed by the same darkness they were fighting against now. But that hadn't stopped him. If anything, it had driven him further, deeper into the shadows where the monsters hid. He and Sage had become inseparable during those first few missions, bonded by the understanding that the system had failed them both. They fought side by side, even after Sage left the task force, even after everything went to hell. The van pulled off the road and into a small clearing at the edge of a dense forest. The headlights cut through the blackness, illuminating a figure waiting in the distance. Sage was there, standing under the dim glow of the moon, which was barely visible through the thick blanket of clouds. Scooby rushed out to join her as the two of them stood side by side, a formidable pair, both marked by the same wars they had fought. Sage's long, fiery red hair cascaded down her back in wild curls, catching the faint light and giving her an almost ethereal presence against the darkness. She was tall, her posture rigid with an air of command, but her beauty was tempered by the hardness of her green eyes.

Those eyes had seen too much. Her pale skin seemed to glow in the dim light, but there was nothing fragile about her. She was a force, a storm contained in a human body. Her past was etched into the lines around her mouth, the set of her jaw, and the scars she bore beneath her clothes. Scooby was beside her, his athletic build silhouetted in the dark. He was a wiry man, all lean muscle, with long, unkempt hair tied back into a ponytail. He looked younger than he was, his boyish features often mistaken for innocence, but that was far from the truth.

Scooby had been through hell and back, and it showed in the way he moved, in the way he sized up every situation, always ready for the fight. He wore the pain of his missing niece like a second skin, but he didn't let it cripple him. It fuelled him, just like Sage's guilt fuelled her.

The back doors of the van swung open; Zander stepped out first. The air was heavy with anticipation, but there was no time for pleasantries. The girls needed to be moved quickly. Zander exchanged a brief nod with Sage before helping the survivors out of the van. They were fragile, broken things, their hollow eyes staring out at the world like it was something they no longer recognized. Sage moved toward them with a quiet, gentle authority, her presence soothing in a way that none of the men on the team could offer.

"You're safe now," she whispered to the first girl, her voice low and steady. "I'm going to take you somewhere they can't hurt you anymore."

The girl looked up at her, tears welling in her eyes, but she didn't speak. She didn't need to. Sage had seen this look before and had held too many girls like her, all of them terrified that the nightmare wasn't really over. And maybe it wasn't. Not yet. But for now, they were free, and that was all that mattered. Scooby stepped forward, helping the next girl down from the van. His movements were careful, his touch light. For all his rough edges, there was a tenderness in the way he handled the survivors, a reflection of the uncle he had once been, the protector who had failed to save the one person who mattered most.

As the last of the girls were safely in Sage and Scooby's care, Zander stood back, watching the exchange with an odd mix of relief and sorrow. He had seen too many of these moments, too many lives saved, too many lost. But it never got easier. Sage turned to him, her expression hard but grateful.

"We'll take them from here. You did good tonight."

Zander nodded, though the weight of what they had done still pressed heavily on his shoulders.

"We wouldn't have been able to get this far without you."

Sage smiled, but it was a sad, distant thing.

"We're all in this together, Zander. Always."

Scooby shot Zander a look, the bond between the two men unspoken but deep. They had all lost something to this fight, but they had found a strange, twisted family in each other. As Sage and Scooby led the girls toward their waiting vehicles, the night closed in around them again. The road ahead was long, the battles endless, but for now, they had a small victory. One more step toward something better, something worth fighting for.

And as Zander watched them disappear into the dark, he couldn't help but wonder if the ghosts that haunted them would ever truly let them go.

CHAPTER 24: DEAD ENDS

There was an oppressive darkness as the truck rumbled through the twisting mountain roads. Zander and his team were weary, their bodies aching with exhaustion, their minds replaying the horrors of the night repeatedly. The snow had begun to fall harder, relentless in its descent, a cold, suffocating blanket that buried the world in an eerie silence.

The headlights of the truck cut through the swirling snowflakes like a knife, casting ghostly shadows across the jagged mountain ranges. Every turn, every incline felt like a battle as they climbed higher into the desolate wilderness. No one spoke. Each of them was lost in their own thoughts, haunted by the memories of what they had just endured. The raid had been brutal. Zander's body was a testament to that, bruises forming where he'd taken punches, and his ribs aching from the bullets that had struck his Kevlar vest. His mind was still buzzing with adrenaline, even though his body screamed for rest. The team had succeeded, but victory never came without a cost. There was always a price to pay, always a toll extracted in blood, sweat, and broken souls. Finally, after what felt like an eternity, the truck came to a stop. They had arrived at their destination, just a mile away from Zander's chalet. Zander stepped out of the truck, his breath visible in the freezing air. His boots crunched against the snow as he made his way to the door, each step heavy with fatigue. He could feel the weight of his exhaustion, threatening to pull him under. As Zander walked through the snow, the soft glow of a fire could be seen flickering through the windows, casting an inviting warmth against the bitter cold of the outside world.

Inside the chalet, the fire crackled and danced in the hearth. The warmth of the flames wrapped around Zander like a comforting embrace, momentarily easing the tension that had coiled in his muscles. The air smelled of wood smoke and something faintly sweet, a welcome reprieve from the metallic tang of blood and sweat that had clung to him all night. The 'House of Asmodeus' had suffered a blow, but it was far from over. Zander knew this. They all did. As he made his way to the bedroom, Zander couldn't help but pause for a moment, taking in the sight of Jules asleep in the soft glow of the firelight.

She lay still, her breathing steady, her face peaceful in a way that seemed almost incongruent with the chaos that raged around him. Zander's gaze lingered on her for a moment longer than he intended. She was beautiful, undeniably so. The curve of her body under the sheets, the way her platinum blonde hair fanned out across the pillow, was intoxicating. For a brief, dangerous moment, Zander allowed himself to imagine a life where they weren't constantly fighting for survival, where they could be together without the shadow of death hanging over them. But that was a fantasy. One he couldn't afford to indulge in. Zander slid into bed beside her, careful not to wake her. His body ached for rest, but his mind wouldn't shut off. The night's events played repeatedly in his head, like a nightmare on an endless loop.

He had seen too much, done too much. Even now, with the girls they had rescued safely relocated, all the suffering cut him deeply. The auction house they had taken down was just one of many. The 'House of Asmodeus' was global, a hydra with many heads. As soon as they cut one off, another would rise to take its place. It was a war without end, and Zander knew it. His thoughts drifted back to the girls they had saved. The looks on their faces, the terror in their eyes. He had seen it too many times before. The scars of what they had endured would never truly heal. And yet, he and his team kept fighting. They had to. There was no other choice. Jules stirred beside him, her eyes fluttering open. For a moment, she looked disoriented, her gaze searching the room before settling on him.

"You made it back," she whispered, her voice heavy with sleep. Zander nodded; his eyes still fixed on the ceiling.

"Yeah. It's done. The girls are safe."

Jules exhaled a breath she hadn't realized she'd been holding. Relief washed over her, but it was fleeting, replaced almost immediately by the nagging sense of dread that had been her constant companion for days. Her mind raced back to her father, to the twisted web of lies and corruption that she had been caught in. She wanted to believe that there was some part of him that still cared. Maybe his involvement with the criminal organization was a misguided attempt to protect her. But deep down, she knew better. Her father had always been a monster. Zander's arm draped over her, pulling her closer to him. She stiffened at first, but then allowed herself to relax, if only for a moment. His touch was reassuring, a lifeline in the storm of emotions that threatened to pull her under.

"What happened last night?" she asked, her voice barely above a whisper. "Did everything go according to plan?" Zander's jaw tightened.

"More or less. We got them out, but it was close. Too close. We need to be careful now. They're going to be watching us more closely than ever. I've got Tek working on a cover story, but we still need to keep a low profile. They're not going to let this go."

Jules nodded, her mind already spinning with the implications. They had struck a blow, but it was only a matter of time before the enemy regrouped. They were dealing with a global syndicate, a network of powerful people who would stop at nothing to protect their interests. It was like cutting the head off a snake, only to find another one waiting in the shadows.

A knock at the door interrupted her thoughts, jolting both of them out of the moment. Zander frowned, glancing at the clock. It was early, too early for anyone to be up.

"I'll get it," he muttered, pulling on a t-shirt and heading to the door.

Phillip stood there, his face pale and drawn, a look of unease etched into his features.

"We need to talk," he said, his voice low and urgent. "There's been a development."

Zander sighed, his shoulders sagging with tiredness.

"Give me a minute." As Phillip turned and walked away, Zander looked back at Jules. She was sitting up now, watching him with a worried expression.

"What is it?" she asked, her voice tinged with apprehension.

"I'm not sure yet," Zander replied, running a hand through his hair. "But it's never good."

He leaned down and kissed her on the forehead before turning to leave. Jules watched him go, her heart heavy with a mixture of fear and uncertainty. She knew that whatever was coming next, it wasn't going to be easy. As Zander made his way down the hallway, his mind was already racing through the possibilities. His gut told him that this was far from over, that the storm they had stirred up was only just beginning. The 'House of Asmodeus' wasn't going to take this lying down. They were ruthless and relentless. And they had resources far beyond anything Zander's team could match. He didn't care. He had dedicated his life to this fight, and he wasn't going to back down now. No matter how many enemies they made, no matter how many sleepless nights lay ahead, Zander and his team would keep fighting. Because they had to. Because no one else would. The war against the 'House of Asmodeus' was just beginning. Zander knew, deep down, that there would be no end until one of them was destroyed.

CHAPTER 25: CRUEL INTENTIONS

Jules awoke with a sharp intake of breath, her chest heaving as if she had been pulled from the depths of an endless abyss. The room was quiet, too quiet, but the remnants of her nightmare lingered like a shadow in the corner of her mind, twisting and curling around her thoughts. Her body felt clammy under the sheets, drenched in cold sweat. Zander's bed, she knew it by the scent of him that clung to the fabric, but the bed was empty. He was gone again. She pressed a trembling hand to her forehead, trying to chase away the horrors that had haunted her sleep. But the memories, the images from her past, wouldn't let go. They wrapped around her throat like invisible hands, squeezing tighter with every breath she took. Her father's face loomed large in her mind, *'the devil in God's uniform,'* she thought, bile rising in her throat.

'He had hidden behind the facade of a pious man, a preacher to the masses, but underneath it all he was a monster. A monster who had sold his own daughter, time and time again, to pay for his gambling debts and indulgent lifestyle. And her mother, weak, terrified, always turning a blind eye. She had never protected her. She had never stood up to him.'

Jules's body trembled, the memories too vivid, too raw. She could still hear her father's voice, that sickeningly sweet tone he used when speaking to the congregation, preaching about salvation and righteousness. It was a grotesque joke, an abomination. How could someone so vile, so utterly twisted, wear the cloak of God's grace? It was as if her entire life had been a carefully constructed lie, a nightmare she couldn't escape from. And now, the cult, this secret society, the same one her father had led her into, the one that had scarred her soul, had resurfaced. *'How had he been involved for so long?'*

She had run from her past, cut ties, changed everything about herself to escape, and yet it was as if she were destined to forever be caught in their web. She thought she had escaped, but now the darkness had found her again. The thought of his involvement made her sick to her stomach. Her father had been a willing participant, a leader in this cult of evil that thrived on human suffering. She had always known he was cruel, but this, this was beyond cruelty. This was sadism, pure and unfiltered. She clenched her fists, the knuckles white against the sheets. She wished, more than anything, that she had been adopted by normal people. Loving people. Not the monsters who had raised her. Tears stung at the corners of her eyes, but she blinked them away. She had cried too much already. What good had it done her? Her mother had been too scared to fight back, too scared to protect her, and Jules had promised herself she would never be that weak. But now she wasn't sure if she was any stronger.

'Zander. Where was Zander?'

Her thoughts shifted to him, but it only brought more confusion, more frustration. He had been disappearing more frequently lately. He told her he was spending time with his team, at the chalet a mile away. He said they were working on their plans, strategizing. But she knew there was more to it. *'There had to be.'*

She could feel him slipping away from her, piece by piece, every time he left without a word. She lay there, staring at the ceiling, trying to make sense of everything. The cult. Her father. Zander's absence. It was all too much. Her head spun with the weight of it. The longer she stayed in this bed, alone, the more her mind wandered to dark places. She couldn't stay still. She needed to move, to do something, anything, to keep the thoughts from consuming her.

Her feet touched the cold floor, and she shivered as she crossed the room. She stood in front of the mirror, her reflection staring back at her. Hollow eyes. Red-rimmed from lack of sleep and too many tears. Her hands trembled as she ran her fingers through her hair, trying to tame the wild mess, but it didn't matter. The person staring back at her wasn't the person she used to be. She didn't even recognize herself anymore.

Zander hadn't said when he'd be back. But lately, his absence felt heavier, like it wasn't just the physical distance between them. '*He was hiding something from her. She could feel it.*'

The nightmares had been getting worse. Every night, she was plagued by the same horrific visions, the cult's ceremonies, the faces of the girls who had been sacrificed, and the sounds of their screams. And then, always, her father, standing there, watching, smiling. As if he were proud of the chaos he had wrought.

But Zander was her anchor. Or at least, he had been. Now, she wasn't so sure.

There was a knock at the door. Jules tensed, her heart jumping into her throat, but then she heard Zander's voice on the other side.

"Jules, it's me. Are you awake?"

She exhaled, relieved but also tense. She opened the door, and there he stood, his face lined with exhaustion, shadows under his eyes. He looked worn like he had been carrying the weight of the world on his shoulders.

"Where were you?" she asked, trying to keep the edge out of her voice.

"Working," he said, his voice soft, almost apologetic. "We're getting closer. Tek sent me a new video from the basement cameras..."

Jules's stomach dropped. She knew what that meant. More girls. More sacrifices. More death.

"Two more," Zander continued, his voice thick with guilt. "We watched it all happen. We couldn't stop it, Jules. We couldn't..."

She turned away from him, her hands shaking. She didn't want to hear it, didn't want to know the details. The images from her nightmares were bad enough. She didn't need more fuel for the fire. But the guilt in his voice gnawed at her, pulling her back.

"There's more, isn't there?" she asked, her voice barely above a whisper.

Zander hesitated, and that was all the confirmation she needed.

"What are you not telling me?" she demanded, turning to face him.

He looked away, running a hand through his hair. "Jules, I..."

"Just say it."

His jaw tightened, his eyes filled with something she couldn't quite place, fear, shame, guilt. "That night... the night you almost, when you blacked out... It was me."

Her breath hitched. "What?"

"I knocked you out, Jules," he said, his voice cracking. "You were about to be taken. They were going to sacrifice you. I had no choice."

Jules staggered back, the room spinning. He had done what? The memories from that night were hazy and fragmented. She remembered the panic, the screams, the terror, but she had blacked out. She had always assumed it was because of the chaos, the fear. But now, hearing this...

"You knocked me out?" she repeated, disbelief dripping from her words. "You didn't think to tell me this before?"

"I was trying to protect you!" Zander said, his voice rising with frustration. "You don't understand, Jules. If they had taken you, if I hadn't done what I did, you wouldn't be here right now."

"I trusted you!" Her voice cracked, filled with betrayal and anger. "You should have told me!"

"And risked losing you?" Zander's eyes were filled with desperation. "I couldn't. I couldn't tell you because I was afraid. Afraid you'd never forgive me."

Jules turned away, her hands pressed to her face as she tried to make sense of it all. Her father, the cult, Zander's secrets. Everything was unravelling. The world she had fought so hard to escape from was dragging her back, piece by piece.

"Jules..." Zander's voice was soft now, pleading. "I did it to save you."

"I don't know if I can trust you anymore," she said, her voice hollow. "You've been keeping secrets from me. I thought we were in this together, but now..." Her voice trailed off.

Zander took a step toward her, his hand reaching out.

"Jules, please. You're the reason I'm still fighting. I'm doing this for you. For us."

She shook her head, backing away from him. "I don't even know who you are anymore."

Zander's face fell, the pain in his eyes clear as day.

"I'm sorry," he whispered. "I'm so sorry." But Jules wasn't sure if she could forgive him. The darkness that surrounded them was suffocating, and with every new revelation, it seemed to pull them further apart. Outside, the wind howled, rattling the windows, as if the world itself was mirroring the storm brewing between them. Jules stood there, staring at Zander, unsure of what to say, unsure of what to feel.

"I need time," she finally whispered, her voice barely audible over the wind. "I need to think." Zander nodded, though the defeat in his eyes was unmistakable. Without another word, he turned and walked out of the room, leaving Jules alone once more, consumed by the dark thoughts that had become her constant companion.

As she tiptoed into the kitchen, each step echoed in the quiet chalet. The walls felt like they were closing in, shadowy figures lurking just beyond the edges of her vision. She swallowed hard, pushing down the surge of panic threatening to consume her. Zander was in the kitchen, and she could hear the soft clink of dishes as he cleaned up. She took a deep breath, steeling herself for the confrontation ahead. When she entered the kitchen, the bright light above, illuminated Zander's back, and he turned at the sound of her footsteps. His expression was a mix of hope and despair, and her heart twisted at the sight of him. She could see the tension in his shoulders, the way he clenched his jaw as he waited for her to speak.

"I need you to tell me everything," she said, her voice steady but edged with urgency. "No more secrets, Zander. I can't fight this alone."

He nodded, his eyes widening with relief. "Okay. Just... let me explain."

As they sat at the small kitchen table, the atmosphere shifted. The bright light above seemed to hum with an unsettling energy, amplifying the silence that hung between them. Zander reached for her hand, but she pulled away, not ready for that kind of intimacy, not yet.

"Start from the beginning," Jules urged, her heart pounding in anticipation of the truth that was about to unfold. Zander took a deep breath, his expression grave.

"I found out about the cult before I met you. I was investigating some disappearances, and it led me to their activities. At first, I thought it was just a group of extremists, but then I realized how deep it ran. They had connections everywhere, law enforcement, politicians, even people in the church."

Jules shivered at the mention of the church. "My father..."

"He's not just involved," Zander continued, his voice steady. "He's one of their leaders. He's been orchestrating these rituals for years, using his position to hide in plain sight."

"Why didn't you tell me?" Jules asked, her voice trembling. "I needed to know. I thought you were protecting me, but it feels like you were just lying to me."

"I was scared, Jules," Zander admitted, his eyes darkening. "I didn't want to put you in danger. The night I knocked you out..."

"Stop." Her voice came out sharper than she intended, cutting through the tension like a knife. "You keep saying you were protecting me, but what you did, what you didn't tell me, put me in even more danger. You should have trusted me."

"I know," he said, a flicker of regret crossing his face. "But I thought I could keep you safe, that I could handle this on my own. I didn't want you to have to face it. Not like this."

Jules leaned forward, her elbows on the table. "But I *am* facing it. We're facing it together. I'm not going to hide anymore, and I need you to stop treating me like a child."

Zander looked like he wanted to argue but held his tongue. Instead, he stared at his hands, rubbing his palms together as if to ground himself.

"The video Tek sent... it was worse than anything we've seen before. They sacrificed those girls in the basement under the resort. It was ritualistic, demonic."

A chill ran through Jules, the words wrapping around her like icy fingers.

"What do we do? How do we stop them?"

"We need to expose them," Zander said, his voice filled with determination. "But we must be careful. They have eyes everywhere, and if they find out we're onto them, they'll come for us. They won't stop until we're silenced."

"Then we won't give them that power," Jules said, her resolve hardening. "I refuse to be afraid anymore. I've lost too much already."

He looked at her, a mix of admiration and concern in his gaze.

"You're brave, Jules. But you don't have to carry this alone. Let me help you."

Jules nodded, her heart racing. "We need to find out who else is involved. We need evidence, witnesses, something that can bring them down."

CHAPTER 26: THE BEAST

Zander needed more time, time to gather more evidence, to infiltrate deeper into the cult's inner circle. Tek had uncovered something, but it wasn't enough. Underground tunnels beneath the resort needed mapping, and the encrypted files were taking too long to crack. The cypher text was complex, almost as if it had a life of its own, slithering through their systems like a serpent, resisting every attempt to decipher it. They were running out of options.

Deep inside the cult's hidden sanctuary, Zander and Jules found themselves engulfed in an oppressive darkness. Flickering torchlights cast eerie shadows across the cold stone walls, the stench of dampness and decay suffocating them with every breath they took. The basement beneath the compound felt more like a tomb, a grotesque reminder of the atrocities committed there. Jules shivered, her mind replaying the horrors she had seen, the nightmares that had chased her in her sleep. Her father's face lingered like a demon lurking at the edge of her vision. She had always known there was something sinister beneath the resort, but this...this was something else. She could feel her stomach churn, the bile rising in her throat as she remembered the video Tek had sent, a grotesque ritual in the basement, another pair of girls sacrificed for the cult's twisted desires. No matter how far they ran, they couldn't escape it. The cult was always there, like a shadow, waiting to strike.

Zander moved beside her, his face a mask of tension. He hadn't told her everything, she knew that much. He'd been distant lately, slipping away to his team's chalet under the guise of needing space to work. She didn't blame him, but the silence between them felt like a growing chasm, something deeper and darker than the tunnels beneath their feet. The dim torchlight flickered, casting long, twisting shadows on the walls as they made their way deeper into the underground labyrinth. Their footsteps echoed ominously; the sound swallowed by the oppressive silence. Ahead of them, the basement gave way to something darker, more ancient. The cult's sanctuary, where the masked figures performed their vile ceremonies, was eerily silent, save for the occasional soft chant of unnatural voices, carried on the cold air. Zander motioned for her to stop. Jules's heart raced as she peered into the distance, where cloaked figures gathered in ritual, knives raised, their sinister chants rising and falling like the tide. She wanted to run, to flee, but she was rooted to the spot, paralyzed by the sight before her. Above them, the bodies of three young girls hung from iron hooks, nude and bloodied, their once beautiful faces twisted in agony. Their eyes were wide with terror, their mouths open in silent screams. It was too late for them. Jules pressed a hand to her mouth, swallowing back a scream. She wanted to save them, but it was too late. She was always too late.

"We have to move," Zander whispered, his voice tight. "We can't be seen."

Jules nodded, her throat tight, but as they turned to retreat into the tunnels, her trembling hand brushed against a tall candelabra. It toppled over, crashing to the ground and setting the long red velvet curtains ablaze. For a moment, the world seemed to stop.

The fire roared to life, spreading quickly, casting a hellish glow over the macabre scene. The masked figures turned in unison, their dark eyes narrowing behind their faceless masks. The leader of the cult, Vanessa, stood in the centre, her lips curling into a cruel smile. She stepped forward, her voice dripping with venom.

"I see you, little lambs. Did you think you could hide from me?"

Jules's blood ran cold.

"Run!" Zander shouted, grabbing her arm, and yanking her back toward the tunnels.

But Vanessa wasn't done.

"Don't just stand there," she snarled to her minions. "Go get them!"

The cultists surged forward, and Zander and Jules bolted through the darkened corridors, their footsteps echoing off the stone walls. The tunnels twisted and turned, a maze with no end in sight. The dim light from the torches flickered, casting grotesque shadows that danced and writhed like demons along the uneven stone walls. Zander cursed under his breath. He should have studied the maps better, should have known every twist and turn, but now they were trapped in a labyrinth of fear, with the cult hot on their heels. They ran through a narrow passageway, the air growing colder, and thicker with the stench of damp earth and rot.

The sound of chanting faded behind them, replaced by the relentless echo of their ragged breathing. Jules's chest heaved, her legs were burning from the effort, but she couldn't stop now. They couldn't stop now. Suddenly, the tunnel opened into a large chamber, ancient artefacts and treasures scattered around like forgotten relics from a bygone era. The flickering light from their torch illuminated the grotesque forms of the objects, their shapes twisted and malformed as if cursed by dark forces. Jules froze, an unnatural chill creeping up her spine. There was something in the air, something alive. And then she saw it.

From the shadows, a figure emerged, a towering, grotesque beast with glowing red eyes.

Its skin was slick with decay, its grotesque form barely human, its face hidden behind a twisted iron mask. The stench of rot and death clung to it like a second skin, filling the chamber with the foul odour of rotting flesh and something far worse.

Zander's breath caught in his throat.

"Stay back," he hissed, pulling Jules behind him.

The creature growled, low and guttural, the sound vibrating through the chamber like a death knell. It stepped forward, its massive form filling the narrow space. Jules's heart raced, her pulse pounding in her ears. This wasn't something they could fight.

The creature lunged, its massive arm swinging toward Zander with terrifying force. He barely had time to react before the blow sent him crashing into the stone wall, ancient artefacts shattering around him as his body slumped to the floor, motionless.

"Zander!" Jules screamed, rushing toward him. But the creature was too fast. Its red eyes glowed with malevolent intent as it loomed over Zander's unconscious form, its breath hot and foul on her skin. Jules was terrified. She mustered every inch of her inner strength to fight back. With trembling hands, she grabbed the nearest object, a rusted, metallic staff, and swung it wildly at the beast. It barely flinched as the weapon glanced off its armoured skin, but Jules didn't stop. She struck again and again, her arms burning with the effort, her rage and fear blending into a single, desperate fury. The creature roared, its voice like thunder in the enclosed space, but instead of striking back, it stepped away, its red eyes flickering.

It was almost as if something held it back as if it were bound by forces unseen. And then, as suddenly as it had appeared, the beast was gone, vanishing into the shadows without a trace, leaving behind only the lingering stench of death. Jules stumbled back, her breath coming in ragged gasps, her hands shaking violently. She glanced down at Zander, his face pale, his body still. She dropped to her knees beside him, cradling his head in her lap.

"Zander," she whispered, her voice breaking. "Please wake up."

For a long, agonizing moment, nothing happened. Then, slowly, Zander's eyes fluttered open. He coughed, a pained groan escaping his lips.

"Jules..." His voice was weak, barely a whisper, but it was enough. He was alive.

Jules let out a shaky breath, tears spilling down her cheeks.

"Don't ever do that again," she muttered, her voice trembling.

Zander managed a weak smile. "Did we...did we win?"

"The beast vanished," Jules replied, her voice hollow. "But we need to go. We need to get out of here." Zander nodded, grimacing as he pushed himself up, his body aching from the blow. "Let's go."

Together, they rose, supporting each other as they moved deeper into the tunnels, the darkness closing in around them like a shroud. The cult was still out there, still hunting them, but the beast...the beast was something else. Something they hadn't yet begun to understand.

CHAPTER 27: CHAINS

The room echoed with cruel, chilling laughter, bouncing off the stone walls like the jagged remnants of a nightmare. Vanessa's voice slithered through the chilly air, mocking the trembling girls before her.

"Don't kill me! Spare me! Please don't hurt me!" she mimicked in a high-pitched tone, her smile twisted into something monstrous. "You're pathetic. All of you. Beg all you want but you're not getting out of here alive. None of you will. You're prey, and we are the hunters." Her words oozed with venom, each syllable sinking deeper into the girls' terror. But Jules had reached her breaking point. Something snapped within her, a burning fury that had been smouldering beneath the surface.

"You bitch! I'll kill you!" she screamed, her voice a raw snarl of rage. She lunged forward, torch raised like a weapon of war, her eyes wild with desperation. Zander tried to grab her, to pull her back, but she slipped through his fingers. Then, with a sickening crack, Zander was struck from behind. Darkness consumed him as he collapsed, his world shrinking to the sound of Vanessa's laughter, a sound that would haunt him.

Jules awoke to the smell of blood and the clinking of chains. The fog in her mind slowly lifted, revealing the cold, damp room that surrounded her. She was restrained, her wrists bound by chains, her neck collared like a caged beast. A harsh beam of light cut through the darkness, searing her eyes, and distorting her vision. She felt the cold bite of steel against her skin. She was naked, chained to a medieval rack. Her body trembled with a combination of pain and fury. Her heart pounded in her chest. She could hear muffled screams, faint and distant, as though coming from deep within the earth. The cries of the other prisoners.

The walls, cold and oppressive, seemed to close in around her. Every breath she took was a battle, her lungs freezing in the damp air. Fear gnawed at her insides, but she refused to let it consume her. The smell of blood and rot filled her nostrils. She gritted her teeth, with only one thought in her mind. *'Where was Zander? Was he still alive?'*

Zander woke to agony. He was nailed to an inverted cross. The sensation of cold iron biting into his flesh was unbearable. Rusty nails had been hammered through his hands and feet, pinning him like a grotesque sacrifice. His muscles screamed in agony, and the overpowering stench of blood filled his senses. It dripped slowly, relentlessly, from his wounds.

He glanced around the room, but darkness swallowed everything except the harsh spotlight blinding him. His thoughts were muddled by the overwhelming pain, but somewhere deep inside, a savage will to survive clawed its way to the surface. He gritted his teeth, his body trembling with exertion, as he noticed a jagged stone within reach. Stretching out, his fingers barely brushed it. But he didn't stop. He refused to stop. His flesh tore, the nails biting deeper into his skin, but he finally grasped the rock. Slowly, painfully, he began to chip away at the wood surrounding the nails. Every strike sent waves of torment through his arms, but he pushed through it. He had to get free. For Jules. For the others.

Jules's heart thundered in her chest as she heard the faint whispers of the other prisoners. She wasn't alone. The sound of their chains, the broken murmurs of despair, filled the room. Her breath caught in her throat, but it wasn't fear that gripped her, it was a flicker of hope. She had to get them out. She strained against the heavy chains, but they were unyielding. Her body ached, her wrists raw from the cold bite of iron. The stench of blood and filth choked her. But she wouldn't give in.

"Zander?" she whispered, her voice weak but determined.

Zander's screams pierced the silence, his raw voice echoing through the stone walls. His body was broken, but he fought on, his determination burning hotter than the searing pain. He chipped away at the last nail, the wood finally giving way as he ripped his hand free. Blood gushed from his torn flesh, but he ignored it. He had to move. He had to get to Jules.

Jules' fingers found a shard of broken stone near her feet. With a surge of adrenaline, she gripped it tightly and began to work at the chains. Her hands trembled, but she persisted. She couldn't give up. She wouldn't. The chains rattled with each movement, a haunting reminder of her confinement, but she was getting closer. Suddenly, the whispers grew louder. The other prisoners were stirring, sensing her defiance.

"We're not alone," Jules whispered, her voice cracking.

Zander dragged himself to his feet, his body screaming in protest. His legs buckled beneath him, but he clung to the wall for support. He was drenched in blood, his vision swimming, but he could still hear Jules. He had to find her.

"I'm coming, Jules," he rasped, his voice barely more than a whisper. "I'll get you out of here. I promise."

In the suffocating darkness, surrounded by the stench of death and despair, Jules and Zander clung to one thing, hope. Their bodies were broken, but their spirits burned bright. They weren't victims. They were survivors. And they would fight to the bitter end. In the shadowy depths of the tunnels, Vanessa's laughter echoed once more, a sinister reminder that the real nightmare had only just begun. But she had underestimated them. She had underestimated the strength born of desperation, the savage will to survive.

Somewhere, deep in the darkness, the beast watched and waited.

CHAPTER 28: THE SINS OF THE FATHER

Zander's body screamed in agony, every nerve alight with fire, yet through the haze of pain, he was sure of one thing, Jules had said it. She had whispered those three cursed words, words that brought both salvation and damnation in equal measure.

"I love you."

It was a phantom declaration, barely audible over the torment wracking his body. Had he imagined it? Was it merely a figment of his fevered brain, trying to grasp something beautiful amidst the horror? Either way, it was enough. His battered body responded, clawing at the metal lever beside him, every movement sending electric shocks of pain through his shattered legs. The air reeked of iron and sweat, the dungeon around him echoing with the anguished breaths of the doomed.

"You can do it. I know you can," Jules's voice cut through the torment, trembling yet resolute, from somewhere deep in the blackened abyss.

The shadows shifted, as the footfalls of the masked men neared the cell holding Jules and the other women. The dungeon, already a tomb of despair, fell deathly silent. The whispers of the captives ceased, replaced by the suffocating sound of hearts beating too fast in the still air. Zander was too far, too broken to help. He cursed himself, his frailty, his failure, as he heard the eerie creak of the cell door. Six figures draped in heavy cloaks, their faces hidden behind grotesque masks, entered like harbingers of death. No one spoke.

Their silence was more terrifying than any threat could be. The women, huddled together like lambs awaiting slaughter, trembled in terror. But not Jules. She stood defiant even as her heart pounded in her chest, it was so loud she swore it would break free from her ribs. Her breath misted in the cold, damp air, and her body was exposed to their hungry stares, but she refused to cower. She would not give them the satisfaction. Two of the masked figures moved toward the corner of the cell where a woman, barely more than a child, began to scream. Her cries filled the dungeon like a chorus of broken dreams.

"No, don't take me! Please, I'll do anything!"

Her pleas were met with the cold indifference of the masked men, who unshackled her wrists and dragged her from the cell. Her sobs echoed down the stone corridors, fading into the dark unknown. Jules stood frozen, her heart a twisted knot of anger and fear, but her face remained a mask of cold defiance. The remaining four figures stood before her, their presence a vile weight in the air. She could feel their eyes crawling over her, devouring her humiliation like ravenous beasts.

"Are you enjoying this, you sick bastards?" she spat, her voice sharp, slicing through the silence. "You like watching me like this? You might as well drop your pants and finish the show." One of the masked men stepped forward, his gloved hand reaching out, gripping her chin with a brutal force that made her skin crawl. He pulled her closer, his mask inches from her face, but it wasn't the touch that sent a chill through her spine. It was the eyes behind the mask, familiar, loathsome. Her breath caught in her throat, a sickening wave of realization crashing over her. The man who held her was not a stranger. He was a ghost from her past, a nightmare that had stalked her through the darkest corridors of her mind.

It was her father.

Time had not softened him. His eyes gleamed with the same cold malevolence that had haunted her childhood. His cruel lips curled into a smile beneath the mask as he tore it away, revealing the face she had prayed she would never see again.

"Hello, Julia," he hissed, his voice a venomous whisper. "You didn't think I'd forgotten you, did you?"

Jules's heart thundered in her chest, bile rising in her throat as her body recoiled from his touch. She had spent years trying to erase him from her life, from her soul. But here he was, the devil himself, risen from the ashes of her worst memories to drag her back to hell.

"You've always belonged to me," he continued, his hand tightening painfully around her jaw. "Did you really think you could escape? Did you honestly believe you could live without my shadow hanging over you?"

She wanted to scream, to lash out, to tear his skin from his bones. But her body betrayed her, locked in place, paralyzed by the suffocating terror that coiled around her heart like a viper. Still, she refused to let him see her fear.

Summoning every ounce of strength left in her, Jules spat in his face.

Her father's smile twisted into something darker, more dangerous. He wiped the spit from his face, his fingers tracing the outline of his jaw with eerie calm.

"Still the same little whore, aren't you?" he sneered. "Phillip told me you were a lost cause, that he'd tried to make a lady out of you. I see he was right. You're nothing but filth."

The words cut deep, each one a blade carving into her soul. She had been fighting her whole life to escape him, to prove that she wasn't his possession, that she wasn't the broken thing he had tried to make her believe she was. And now, he was here to finish what he started.

"I'll make sure you remember your place," he whispered. "When I'm done with you, you'll beg for the mercy I'll never give."

Jules's skin crawled with the promise of his words, but her eyes never left his. She would not break. Not ever. She had endured him once, and she had survived. She would survive again. With that, her father and his minions turned on their heels and left. In the darkness, the other women cowered, their hope slipping away like water through their fingers. The screams of the girl dragged away, faded into silence, leaving only the oppressive weight of despair hanging in the air. But Jules wasn't done fighting.

"Zander," she whispered into the void, her voice barely audible. "Zander, can you hear me?"

From the shadows, his voice came, broken and strained but alive.

"Yes, Jules. I heard everything."

His words were like a lifeline, a fragile thread connecting them through the darkness. But she knew it wouldn't be enough.

"Zander, you have to leave me," she said, her voice trembling but firm. "Go. Get your team and come back for us. You can't save me now."

"I can't leave you!" Zander's voice cracked with pain, the sound of his struggle echoing through the dungeon. "I won't!"

"You must!" Jules's voice rose, her desperation spilling over. "They'll kill you, Zander! You have to save yourself!"

"And what about you?" Zander's words were laced with anguish. "Do you think they'll let you live?"

A bitter laugh escaped her lips. "My father won't kill me. Not yet. But he'll make me wish he had." The silence that followed was suffocating. Jules could feel Zander's agony, the weight of his decision pressing down on him. She could hear his laboured breathing, the pain in every gasp as the collar around his neck tightened its grip.

"Promise me," she whispered, her voice barely more than a breath. "Promise me you'll come back."

"I swear it," Zander rasped. "I will come back for you."

But Jules knew the truth. She knew the chances of Zander surviving were slim, the odds stacked against him in this wretched place. Still, she clung to that small flicker of hope, that tiny spark that had kept her alive all these years.

As Zander struggled through the tunnels, blood pouring from his hands and feet, the collar choking him with every breath, he thought of her. Naked, broken, but still fighting. And that thought drove him forward, through the labyrinth of horrors that lay in his path.

The collar tightened, its metal edges biting into his flesh. He could feel the life draining from him, his vision darkening as he fought against the suffocating weight. But he wouldn't stop. He would break free, for her.

"Think, Zander," he muttered through gritted teeth, his hands slick with blood as they searched for any weakness in the collar's design. "There has to be a way."

His mind raced, recalling his training, the lessons drilled into him over the years. Metal could break under pressure. He just had to find the right angle, the right force. With a final, desperate push, Zander twisted the collar with all his remaining strength. A sharp crack echoed through the tunnels as the collar snapped, its grip finally shattered. He fell to the ground, gasping for air, the taste of blood and iron thick in his mouth. For a moment, he lay there, broken but free. Then, slowly, painfully, he rose to his feet. He wasn't done yet. Jules's face filled his mind, her voice calling to him from the depths of the dungeon. He had to keep moving. He had to find a way back. Because if he didn't, the darkness would swallow them both.

CHAPTER 29: SKINS & ORGANS

The shadows stretched long over the day's descent, like the black fingers of death itself closing in on Zander's fate. He lay on the cold slab of a bed, caught in a cruel limbo between life and death. His breaths were shallow, irregular, a prisoner of the agony that gripped his broken body. Every pulse of pain surged through him like the echoes of a distant war drum, calling him back to the brink of consciousness only to toss him into the abyss once again.

The team around him moved like ghosts, their voices distant murmurs as they worked in silence, piecing together a strategy to bring down the malevolent empire of the House of Asmodeus. Sage stood apart from the others, her eyes narrowed and hardened, watching every rise and fall of Zander's chest, knowing that each one might be his last.

In the background, Tek's fingers danced across the keyboard, a man possessed by the thirst for justice. His screen flickered with encrypted files, the secrets of devils hidden beneath layers of digital darkness. The deeper he dug, the more grotesque the revelations became, until they formed a tapestry woven from the bodies and souls of the countless innocents who had been consumed by the cult.

"This... this is beyond anything I've ever seen," Tek muttered, his voice tight with disbelief. His screen was a graveyard of horrors, the names of the wicked, the vile, and the corrupt, interspersed with photographs of the damned, those taken, tortured, sold, and discarded like pieces of flesh in a macabre trade.

Sage turned her head slightly, her eyes dull with exhaustion.

"Keep going. We need everything."

Through the dim light of the makeshift medical area, Sage moved to Zander's side again, her voice breaking the uneasy silence. "Zander... It's Interpol. They're in."

His eyelids fluttered, barely responsive. The words seemed to rattle in the air, trying to reach the man buried beneath layers of pain. The mention of Interpol stirred something within him, but it was not enough. Sage felt the pressure build like an invisible vice crushing her chest. Every moment wasted was another heartbeat closer to losing Jules, another breath wasted on a world drowning in the stench of betrayal and filth.

"They know about the auctions, about the organs," Sage whispered, though it was more for her own benefit than Zander's. "We have the names, people you wouldn't believe. Celebrities, politicians, the untouchables. But we're going to take them all down."

Her voice faltered, for just a moment. Doubt flickered like a dark moth in her mind. She had seen too much to be so naive, she had watched the powerful escape punishment time and time again. And now, with the House of Asmodeus unmasked, the stakes had never been higher. Too many lives hung in the balance. Her thoughts were interrupted by a low groan from the bed. Zander was stirring, his fingers twitching like dying spiders.

"Zander," Sage whispered again, leaning closer, her voice trembling with the urgency that roared inside her. "We have to end this. Now."

His eyelids cracked open, his gaze unfocused but slowly sharpening as reality clawed its way back into his consciousness. Sage pressed a hand to his shoulder, grounding him.

"We need you."

The words hit him like a cold flannel on his face. Zander's mind wrestled its way out of the haze, grasping at the world with trembling hands. Pain surged through his body in violent waves, but there was something stronger than pain now, a hatred, a fury so deep that it ignited his bones.

'The others...' His voice was hoarse, like the death rattle of a soldier left for dead on a battlefield. "Jules... Are they safe?"

Sage exchanged a glance with Andy, who had quietly stepped into the room. His jaw clenched.

"We're making progress, but we need you fully conscious. We need your mind, Zander. Interpol is ready to move, but we can't do this without you."

Zander's eyes snapped open fully now, his gaze finding Andy's and locking there, filled with a grim, almost murderous determination. Every part of him screamed in agony, but it didn't matter. Not anymore. The memories of Jules being dragged away, of the other captives, the women, their cries seared into his mind. He had to fight, had to claw his way back from the darkness. With a groan, Zander struggled to sit up. Sage gently placed a hand on his chest, pushing him back.

"You're not ready."

But he was. Ready or not, he had to be. The cold metal bite of the collar, the weight of blood on his hands, the smell of death all around him, he had come too far, seen too much.

"I'll never be ready," Zander whispered, his voice ragged but resolute. "But that doesn't matter now. What matters is bringing those bastards down. We can't wait. We don't have time."

His words carried a dark, solemn vow, one that the others knew too well. Time was their greatest enemy. Any delay would mean more lives lost, more bodies auctioned off to the highest bidder in this twisted underworld of suffering and profit. Sage looked into Zander's eyes, and in them, she saw the fire that had never really left, the iron resolve that had always been there, waiting to be forged in the flames of battle once again. Andy spoke quietly, though the words felt like they came from some far-off, darker place.

"We've breached their system. We know where they are. Tek found... everything. It's worse than we thought."

"Worse how?" Zander growled, his voice low, dangerous.

"The leaders... They're not just some criminals. They're untouchables. They've got people in their pockets everywhere, Hollywood, the government. Even a former president."

Andy said, the words cutting through the tension like a jagged blade. "They've been pulling the strings for years, controlling the flow of lives like it's all some sick game."

Zander's face twisted with rage, the fury rolling off him like a black storm. His fingers curled into fists, despite the sharp pain that shot through his broken hands.

"Then we tear them apart. Piece by piece."

Sage's voice broke through, colder than usual, her eyes hard.

"Interpol's on board. But we both know how this works. They'll try to keep the big names clean, sweep this under the rug if it gets too messy. We need to be smart about this."

Zander's mind whirred, his military training kicking in through the pain. The plan. The assault. He envisioned every step, every gunshot, everybody falling as they ripped through the House of Asmodeus's stronghold like the vengeful reapers they had become. There would be no mercy.

"I'll brief you on the layout," Andy said, pulling up the holographic map Tek had created of the sprawling complex that housed the House's unspeakable horrors.

"There's no room for mistakes. The place is a fortress."

The map displayed a web of tunnels and fortified walls. It wasn't just a den of criminals, it was a labyrinth of evil, carved into the earth like some kind of ancient tomb. The stench of death was practically palpable even from the digital display.

"We're going in at night. Less patrols. Tek will disable the cameras. We get in, extract Jules and the others, and we burn that place to the ground." Andy said, the cold finality in his voice slicing through the room. Zander forced himself to stand, every muscle screaming in protest, every breath laboured. But his eyes were clear now, his purpose sharper than ever. His mind locked onto the thought of Jules, the moment she had spat in her father's face, those defiant eyes, refusing to break even as the world tried to crush her. He would not fail her.

"We don't leave anyone behind," Zander said, his voice dark and venomous. "And we don't stop until every last one of them is dead."

Sage met his gaze, and for a moment, the room fell silent, as if even the walls were holding their breath. They had been on this path for too long, seen too many nightmares unfold before them. Now, they stood on the edge of the abyss, ready to descend into the darkness and tear it apart from the inside.

"Let's bring these bastards down," Sage whispered, her voice filled with the quiet fury of someone who had spent a lifetime fighting battles she was never meant to win.

The team geared up in silence, their movements quick and efficient. Each of them knew what was at stake. There were no second chances, no do-overs in this game. The House of Asmodeus had built its empire on blood and pain, but soon, they would taste both.

As Zander fitted his weapons and strapped his gear in place, a single thought burned in his mind, brighter than any pain, any fear. Jules was still out there. Alive. Waiting for him.

And God help anyone who stood in his way.

CHAPTER 30: HOSTAGES

The sun had long since bled out behind the mountains, dragging the last slivers of light down with it. The forest lay suffocated under a blanket of oppressive darkness, thick and inescapable, like the fingers of the dead clawing at the sky. Inside the chalet, Andy's team moved with grim precision. The cold, clinical hum of machinery was the only sound, save for the occasional metallic click of weapons being assembled. The air was thick, oppressive, charged with an unspoken understanding of the hell they were about to walk into.

Zander, weakened but unbroken, insisted on joining them. His skin was pale, his face shadowed with the weariness of a man too close to death, yet his eyes burned with a fevered intensity. This was personal. The House of Asmodeus had taken everything from him, his strength, his sister, and possibly Jules, the woman he barely knew but couldn't shake from his thoughts. Now, it was time to take something back.

"We're just doing recon tonight," Andy reminded them, his voice low but firm. "We only have 24 hours before Interpol lands. We need to map out the place, figure out their defences. No heroics. Stick to the plan, stay silent, and stay alert. If you see something... dark, we don't intervene. Not tonight."

Noah, Mick, and Scooby all nodded, their faces devoid of emotion. They had seen horrors before, but this, this would be different. They weren't just going up against traffickers and murderers. They were facing something far more insidious, a cult that thrived on agony and despair, where human lives were mere currency. Mick's fingers twitched near his weapon, a subtle sign of the anxiety that bubbled up inside of him.

"Sage," Andy said, his eyes flicking toward her. "Are you set?"

She nodded, though her gaze was fixed on Zander, who was struggling to zip up his combat vest.

"Are you sure you're up for this?" she asked, her voice tight. "You should rest and save your strength for tomorrow."

Zander's lips twisted into a grim smile, bloodless and cold.

"I know this place better than anyone. And I need to know if Jules is still alive."

Sage opened her mouth to protest, but the fire in his eyes silenced her. There was no turning back. They were all in too deep. They moved out, fading into the forest like ghosts. The trees loomed over them, gnarled and ancient, as if watching. Every rustle of the wind through the branches felt like whispers, warning them to turn back, to flee before it was too late. But they pressed on, the heavy crunch of their boots swallowed by the endless darkness.

The entrance to the tunnels was hidden beneath a mess of vines and rotting foliage. The iron gate that once blocked it was long abandoned, rusted and twisted with age, as if it too had been consumed by the malevolence that festered within. Andy signalled for the team to split. Team A, led by him, would take the northern passageways. Zander, Noah, and Scooby would explore the southern routes, their goal, to map out the lower chambers where the House of Asmodeus held its captives. Sage stayed with Andy, her medical kit strapped to her back, her fingers trembling slightly as they hovered near her weapon. The tunnels were alive with the stench of rot and decay, the very air thick and cloying, pressing down on their lungs.

Their flashlights flickered weakly against the walls, illuminating grotesque carvings etched into the stone. Mick noticed what seemed like faces twisted in agony, bodies contorted in torment, relics of the cult's sadistic devotion to pain. Each step felt like a descent further into hell. Zander's team moved quietly, their senses heightened, every breath a risk, every sound a potential threat. As they turned a corner,

Zander froze, his heart pounding in his chest. Voices. Low, guttural whispers carried through the tunnels, rising, and falling like the chanting of demons. Zander signalled for the others to stay back as he crept forward, pressing his body against the cold stone. Ahead, the tunnel opened into a vast chamber, dimly lit by flickering torches that cast monstrous shadows on the walls. Guards stood at attention, their faces hidden behind black masks, their weapons gleaming in the low light.

But it wasn't the guards that caught Zander's attention. It was the cages. Rows upon rows of rusted iron bars, each one containing a woman, young, broken, eyes wide with terror. Some wept silently, others stared vacantly into the darkness, their spirits crushed, their bodies barely clinging to life. Zander's stomach twisted, bile rising in his throat. This was worse than he had imagined. The House of Asmodeus wasn't just trafficking women, they were breaking them, piece by piece, until nothing remained but husks. He motioned for Noah and Scooby to retreat. They couldn't risk being seen. As they slipped back into the shadows, Zander's mind raced. Jules had to be here, somewhere in the maze of suffering and despair. He would find her, and when he did, he would burn this place to the ground. Back at the chalet, the team gathered around the table, the map spread out before them like a battlefield. Tek, their tech expert, laid out what they had discovered.

"The place is a fortress. Armed guards everywhere, surveillance cameras in nearly every hallway. But the real issue is the hostages. We counted at least thirty, maybe more. If we're going to get them out, we'll need a solid plan and perfect timing."

Andy's brow furrowed as he traced the routes on the map.

"The trucks will be arriving Saturday night. We'll have to move before then. If we can hit them hard and fast, we might be able to create enough chaos to get the hostages out before the reinforcements arrive. But we can't afford any mistakes."

Sage, her eyes fixed on the map, spoke softly.

"Some of those women can barely stand. We'll need to secure medical help immediately after the extraction. We have to account for that." Zander, leaning heavily against the table, nodded. His voice was a rasp, but it held an edge of steel.

"We need explosives. Tear gas, grenades, anything that will disorient them. We hit them in the basement first, where they're holding the rituals, then we split into two teams. We clear the dungeons, secure the exits." Andy glanced at Zander.

"We'll have Interpol with us, seven agents. They've been briefed. Once we breach the tunnels, they'll make the arrests and ensure no one slips through our fingers."

Noah leaned back, cleaning his Glock with slow, deliberate motions.

"We're walking into a nightmare. These aren't your typical criminals. They're fanatics, with enough money and power to bury us if we screw up. We have to be smart."

Zander's jaw tightened. "We don't have a choice. This ends tomorrow."

The room fell into a heavy silence, each member of the team lost in their thoughts. Months of planning, gathering intel, enduring the nightmares of the things they'd seen, this was the moment everything had been building toward. The House of Asmodeus had to fall, and the screams of the innocent would be silenced once and for all.

As the first pale light of dawn seeped through the windows, they knew that the night ahead would be long and bloody. Hours later, Zander found himself in the chalet's armoury, where Noah meticulously prepared the arsenal. The dim light cast long, eerie shadows across the room, giving the weapons an almost sentient gleam, as if they too understood the violence they were about to unleash. Sage entered, her footsteps soft, her expression unreadable. She moved to

Zander's side, her hands gentle as they worked to bandage his wounds for what felt like the hundredth time.

"You're in no shape for this," she whispered, her voice barely audible above the quiet hum of the room.

"I don't have a choice," Zander replied, his voice like gravel, worn and rough. "This is our last shot. If we don't stop them now, more will die."

Sage didn't argue. She knew better. Instead, she placed a small syringe on the table beside him. "Adrenaline," she said. "Use it when you need it."

Zander gave her a grim smile, his fingers brushing hers for a brief second before he turned back to the weapons laid out before them. "Thank you."

CHAPTER 31: MISCONCEPTIONS

The room was heavy with tension as the door creaked open, revealing six figures in suits. Their presence was a storm waiting to break, a whirlwind of secrets, hidden agendas, and the cold, distant air of authority. They walked in, each step punctuated by the unspoken weight of what was to come. Every man and woman in the room knew that their lives, once separate, would soon be intertwined in a deadly game of survival.

Inspector Francesca Rizzo was the first to step inside. She moved with the grace of a predator, her sharp eyes scanning the room. It was a gaze that had broken hardened criminals, and now it sized up potential allies, and threats, with equal ferocity. Beside her was Agent Pedro Santos, all charm, and smooth smiles, but his relaxed air was a façade.

He'd singlehandedly brought down entire criminal empires in Brazil, and his charm was as dangerous as his mind was sharp. Next came Detective Colette Babineux, quiet and unassuming in her entrance. Babineux was the ghost in the machine, an expert in cybercrime whose calm demeanour hid a mind capable of turning any digital landscape into a battleground. Behind her, Officer Khady Diouf from Senegal exuded an air of cool professionalism, her posture rigid, her expression unreadable. Tactical operations were her bread and butter, and there was no one better at orchestrating counterterrorism strikes. Trailing the others, two more figures entered. Special Agent Maverick Martinez from the United States, a hard man with a harder edge, who was known for his precision and cold efficiency. He didn't waste words; his icy demeanour spoke for itself.

Finally, there was Officer Dimitri Popov from Russia, the last to enter and by far the most unsettling. His casual smirk sent ripples of unease through the room. His reputation had preceded him, rumours of corruption, dubious dealings, and moral ambiguity hung over him like a dark cloud. He seemed to bask in the discomfort he caused, his presence a subtle mockery of the team. The members of the task force, already assembled, eyed the newcomers warily. They had every reason to. Zander's team was a group of seasoned veterans, brought together by the most dangerous mission of their lives, to dismantle the House of Asmodeus, a shadowy organization that thrived on chaos and destruction. This was no ordinary criminal syndicate, and failure was not an option. Captain Anne Crowe, the leader of the Interpol team, stepped forward, commanding the room with an undeniable presence.

Tall, imposing, with red hair pulled back into a severe knot, her piercing blue eyes scanned the group. She radiated control and power, with an iron fist beneath a velvet glove.

"Welcome to our task force," Crowe began, her voice firm, authoritative. "We've all been brought together for one reason. To destroy the House of Asmodeus. They are ruthless, well-connected, and will stop at nothing to achieve their aims. Our mission is to ensure they are brought to justice. Every member of this team brings a unique skill set to the table, and we will need to work together if we're to succeed."

Rizzo nodded slightly, already sizing up her new teammates, calculating who would be the most useful. Santos offered a brief smile in Captain Crowe's direction, but his eyes were already searching for the angle, always looking for the next move, even when standing still.

Zander, stood near the back, observing. His gut twisted with unease. Something was off about Popov. It wasn't just the rumours of corruption. It was the way the Russian officer leaned against the wall, looking down his nose at the others. It was the barely concealed disdain in his eyes, the way he smirked as if the entire mission was beneath him.

But this was Interpol. They were supposed to be the best. Why was this man even here?

As the group broke into smaller conversations, Zander's team members began to mingle with the newcomers. Babineux found herself in an intense discussion with Sage, one of Zander's top analysts. Santos struck up an easy rapport with Noah, swapping stories of past operations, while Diouf and Andy discussed the intricacies of coordinating international efforts.

But it was Popov who quickly became a thorn in the group's side. His comments, laced with sarcasm and a subtle superiority, grated on the others. At first, it was trivial things, dismissive remarks about protocol, jokes about the "inefficiency" of certain tactics, but it quickly escalated. During a particularly tense discussion, Andy laid out a carefully thought-out plan to intercept one of the House's shipments.

"We'll need precision," Andy explained, his voice steady. "If we strike too hard, we risk losing critical evidence. We can't afford mistakes."

Popov interrupted, his voice dripping with condescension.

"Or we could just blow the whole thing up, yes? Guns blazing? I'm sure your American method will work." The room went silent, the tension thick enough to cut. Zander's jaw clenched, but before he could speak, Captain Crowe stepped in.

"Dimitri," Crowe's voice was calm, but there was an edge to it, a warning. "We follow protocol for a reason. We're here to save lives, not waste them."

Popov shrugged, the smirk still on his lips.

"Just providing some perspective. Sometimes, you need to get your hands dirty if you want actual results."

Zander's eyes narrowed. There was something deeply wrong with this man. It wasn't just his arrogance. There was a sense of menace in the way Popov dismissed human life, as if it were an afterthought. And Zander wasn't the only one who noticed.

Later, as the team took a break, Rizzo and Noah huddled together, speaking in low voices.

"Is he always like this?" Noah asked, his brow furrowed.

Rizzo nodded. "Popov? Yeah, he's trouble. I don't trust him. The word from higher-ups is that we had no choice. Someone high up forced him onto this mission. But mark my words, he's a loose cannon."

Popov's behaviour only grew worse. During another briefing, he suggested using his "connections" to expedite the mission, a suggestion that made everyone in the room uneasy. Martinez, normally calm and composed, finally snapped.

"We're not using your shady contacts, Popov," Martinez said, his voice icy. "This isn't some back-alley deal. You're putting the mission at risk."

Popov's smirk never faltered. "You're too rigid, Martinez. Sometimes you need to break the rules to win."

Captain Crowe had heard enough. She stood, her posture rigid, her voice cold as ice. "Dimitri, you're off this mission."

Popov blinked, the smirk faltering for the first time. "What?"

"You heard me," Crowe said, her voice unyielding. "You're a liability. I won't have you endangering this team or the civilians we're trying to protect. You're done here."

For a moment, Popov's eyes flashed with anger, but he quickly masked it with a sneer. "Fine," he spat. "Your funeral. But when this mission fails, don't say I didn't warn you."

He stormed out, leaving a palpable sense of relief in his wake.

Zander turned to Crowe.

"That man... He's dangerous. We need to change our plans now. I don't trust him."

Crowe nodded. "I know. We didn't ask for him. He was forced on us by someone high up. But I'm not willing to risk the mission, or anyone's life, just to appease some bureaucrat. Popov is out. Sadly, I am inclined to agree with you, we need to change everything now. I don't feel comfortable going ahead with the plan, with Popov knowing all the details."

Zander felt a surge of gratitude. Crowe wasn't just another cold, distant operative. She cared about the mission, about the people involved. She was a leader he could trust. The rest of her team had been nothing but supportive, eager to work with Zander's group. Rizzo's sharp mind, Santos's charm, Babineux's quiet efficiency, and Diouf's tactical brilliance, they were all assets. The only problem had been Popov. As Crowe looked out into the snowy night, she allowed herself a brief moment of reflection. Removing Popov from the mission had been necessary, but she knew there would be fallout. Higher-ups didn't like it when their orders were disobeyed. But Crowe didn't care. She'd made her decision to protect the mission and her team. As she watched the darkened sky, a part of her knew that this was only the beginning. The real battle was yet to come, and with Popov gone, they could finally face it with unity, not division.

CHAPTER 32: RACES & FACES

The sharp, biting cold of the mountain air clung to everything, filling the spaces between the towering peaks with an eerie silence. It was the kind of cold that felt almost alive, creeping into your bones, whispering promises of a storm brewing. The resort, isolated and majestic, perched precariously on the edge of a jagged mountain range, was about to shut down for the season. But before the last chairlift creaked to a halt and the slopes emptied, there was one more spectacle to witness, a competition that would test not only the competitor's skill, but their very wills to survive. The resort staff and guests mingled in the lodge, the rich scent of pine and smoke from the large hearth mixing with the scent of sweat and snow-soaked gear. A group of the most elite guests had gathered, all invited by special arrangement.

They weren't just here for the slopes, they were here for something far darker, something that lurked beneath the facade of camaraderie and friendly competition. The ten races they would face would be more than just displays of skill, they would be tests, hunts, and sacrifices.

The first race, a lightning-fast downhill dash, was meant to warm up the crowd and set the tone for the day's events. Among the competitors stood Drake Morrison, a Hollywood icon whose celebrity status eclipsed his talent for skiing. He was confident, cocky even, as he took his position at the starting line, eyeing his competition with barely concealed amusement. Tara, one of the resort's most skilled skiers, stood beside him. Her time navigating these slopes gave her the upper hand, but Drake's competitive spirit burned brighter than his regard for safety. The whistle blew, and they were off. Drake pushed hard, his skis cutting through the snow with reckless speed, but Tara's mastery of the terrain soon outpaced him.

She sped through the final stretch with effortless grace, securing the first victory for the staff. A murmur of excitement ran through the crowd. But beneath the surface of friendly applause, darker sentiments brewed. In particular, Henrik Lund, a corporate titan from Denmark, was not one to lose gracefully. The next race was his, a slalom, and he was up against Valerie, another staff member known for her agility on the slopes. But Henrik wasn't just a businessman, he was a predator in every sense of the word. Losing wasn't an option. As the race began, Valerie took the lead, her movements fluid and swift. But in the final moments, Shelley, a waitress at the resort, pulled ahead, securing the victory. Henrik's scowl deepened, his gaze locking onto Shelley with a look that promised retribution. He exchanged a brief glance with Vanessa, a cold, silent nod passing between them. Shelley had won the race, but Henrik had decided she was now to be one of his unwilling victims. He didn't just lose.

He made people pay. Shelley had just marked herself as his next target. As the sun rose higher, the competition continued. The third race was a giant slalom, drawing a crowd eager to watch Mamosita Morales, a famous rapper known for her larger-than-life persona. She was fearless, loud, and brimming with bravado as she prepared to race Megan, a shy and unassuming new employee at the resort. The crowd's energy pulsed around Mamosita, who revelled in the attention. But as the race unfolded, it became clear that Megan's quiet precision would trump Mamosita's aggressive approach. When Megan crossed the finish line first, the crowd erupted into cheers, but there was something else, something sinister, in the air. Behind the celebrations, eyes were watching. Waiting.

The fourth race, a brutal cross-country endurance challenge, brought the Burlington family from Texas into the spotlight. Elijah and Olivia Burlington, along with their two teenage children, EJ and Ava, were the epitome of wealth and power. They were used to getting what they wanted, and they wanted to win. But the staff, led by Monica, head of guest services, had a different plan. The race was gruelling, pushing the competitors to their physical limits. The Burlington's fought hard, but in the end, it was Monica's team that pulled ahead, securing another victory for the staff. The Burlington's seethed with rage, their perfect façade cracking ever so slightly as they accepted defeat. It was the fifth race, the freestyle event, where things began to take a darker turn. Mike Rowlands, a well-known snowboarder and actor, flashed a perfect smile for the cameras as he prepared to take on Pippa, a cleaner at the resort who, to everyone's surprise, was a prodigy on skis. The race was mesmerizing, with Mike showing off his effortless charm and agility. But Pippa's performance was something else entirely. She moved like she was part of the mountain itself, her tricks defying logic and gravity. As she crossed the finish line, the crowd erupted, but a shadow seemed to pass over the festivities. It was subtle, almost imperceptible, but it was there, a shift in the energy.

The guests were no longer just competitors. They were hunters, and the staff were their prey.

As the afternoon progressed, the sixth race, a biathlon combining skiing and shooting, unfolded with the Ivanov's, a wealthy Russian family, squaring off against the bar staff. The Ivanov's were cold and calculating, their skill with rifles unmatched. But the bar staff had something they didn't, teamwork. They skied with precision, shot with accuracy, and in the end, claimed another victory for the staff. The guests were growing restless.

This wasn't how it was supposed to go. They weren't here to lose. Not to the help. The seventh race was a team relay, with Drake Morrison, Henrik Lund, and Mamosita Morales leading the guests' team against Lisa, Nicola, and Hayley from the resort staff. The tension was palpable as the race unfolded, the lead changing hands several times. In the end, a flawless baton exchange between the staff secured yet another victory. Henrik's face was stone-cold as his team trudged back to the lodge, the dark promise of retribution hanging in the air like a thick fog. By the time the eighth race, a parallel slalom began, the atmosphere had shifted from excitement to something far more sinister. James, a local boy, had been invited to participate in this race, a rare exception made by Phillip, the event's organizer. James didn't realize that his inclusion wasn't due to his talent on the slopes, but because Henrik Lund had taken an unhealthy interest in him. Henrik had paid Phillip handsomely to ensure James would compete, but it wasn't for the race. Henrik watched James like a predator stalking prey, his lust and hatred intertwining in a sickening display of inner conflict.

He despised his own desires but couldn't resist them. James, oblivious to the danger, skied with precision and speed, defeating Henrik in the race. But as he crossed the finish line, he had no idea he had just sealed his fate. Henrik didn't just like young, fit men. He liked to break them, consume them, and then wash down their flesh with a fine bottle of Châteauneuf-du-Pape. James's victory had marked him as Henrik's next victim, though he remained blissfully unaware of the dark forces swirling around him. The ninth race, a mogul challenge, saw the Burlington children, Ava, and EJ, face off against two staff members. Ava's agility on the slopes was impressive, and EJ's arrogance nearly won him the race, until Samantha, a member of the staff, sped past him in the final moments, sending EJ into a furious tumble.

As he stormed off the slopes, his face twisted in rage, he spat venomous words at Samantha.

"You little slut, I'll make you pay for that." He hissed, his voice filled with dark promise. Samantha paled, but Phillip assured her that EJ was just being a bad sport. She wasn't convinced. Something in EJ's eyes told her that she hadn't seen the last of him.

The final race of the day was a mixed team event, a thrilling climax to the competition. The elite guests, led by Drake Morrison, Henrik Lund, and the Burlington's, faced off against the staff in a race that would determine the ultimate victors. As the teams hurtled down the course, weaving through slalom gates, speeding down treacherous slopes, and pulling off daring freestyle tricks, the crowd's excitement reached a fever pitch. But underneath it all, there was something far darker at play. The race was neck-and-neck until the final leg, when Connie, one of the staff, faced off against Ava Burlington. The tension was unbearable as the two women raced toward the finish line. Ava's aggressive style briefly gave her the lead, but Connie's calm, calculated approach allowed her to pull ahead in the final moments, securing a triumphant victory for the staff. The crowd erupted into applause, but the cheers felt hollow, empty. The guests had lost, but they were far from finished.

They had come to this isolated resort not just for skiing, but for something far more sinister, something that would unfold under the cover of night, away from the prying eyes. As the sun set over the mountains, casting long shadows across the resort, a sense of dread settled over the lodge. The guests retreated to their rooms, but the darkness they carried within them was far from contained. Henrik's eyes were fixed on James, his hunger barely concealed. EJ's threats echoed in Samantha's mind, and Shelley couldn't shake off the feeling that Henrik's promise of revenge would come sooner rather than later.

CHAPTER 33: THE WATCHER

Captain Anne Crowe stood at the back of the crowd, her fiery red hair hidden beneath a dark woollen hat. The biting mountain wind whistled through the peaks as the final moments of the skiing competition played out on the slopes below. Anne's sharp eyes cut through the commotion, focusing not on the race, but on the faces that intrigued her, faces she had been tracking for years. She had deliberately positioned herself in the shadows, blending effortlessly with the crowd. As the head of Interpol's task force, Anne had perfected the art of remaining unseen. Today, however, she wasn't just a cop, this was personal.

Her daughter Alex had grown up idolizing one of the men in these sick games, Drake Morrison, the Hollywood star who now raced down the slopes with an air of invincibility. The sight of him stirred something deep in Anne's chest. Not admiration like Alex had felt, but an overwhelming sense of sadness. She knew the truth would shatter her daughter's fantasies if she succeeded in what she was about to uncover. But Drake wasn't the most dangerous person here. Her attention shifted to Henrik Lund, the Danish businessman whose presence always seemed to coincide with tragedy. Lund's perfectly tailored jacket and smooth, easy smile masked a trail of disappearances, young boys vanishing wherever he went. He had always managed to escape justice, always slipping away before she could pin him down. But not today. Anne's jaw clenched as her eyes traced his movements. He was laughing, pretending to be just another powerful man enjoying the luxury of the resort. But Anne saw through his act. She always had.

"Captain," came the voice in her ear. Sage was already in position.

"I see him," Anne replied, eyes narrowing on Lund. "Stay sharp. He's not here just for the slopes." A knot of dread formed in her stomach as she noticed the four men surrounding Lund. They weren't ordinary guests, these were his personal guards, and among them, they dragged a boy. No older than sixteen. His face was pale, his movements stiff with fear.

Anne's blood ran cold.

"Sage," Anne whispered, "They've got the boy. They're moving him."

Sage's voice crackled through her earpiece, "Understood. I'm following."

Anne's mind raced. She had been hunting Lund for years, piecing together circumstantial evidence, but she never had enough to catch him. The disappearances had haunted her, young boys taken from across Europe, never to be seen again. Now, Lund was close, but so was the risk. If they acted too soon or without enough proof, he'd slip through her fingers yet again.

As the ski competition continued around her, Anne's gaze never left the group. The boy was terrified, he was being quietly escorted to a back entrance.

Lund himself remained at the festivities, schmoozing with the elite as if he were untouchable. But his men, the ones taking the boy, moved with cold efficiency, leading their captive into the service area of the resort.

"Sage," Anne said, "follow them. Don't engage. I need to know where they're taking him. Stay out of sight."

"On it," Sage replied, her tone steady, professional.

Anne's pulse quickened as she watched Sage move. Everyone knew the risks. They'd been preparing for this moment, but it didn't make it any easier. If Lund caught wind of what they were doing, the consequences would be fatal. Sage trailed the group, her footsteps light, her figure blending into the resort's architecture. The festive atmosphere of the ski competition slowly faded as she entered the quieter service corridors, the hum of the crowd replaced by the mechanical sounds of the resort's operations. Ahead, the boy stumbled, his fear palpable, but the men kept a firm grip on him. They passed through a heavy door labelled

"**Staff Only**," disappearing into the darkness beyond.

Sage paused for a moment, gathering her nerve. She knew what awaited her on the other side, a labyrinth of tunnels beneath the resort, long-forgotten storage areas that few even knew existed. These tunnels had been part of the investigation for months, a hiding place for the cult's grim operations.

"Sage, what do you see?" Anne's voice crackled in her ear.

"They've taken him into the tunnels," Sage whispered, her hand resting lightly on the door. "I'm going in."

"Be careful," Anne's voice was taut with tension. "Get the intel, find out where they are holding him." Sage took a breath and slipped inside, the cold air of the tunnel hitting her like a wall. The atmosphere was stifling. Dim lights flickered, the air was thick with the scent of damp earth and mildew. The tunnel stretched on for what felt like miles, twisting, and turning in an endless maze. Sage kept her distance, her sharp eyes tracking every move the men made as they hauled the boy deeper into the darkness. She was close enough to hear their low murmurs, but far enough to remain unseen. Her heart pounded in her chest, but her movements were methodical, each step precise. She had been in worse situations, much worse, but this felt different. The stakes were higher. The boy's life hung in the balance. Deeper into the tunnels, the group finally stopped at a heavy iron door. Sage edged closer, pressing herself into the shadows as she watched one of the men unlock the door with a key. They dragged the boy inside. Through the small, barred window of the door, Sage saw the room beyond. It was dimly lit, the faint hum of electricity the only sound. The boy was dumped unceremoniously onto a mattress in the corner, his face pale and terrified. He wasn't alone. In the flickering light, Sage could make out the forms of other captives, emaciated, terrified young boys huddled in the corners of the room. Sage's stomach twisted. The door clanged shut behind them, and she slipped away before they could spot her.

"Sage," Anne's voice cut through her thoughts, "What's happening?"

Sage took a shaky breath, keeping her voice steady.

"He's alive. They've taken him into a holding cell. There are others down here, Captain. This is bigger than we thought."

There was silence on the other end, and then Anne spoke, her voice filled with grim resolve. "I had a gut feeling that Lund would be holding more victims somewhere. Come back. We need to inform the team."

"Understood," Sage replied, already retracing her steps through the dark tunnels.

Sage emerged from the tunnel entrance, slipping back into the resort unnoticed. The juxtaposition between the bright, festive atmosphere above and the horror lurking beneath was almost too much to bear. She moved quickly through the crowd, her heart pounding in her chest as she made her way back to Anne. When she found her, Anne was waiting, eyes still locked on Lund.

"What did you find?"

Sage's face was grim. "It's worse than we thought. It's not just James. There are other boys down there, Captain. We need to save them."

Anne's jaw tightened, her mind already working through the next steps.

"We will save them all. But we have to do it right. No mistakes."

Sage nodded, knowing that these next few hours would decide everything. The fight wasn't over yet, but they were closer now than they had ever been.

As Anne turned her attention back to Lund, her resolve hardened. This time, he wouldn't slip away. This time, she would bring him down.

CHAPTER 34: ADAM

Zander lay in a haze of darkness, his pupils dilated, reflecting the faint glimmer of the flickering lights above him. A weak smile danced on his lips, buoyed by the steady flow of morphine coursing through his veins. Each pulse of his heart sent soothing waves of euphoria washing over him, smothering the relentless pain that had become a constant companion. In this altered state, he felt invincible, as if he could rise above the chaos surrounding him.

Yet, deep beneath this chemical induced euphoria, a gnawing dread festered.

The grim reality loomed like a dark cloud. Jules was trapped somewhere in the depths of the tunnels, and the image of her torment haunted him relentlessly. He could almost hear her voice, soft and pleading, echoing in the hollows of his mind. The morphine was both a blessing and a curse, masking his anguish while amplifying his fears. He had to escape, had to find her before it was too late. But the binding chains of helplessness tightened around him, reminding him of the reality he was trapped in. In another dimly lit room, Tek was absorbed in the task of hacking into the security systems that guarded the tunnels.

His fingers tapped across the keyboard with a fervour that belied the cold sweat pooling at the base of his spine. His brow furrowed as he navigated through the chaotic mess of codes and surveillance feeds.

"We're in," Tek whispered, a sliver of hope threading through his tense voice.

Collette Babineux, an Interpol agent with a sharp, calculating gaze, nodded in agreement. Her French accent added a chilling air to her words.

"First, we must deactivate the alarms before manipulating the camera feeds, no?"

As they worked, Special Agent Martinez, Sage, and Officer Khady Diouf readied themselves to venture into the ominous tunnels beneath the resort. Sage's heart raced as she recalled the treacherous path mapped out on the stone walls during their earlier reconnaissance. The entrance lay concealed beneath a dilapidated structure, cloaked in the suffocating stench of dampness and decay.

"Stay sharp," Martinez ordered, his voice cutting through the thick air as Sage took the lead. The dread that enveloped her only intensified with every step they took into the gaping maw of darkness. The tunnels were a graveyard of secrets, their cold, moist air wrapping around them like a shroud. The narrow beam of Sage's flashlight sliced through the oppressive darkness, illuminating the slick, glistening stone walls. Each footfall echoed ominously in the silence, amplifying the rapid thrum of her heart. The atmosphere grew heavier with each passing moment, thick with foreboding and the faint, sorrowful moans that reverberated through the labyrinthine depths. Determined, Sage pressed on, driven by an insatiable need to uncover the source of the mournful cries. They resonated like ghostly whispers, pulling her deeper into the abyss. As she rounded a bend, a chilling sight awaited her, a cell door loomed ahead, its iron bars radiating a sense of coldness that penetrated her bones. The eerie sounds intensified, sharpening her senses, and sending shivers cascading down her spine.

With a trembling hand, Sage cautiously directed her flashlight into the darkness of the cell. At first, her eyes were drawn to a colossal figure huddled in the corner.

Fear gripped her heart, compelling her to step back. The figure stirred, and as the light flickered over him, the horrifying details emerged from the shadows. What she had initially perceived as a monstrous creature was a man, tall and robust, his body contorted and scarred by festering wounds. The grotesque sight unfolded before her like a nightmare, each detail blending with horror and sorrow. His face was shrouded in darkness, revealing only hints of disfigurement that marred what might have once been a handsome visage. His skin was unnaturally sallow, stretched tightly over his muscular frame. It bore witness to the torment he had endured. Nearby, lay a discarded helmet, its glowing eyes dimmed and lifeless, a relic of the terror that had once filled the hearts of Zander and Jules. The sight of it, stripped of its power, left Sage feeling hollow. The realization hit her like a blow to the gut, this poor man had been reduced to a figure of fear by the very monsters who had imprisoned him.

Suddenly, the sadness surged within her, leaving her breathless. This was no monster, this was a man, dehumanized and broken. She stepped closer, drawn by a magnetic pull of empathy and understanding.

"Hello?" she whispered, her voice trembling with a mixture of fear and compassion.

The man jerked at the sound of her voice, his weary gaze snapping toward her. Despite the sunken hollows beneath his eyes, a flicker of life sparkled within them, a glimmer of hope buried beneath layers of despair. Their eyes locked, and an unspoken connection formed between them, heavy with shared pain and unvoiced fears.

Sage's throat felt dry as she swallowed hard.

"I'm not here to hurt you," she assured him softly. "I want to help."

He stared at her, suspicion, and hope warring in his gaze. Slowly, he shifted, moving into the dim light of her beam. The full extent of his suffering unfolded before her, the rags he wore soaked in blood and filth. His massive hands were shackled to the wall, the metal biting deep into his flesh, leaving angry welts that glistened with infection. A single tear slipped down Sage's cheek, betraying her anguish at his plight.

"My name is Sage," she continued, her voice shaking with an unsettling intensity. "I'm with a team. We are here to rescue the hostages. I promise to come back for you."

The man blinked, his lips parting as if to speak, but no sound escaped his cracked mouth. He glanced at the shackles that bound him, eyes filled with a raw mixture of longing and despair. Sage inched closer, her hand reaching through the bars as she extended her fingers toward him. "We're going to get you out of here," she promised. "But we need to free the other hostages first." His gaze locked onto her hand, and with a flicker of uncertainty, he extended his own, the rough skin brushing against her fingers in a fleeting moment. Sage gently squeezed his fingers, her heart brimming with compassion for the pain he had endured.

"I need to know your name," she whispered urgently, her voice a mere breath.

He looked at her, his expression shifting as if battling an internal storm.

Finally, with a voice rough from disuse, he whispered, "Adam."

Sage nodded, tears slipping silently down her cheeks.

"Adam, I promise you, we're going to get you out of here. But I need you to hang on just a little longer."

His eyes held hers, a potent blend of anguish and gratitude swirling in the depths of his gaze. He gave a subtle nod, barely perceptible yet profoundly meaningful. As she withdrew her hand, a reluctance hung in the air, a silent promise exchanged between them.

"I will be back," she vowed, her heart heavy with the burden of her mission.

Before she could turn away, her eyes were drawn once more to the helmet, its crimson eyes now dulled, a ghost of the terror it had once instilled. In that moment, the helmet transformed from a symbol of fear to a reminder of Adam's humanity, a reminder that beneath the grotesque exterior lay a man deserving of rescue, not a monster to be feared.

Sage darted through the tunnels, her mind racing with the urgency of her discoveries. The need to alert her team about Adam surged within her, propelling her forward with a frantic energy. The cries of the other hostages rang in her ears, merging with the memories of Adam's haunted gaze, intensifying her determination. She refused to abandon him.

Upon reuniting with the team, Sage wasted no time in sharing her findings. Martinez listened intently, concern etching his features as she recounted the plight of the man she had encountered.

"We will ensure his safe release," he assured her, his voice steady and resolute. "First, we secure the hostages, and then we return for him. We cannot risk altering our plan now."

Sage nodded, her resolve only hardening. They moved with a sense of urgency, the weight of Adam's suffering heavy on their shoulders as they pressed deeper into the oppressive darkness. The air grew thicker, infused with the stench of decay and despair, each breath a reminder of the urgency that drove them forward.

Meanwhile, Noah and Samson were hidden away in their makeshift command centre, quietly finalizing their plan. The explosive devices were set, ready to unleash chaos during the sacrificial ceremonies that would provide the team with a crucial diversion. Every detail had been meticulously arranged, timers primed, wires connected with precision.

"This had better work," Noah muttered, unease threading through his words.

Samson, sensing his partner's anxiety, offered a steadying touch on his shoulder.

"It will. Every step has been executed flawlessly. Now, we just need to trust in the plan."

In the tunnels, the oppressive conditions weighed heavily on the team. Each step they took echoed like a heartbeat in the oppressive silence. Martinez took the lead, his authoritative voice cutting through the air.

"Stay close. We must save them all."

CHAPTER 35: THE GIRLS

The air in the tunnels thickened with the stench of rot and despair, clinging to Sage's skin like a second layer. As she followed Martinez, her flashlight piercing the oppressive darkness ahead, but it did little to push back the overwhelming sense of dread that seemed to seep from the very walls. Every step echoed through the narrow passageways, the sound bouncing off the damp stone as if mocking their approach. The further they ventured, the more the darkness seemed to close in around them, swallowing the light, muting the world.

The moans began softly at first, faint, almost imperceptible amid the suffocating silence. But as the group pressed deeper into the twisted belly of the tunnels, those sounds grew louder, sharper. They were not just cries of pain, but the broken, ragged wails of the damned.

Sage's stomach churned. The echoes wrapped around her, sinking into her bones, filling her with an overwhelming sense of foreboding. Martinez, stone-faced and resolute, moved in sync beside her, his gun drawn, its barrel gleaming faintly in the light. Diouf followed closely, her eyes darting from shadow to shadow as if expecting the darkness itself to rise up and consume them. The oppressive atmosphere weighed heavily on them all, but the mission kept them moving.

"We're close," Sage whispered, her voice barely audible. There was something up ahead, just around the next bend. The cries had intensified, now tinged with an edge of hysteria that sent icicles through her heart. They rounded the corner, and the tunnel widened into a large chamber. The light from Sage's flashlight danced across the damp walls, casting eerie, shifting shadows that seemed to writhe and slither across the floor. And then she saw them, cages, dozens of them, lined up like grotesque zoo enclosures. Inside the cages were women, girls, really, huddled together in tattered, blood-stained clothing. Their skin was pale and bruised, smeared with filth. Some had hollow eyes that stared out blankly into the darkness, while others were curled in on themselves, trembling, rocking back and forth as if trying to escape into the recesses of their own minds. The air was thick with the foul stench of human suffering, a nauseating blend of sweat, urine, and blood. Sage's heart clenched in her chest. They had known it would be bad, but nothing could have prepared her for this. These girls had been brutalized, stripped of their humanity, their hope.

"Dear God," Martinez breathed beside her, his steely composure momentarily slipping as his eyes swept over the horrific scene. Diouf cursed under her breath, her usually unshakable demeanour faltering. Sage's hand trembled as she lifted the flashlight, illuminating the cage closest to her. Inside, a girl, no older than fifteen, lay sprawled on the floor, her limbs twisted at unnatural angles. Her once-blonde hair was matted with blood and dirt, her face swollen and discoloured from countless blows. She wasn't moving.

"Is she...?" Diouf asked, her voice tight with dread.

Sage knelt by the cage, pressing her fingers against the girl's neck, feeling for a pulse. There was nothing. Her heart sank. Another life, snuffed out by the cruelty of the monsters that had turned this place into a living hell.

"Dead," she confirmed, her voice hollow.

A low, whimper rose from the cage beside her, and Sage snapped her attention to the haunting sound. Another girl, this one barely clinging to consciousness, lay slumped against the bars. Her eyes were wide with fear, her lips cracked and bloodied. She was so gaunt, so frail, that it looked as though the very air might crush her.

"We need to get them out of here," Sage said, her voice barely holding steady. She could feel the panic rising in her chest, but she forced it down. These girls needed her to be strong. She couldn't afford to lose it, not now. Martinez was already at one of the cages, his fingers deftly working at the lock.

"Diouf, help me with these," he ordered, his voice grim and focused.

Diouf moved to the next cage, pulling out a small set of tools from her belt. The locks were old, rusty, whoever had put these girls here hadn't bothered with anything high-tech. After all, the monsters that ran this place didn't expect anyone to come for them. They believed these girls were forgotten, discarded, left to rot in the dark. Sage crouched down in front of the girl still conscious, her heart aching as she looked into her terrified eyes.

"We're here to help," she said softly, though she doubted her words would mean much in the face of the horrors this girl had endured. "We're going to get you out of here. You're safe now."

The girl blinked, her lips parting as if she wanted to speak, but all that came out was a hoarse, ragged whisper.

"Please... don't leave us..." Her voice cracked, tears spilling from her bloodshot eyes.

"We won't," Sage promised, reaching through the bars to take her hand. The girl's fingers were ice-cold, her grip weak. "We're going to get you all out."

Diouf's lock clicked open, and she pulled the door free with a loud creak. Inside, the girls flinched at the sound, their bodies instinctively recoiling as though expecting another round of torment. But when the door swung wide, they hesitated, unsure of whether to trust this unexpected moment of freedom.

"It's okay," Diouf said gently, stepping aside to let the girls crawl out. "Come on. We're here to help." The first girl, a skeletal figure with hollow cheeks and sunken eyes, moved tentatively forward. Her steps were shaky, as though her legs might give out beneath her at any moment. Behind her, the others followed, each one as broken and fragile as the next.

Martinez worked quickly, freeing one cage after another. The more girls they freed, the clearer it became just how badly these girls had been treated. Some had fresh wounds, whip marks, burns, bruises in the shape of hands around their throats. Others bore older scars, faded but no less sinister, proof that their suffering had been drawn out over weeks, maybe months. One girl's wrists were bound in bloody bandages, the crude wrappings barely concealing the raw, infected flesh beneath.

"How could anyone do this?" Diouf muttered under her breath, her voice thick with revulsion. Sage didn't have an answer. She didn't think there *was* an answer that would ever make sense. The evil that had been wrought in this place defied reason. The last cage was the hardest. Inside, two girls clung to each other, their limbs tangled together in a desperate embrace. They were shivering violently, their faces hidden against each other's shoulders, as if by shutting out the world, they could deny what had been done to them. Sage knelt by the door, her heart aching as she looked at them.

"Hey," she said softly. "It's over now. We're going to take you home."

One of the girls lifted her head, her eyes red and swollen from crying.

"Home?" she rasped, her voice so small, so broken. "There's no home..."

Sage's chest tightened.

"Yes, there is," she insisted, though she could feel the weight of the lie. For these girls, there would never be a real home again. Not after this. Not after what had been stolen from them. But they had to try. They had to give them *something* to hold on to.

The girl hesitated, then slowly, she and her companion untangled themselves and crawled forward, their movements stiff and pained. As they crossed the threshold of the cage, Sage reached out, gently taking their hands. Their skin was paper-thin, their bones fragile beneath her fingers. She had never felt so helpless.

"We have to move fast," Martinez said, his voice cutting through the heavy silence. He cast a glance toward the tunnel behind them. "We don't know how much time we have before someone realizes we're down here." Diouf nodded, helping one of the girls to her feet.

"We can't carry all of them."

Sage glanced around at the girls they'd freed, there were at least thirty, and every one of them was in desperate need of medical attention. Some of them could barely stand.

"We don't have a choice," she said, her voice hardening with determination.

"We get them out, all of them, or we die trying." Martinez met her gaze, his eyes narrowing slightly.

"We won't let that happen. Let's move."

They began herding the girls toward the tunnel entrance, Martinez and Diouf taking point while Sage stayed at the back, making sure none of the more fragile girls lagged behind. Every step was agonizingly slow, the injured girls stumbling over the uneven ground, their legs barely able to hold them up. Sage felt her frustration rising, time was running out, and they weren't moving fast enough. Halfway through the tunnel, one of the girls collapsed. Sage was by her side in an instant, kneeling and gently lifting her limp body into her arms. The girl weighed almost nothing, her frail frame barely filling Sage's arms. She couldn't have been older than seventeen, but the haunted look in her eyes made her seem decades older.

"I've got you," Sage whispered, cradling the girl's head against her shoulder. "Just hold on a little longer." But even as she said it, she knew the girl was fading. Her breaths were shallow, her eyes unfocused. Sage felt a wave of panic rise in her throat. She couldn't let this girl die. Not here. Not after they had finally freed her.

But as the tunnel stretched on, the girl's breathing grew fainter, her grip on Sage's arm loosening. And in that moment, Sage felt it, the life slipping away from her, leaving only a hollow shell behind.

"Stay with me," she whispered, her voice cracking with emotion. But it was too late. The girl was gone. Sage squeezed her eyes shut, her heart breaking. Another life lost. Another soul claimed by this godforsaken place.

"We need to keep moving," Martinez called from up ahead, his voice tense.

Sage gently laid the girl's body on the ground, her hands trembling. She wanted to scream, to rage against the injustice of it all. But there wasn't time. She had to keep going.

She stood, wiping the tears from her eyes. There would be time to mourn later. Now, she had to save the others. As they pressed on, the air around them seemed to grow colder, heavier, as if the very walls were closing in. The darkness was alive here, watching, waiting, hungry. Sage could feel it, a malevolent presence that lurked just beyond the edges of the light, ready to pounce. But they were almost there. Almost free.

CHAPTER 36: THE BOYS

The heavy door of the chalet creaked as Sage, Martinez, and Diouf slipped inside. The air was thick with tension, their nerves frayed from what they had just witnessed in the tunnels. Sage could still feel the weight of the girls' fragile bodies in her arms, the haunting whispers of their suffering echoing in her ears. But there was no time to process the horror. They had rescued the girls, yes, but the mission was far from over. Collette Babineux stood waiting for them, her sharp, calculating eyes scanning the haggard team. Her face betrayed nothing, but Sage could sense her unease. She knew what kind of nightmares lurked beneath this place, even if her stoic demeanour masked it.

"Are they stable?" Babineux asked, her French accent slicing through the air as she turned her attention to the group of broken girls huddled together on the floor. Mick, who had medical field training, knelt beside the closest one, checking her vitals.

"They need immediate attention," Mick insisted, his voice tight. "Some of them are in shock. A few of them might not make it through the night without proper medical care."

Babineux nodded, her mouth set in a grim line.

"I'll radio for backup. Get a team in here to evacuate the girls."

"We don't have time," Martinez interjected, wiping sweat from his brow. "There are more hostages, boys, held deeper in the tunnels. We need to move before they realize we've been down there."

Sage straightened, her muscles aching from the ordeal but her mind sharpening with the urgency of the situation. She couldn't leave those boys down there. Not after what they'd just seen.

"Mick, stay with the girls. You're the only one with the medical field training. Keep them alive until help arrives."

Mick nodded, though hesitation flickered in his dark eyes.

"Be careful," he warned, glancing between Sage, Martinez and Diouf. "The deeper you go, the more dangerous it's going to get. We might have caught them off guard with the girls, but they'll be ready now."

Sage and Diouf nodded, already moving toward the exit. Martinez was right behind them, his hand gripping his weapon tightly. They exchanged a glance, no words needed. They all knew what they were walking back into. The tunnels were waiting.

The descent into the darkness felt more suffocating this time. Every step they took felt heavier, slower, as if the shadows themselves were alive, thickening around them, swallowing their light. The walls dripped with moisture, the air heavy with the stench of mold and decay. As they moved deeper into the labyrinth, the sounds of the outside world faded, replaced by the faintest whispers of misery carried on the stagnant air. Somewhere ahead, the boys, scared, abandoned, and broken, waited for them.

"They've moved them, how much farther do you think we have to go?" Sage asked in a low voice, her eyes darting around as they crept forward.

"Hard to say," Martinez muttered, scanning the tunnel with his flashlight. "The layout's a mess, but we're tracking the same patterns as where the girls were kept. I'd guess they're holding the boys in a different section of these tunnels, somewhere further in."

Sage swallowed the lump of dread building in her throat. She couldn't imagine what horrors these boys had endured. And she didn't want to. All that mattered now was getting them out, alive. The tunnels seemed to stretch endlessly before them, the damp stone walls narrowing and widening unpredictably, forcing them into a constant state of hyper-vigilance. Every twist and turn could reveal another horror, another trap. Sage's heart raced in time with her footsteps. Then, they heard it, a faint sound. Crying. Not the broken sobs of the girls they'd rescued earlier, but the stifled, terrified weeping of children. Sage's pulse quickened.

"They're close," she whispered, motioning for Martinez to stay low. They moved forward cautiously, their flashlights barely skimming the walls, trying to remain as invisible as possible. The crying grew louder, more distinct, until they reached a narrow passage that opened up into a small, dimly lit chamber. Sage felt her stomach turn.

There, huddled together in the far corner of the room, were the boys. Around a dozen of them, ranging from what looked like seven to thirteen years old. Their clothes were torn, hanging off their small bodies in rags. Some had shackles around their ankles, binding them to the stone wall. Their faces were hollow with fear and hunger, eyes wide and glassy, as if they had seen too much to understand what was happening anymore.

One of the boys, barely older than ten, had a deep gash running down his arm, the blood dried and crusted over. Another had his head buried between his knees, rocking back and forth, muttering something unintelligible. The sight of them, so small, so defenceless, made Sage's chest tighten with rage. Sage crouched low, whispering to Martinez,

"We need to get them unchained. We'll take them out the way we came, quietly. If they've doubled back with more guards...."

The sound of heavy boots echoed down the tunnel before she could finish her sentence.

Martinez swore under his breath, his hand flying to his weapon.

"They know we're here."

Sage's heart skipped a beat. They didn't have time to free all the boys before the guards arrived. She could hear them coming, maybe four or five, but it was hard to tell in the labyrinthine acoustics of the tunnel.

"We fight," Martinez said grimly, standing up straighter and motioning for Sage to take cover behind the pile of crates in the corner. "When they come through, we take them out fast, quiet if we can." Sage nodded, her hand tightening around the grip of her pistol. Her pulse thrummed in her ears as the footsteps grew closer, reverberating off the walls. She peered over the crates, her eyes locked on the entrance. Then they appeared, five of them, armed and dressed in black tactical gear. Their faces were hard, emotionless. Mercenaries. Trained killers. They moved with precision, their weapons drawn, sweeping the room as they entered. Diouf held her breath. One of the guards motioned to the boys, barking something in a language none of the team had heard before. The boys flinched, pressing themselves further against the wall, their fear palpable. Martinez struck first. In a swift, fluid motion, he lunged from his hiding place, his silenced pistol snapping off two quick shots. The first guard dropped instantly, a hole between his eyes, his body crumpling to the floor. The second took a step back, startled, but it was too late. Martinez's second shot hit him square in the chest, sending him toppling into the stone wall with a sickening thud.

But the element of surprise didn't last. The remaining guards reacted instantly, raising their weapons and firing in a frenzy of bullets and chaos. Diouf stepped out from behind them, snapping one of their necks, his body crumpled to the floor. Sage ducked behind the crates, her heart pounding as rounds ricocheted off the stone walls, sparks flying in every direction. She fired back, her shots precise. One guard fell, clutching his throat as blood poured from the wound. But the final guard, larger and faster than the others, lunged toward Martinez, tackling him to the ground. Sage's breath caught in her throat as the two men grappled, fists flying, weapons forgotten in the vicious struggle. Martinez's face twisted in pain as the guard landed a brutal punch to his ribs, the sound of cracking bone echoing through the chamber. Sage didn't think, she just reacted. In one swift motion, she aimed her pistol and fired, the bullet hitting the guard square in the back. He stiffened, his body going limp as he collapsed on top of Martinez. Then there was Silence.

For a moment, all Sage could hear was the sound of her own ragged breathing, the adrenaline coursing through her veins. She lowered her gun, her hands trembling slightly as the reality of what had just happened sank in. Martinez groaned, pushing the dead guard off him with a grunt.

"You always have to be the hero, don't you?" he muttered, though there was a hint of a smile in his voice. Sage let out a shaky breath, offering him a hand to help him to his feet.

"You looked like you could use a hand." She quipped.

Martinez winced as he stood, clutching his ribs. "I'll live."

They all turned their attention to the boys, who were staring at them with wide, terrified eyes. Some of them were trembling, others too shocked to move. Sage approached them slowly, lowering her weapon and holding up her hands in a gesture of peace.

"It's okay," she said softly, her voice gentle. "We're here to help. We're going to get you out of here." The boys hesitated, but eventually, one of the older ones, barely twelve, nodded and stepped forward.

"You... you're not with them?" he asked, his voice trembling.

Sage shook her head. "No. We're here to rescue you."

Martinez moved quickly, using a set of bolt cutters he'd found in the corner to snap the chains binding the boys to the wall. One by one, the boys stood, their movements slow and pained, as though they hadn't been allowed to move freely in days.

"We need to move," Diouf said, her voice urgent. "There could be more guards."

Sage nodded, her heart still racing. She turned to the boys, her eyes scanning their faces, each one a portrait of fear and resilience.

"Stay close to us," she instructed. "We're going to get you out of here."

The journey back through the tunnels felt longer than it had before. The boys followed in silence, their eyes darting nervously around the dim passageways. Sage kept her flashlight low, trying to avoid drawing attention to their movements. They passed the bodies of the guards they had killed, their lifeless forms slumped against the cold stone walls. Sage felt a pang of guilt twist in her chest, but she pushed it down. There was no time for remorse.

As they neared the tunnel's exit, Sage could feel the tension in her muscles easing, just a little. They were almost free. And then she heard it, another set of footsteps.

"Shit," Martinez hissed, his hand flying to his weapon. "More of them."

Sage's heart skipped a beat. They couldn't afford another fight, not with the boys in tow.

She scanned the tunnel, her mind racing.

They pressed themselves against the walls, the boys huddled together in terrified silence, as the footsteps grew closer. Sage held her breath, praying they wouldn't be discovered. But the footsteps passed by, fading into the distance.

Sage exhaled, her body sagging with relief. They had made it.

CHAPTER 37: MAN DOWN

The basement of the resort was a place where nightmares were born, where despair had festered for years, untouched by the warmth of daylight. Darkness did not merely fill the air, it suffocated it, clung to every stone, coiling around each rough-hewn surface like a living thing. The walls dripped with moisture, but it was more than just the cold sweat of a forgotten place, it was as though the very stones themselves wept, bled with the pain of those who had been lost within these walls. Ancient symbols, etched deep into the stone with sharp precision, seemed to pulse and writhe in the faint flicker of torchlight, like living scars that breathed with a malevolent hunger. These were not symbols meant for mortal eyes, they were the remnants of dark rituals, of prayers whispered to gods long forsaken, of sacrifices too vile to be remembered in any sane world. The air itself was thick with the stench of damp rot, mingled with something far worse, a cloying, metallic tang that filled the lungs and turned the stomach. The distant, irregular hum of rusted machinery added a discordant soundtrack to the creeping horror, while the faint but incessant drip of unseen water played the role of some forgotten clock, counting down the seconds until madness claimed another soul.

Here, light was an intruder. Even the faint glow of their flashlights seemed hesitant, casting long, jagged shadows that moved on their own, devouring hope and leaving only the abyss. In the bowels of this forsaken place, Zander, Andy, and Captain Anne Crowe crouched in silence, their bodies tense and coiled like predators waiting for the moment to strike. Every second stretched impossibly long, the weight of the oppressive darkness pressing down on them, squeezing the breath from their lungs. Time had become meaningless here. Zander's heart hammered in his chest, each thud a cruel reminder of the horrors that awaited them in the chamber ahead. The sound of his own heartbeat filled his ears, a rhythmic echo that only deepened the dread pooling in his gut. Andy stood close, his tall, muscular frame a silhouette of readiness, his hand resting on the hilt of his blade, fingers twitching as if anticipating the violence to come. His eyes never wavered from the heavy wooden door at the end of the corridor, where the dim light of torches flickered from beneath the crack, illuminating the edges in an eerie red glow. Captain Crowe, ever the tactician, observed her surroundings with cold, calculating precision. Every creak of the floor, every rustle of distant movement was catalogued, assessed for threats. Her mind worked like a machine, sharpening with each second that passed. She had seen hell before, but even here, in this rotten crypt, something felt wrong. Darker. More twisted. Then, the door groaned open, a sound like the moaning of a dying beast. It sent a shiver through the group, as though the very air itself recoiled from the noise. Six guards swept in, their movements eerily synchronized, like they were part of one singular entity. Their crimson cloaks billowed behind them like fresh blood spilling onto the stone floor, and their black masks, smooth and featureless, were devoid of humanity. The masks gleamed in the torchlight, casting reflections that shimmered like the glint of polished bone. They were an unsettling reminder that the men beneath those masks had long since surrendered their souls. In their midst, they dragged a figure, bound in chains so thick they looked as if they had been crafted to bind a god. The chains clanged heavily against the floor with every movement, echoing through the chamber like a death sentence. This was no man, no prisoner, this was a creature pulled from the darkest nightmares. It towered over the guards, its muscles bulging grotesquely against the iron shackles, straining with unnatural strength. But the chains held, binding it like an animal, as though the metal had been forged in hellfire itself. Its helmet was a grotesque thing, adorned with glowing red eyes that cut through the dim light like twin embers burning in the heart of an inferno. The creature snarled and thrashed, its movements violent and uncontrolled, but the guards did not flinch.

They moved with the cold efficiency of predators who had broken beasts far worse than this. The beast was pushed toward the throne that dominated the far end of the room. The throne was a monstrosity, carved from ancient stone blackened by centuries of sacrificial blood. Its surface gleamed wetly in the dim light, slick with a sheen that spoke of countless rituals performed in the name of gods long forgotten. The back of the throne twisted upward like the gnarled branches of a dead tree, each twist and curve adorned with grotesque figures, faces frozen in expressions of terror and agony, as though the stone itself had been moulded from the souls of the damned. One of the guards stepped forward, pulling out a syringe filled with a thick, viscous liquid that glimmered in the torchlight like oil on water. The liquid was noxious, unnatural, a dark substance that seemed to pulse with its own malevolent energy. Without hesitation, the guard plunged the syringe into the creature's thick neck, the needle disappearing beneath the taut skin. The beast roared, a guttural, primal sound that reverberated through the chamber, shaking the very walls. Its body convulsed violently, muscles rippling beneath its scarred skin as the foul concoction coursed through its veins. For a moment, it seemed as though the chains would not hold, as though the creature might break free and tear its captors apart. But then, its movements slowed. Its roars became a low, pitiful moan, and finally, it collapsed, slumping against the throne, its massive body going limp.

Whatever foul magic had been injected into its veins, it had taken hold. The beast was subdued, for now. The guards worked quickly, securing the creature with thick ropes and additional iron cuffs, as though they feared the chains might not be enough. They bound it not just to the throne, but to the very floor itself, as though they sought to chain it to this cursed place, ensuring it could never leave. And then, just as silently as they had entered, the guards vanished, leaving the room steeped in an oppressive, suffocating silence. Zander's eyes were wide, his breath shallow. Curiosity gnawed at him, a dark compulsion urging him forward, toward the slumbering beast. He inched closer, each step heavy with dread, as though the very air grew thicker, the nearer, he came to the creature.

Crowe and Andy exchanged wary glances, their muscles tensed, but they did not stop him. There was an unspoken understanding between them, they had come too far to turn back now. With every step, the temperature seemed to drop, the air growing colder, heavier. Zander's breath fogged in the dim light, and a chill crawled up his spine. The creature, no, the man, was larger up close, his chest heaving with laboured breaths even in his unconscious state. As Zander drew closer, the helmet with the glowing red eyes slipped from the man's head, falling to the ground with a dull clang. The face beneath was not a beast at all. It was human. Twisted and mutilated beyond recognition, but unmistakably human. His skin was a patchwork of scars and lesions, his flesh pulled taut over bones that jutted out at unnatural angles. His lips were cracked and split, his eyes sunken deep into hollow sockets that spoke of endless torment. His face had been contorted into a grotesque mask of suffering, a man who had been pushed beyond the limits of human endurance, broken, and remade into something monstrous. Zander's hand trembled as he reached out, fingers just inches from the man's disfigured skin, when the door to the chamber burst open with a deafening crash. The sound ripped through the heavy silence, sending a jolt of terror through Zander's body. He spun around, eyes wide, as more guards flooded the room. Their crimson cloaks billowed behind them, the black masks reflecting the flickering torchlight with a predatory gleam. At their head was a figure far more terrifying than the guards, a man whose presence filled the room like a black cloud. Dimitri Popov, the Russian Interpol agent turncoat. His eyes were dark, cold, and soulless, his face a mask of cruel amusement. His lips curled into a twisted smile that showed far too many teeth.

"(Вот он!) There he is!" Popov's voice echoed through the chamber, his words sharp and commanding. His voice carried the weight of authority, and the guards reacted instantly, surging forward like a pack of wolves. Zander barely had time to react before the guards were upon him. Hands like iron clamped down on his arms, dragging him away from the throne. He fought, his fists flying, his adrenaline spiking as he thrashed against their grip, but it was like fighting the ocean, overwhelming, relentless. For every guard he struck down, two more replaced them, their strength unyielding.

They forced him to his knees before Popov, his chest heaving, his mind racing for a way out. But the Russian stood over him like a dark god, his eyes gleaming with sadistic delight.

"(Ты попал в медвежий угол, мой друг). You've walked into the bear's den, my friend," Popov said, his voice thick with mockery.

Zander spat at his feet, defiance burning in his chest like a fire.

"I'm not your friend."

Popov's smile widened, but it was a cold, humourless thing. His eyes gleamed with something dark, something that whispered of death.

"(Терпение и труд всё перетрут) Patience and work grind everything down, but I see you're not one for patience, are you?"

Zander's mind raced, searching desperately for something to stall Popov, to give Andy and Crowe a chance to act. He needed to buy time, just a few seconds more.

"You think you're in control here, Popov?" Zander said, his voice steady despite the terror clawing at his insides. "You're nothing but a puppet in this sick game. You're not the one pulling the strings."

Popov's smile vanished in an instant, replaced by a cold, deadly stare. He took a step closer, his breath cold against Zander's face.

"You don't understand, Zander. You're already dead."

With a flick of his hand, the guards yanked Zander to his feet, their grips unbreakable. Popov leaned in, his voice a low whisper filled with malice. "You will watch your friends die, one by one. And when there is nothing left, I will end you myself."

Zander struggled against their hold, but it was futile. The guards dragged him away, his mind reeling with a desperate need to escape. The walls of the resort seemed to close in, the darkness pressing in on all sides, suffocating any hope of freedom.

In the shadows, Andy and Captain Crowe watched, their jaws clenched with barely contained rage. Andy's voice was a harsh whisper. "We need to get him back."

"We will," Crowe replied, her voice sharp and precise. "But one wrong move, and we're all dead." The weight of their decision hung in the air as thick and suffocating as the darkness around them, their only chance of survival resting on the edge of a knife.

CHAPTER 38: EMPTINESS

They melted deeper into the shadows, becoming one with the darkness that clung to every corner of the labyrinthine tunnels beneath the resort. The air was thick, suffocating.

Every step they took was a calculated risk, each movement deliberate and silent, as if the very walls were listening, waiting to betray them. The mission had shifted, this was no longer about stopping a ritual that promised untold horror. This was survival, a desperate fight against forces they barely understood but could feel creeping ever closer, like the cold fingers of death brushing against their skin.

Below, in the endless maze of tunnels that twisted and turned like the intestines of a slumbering beast, Sage and her team raced through the oppressive blackness. Their breath came in ragged gasps, the sound muted by the overwhelming silence that filled the space around them. The air was stale, thick with the scent of damp earth, mildew, and something far more sinister, an underlying note of death, as if the walls themselves had absorbed the suffering of countless souls who had perished in this forsaken place.

The darkness was so complete, so impenetrable, it felt alive, as if it were actively swallowing them whole. Sage's heart pounded in her chest, the adrenaline coursing through her veins like fire, urging her to move faster, to escape the creeping dread that chased them with every step. The walls pressed in on them, the narrow passageways feeling more like a grave than a tunnel. When they finally emerged into the cold, open night, it was as if the world itself had changed. The air hit their faces, cold and sharp, biting against their skin, pulling them out of the suffocating claustrophobia of the tunnels. For a moment, they all stood still, sucking in the fresh air with greedy gulps, trying to shake off the oppressive weight that still clung to their shoulders. The hostages had been saved, but the night was far from over. The success of the rescue did little to lift the tension in the air, the weight of the unfinished mission still hanging over them like a guillotine waiting to drop. There were still two missing, Jules and James. And Adam. Adam, the tortured soul they had found in the depths of the tunnels, bound in chains, his mind shattered by unspeakable horrors. Sage had promised him she would save him, and now that promise weighed on her like a lead weight. The brief moment of relief was shattered as Captain Crowe's voice crackled through their earpieces, sharp and commanding.

"We need to blow the tunnels."

The words hit Sage like a punch to the gut. Blow the tunnels? With Adam still down there? She couldn't let that happen. Her heart lurched in her chest, panic seizing her throat. She glanced at her team, their faces lit by the cold moonlight, pale and strained, waiting for her command.

"We can't," Sage blurted out, her voice tight with urgency. "Adam's still in there. We can't leave him behind. I promised him I would save him. And we haven't found Jules or James yet either. We need more time."

The silence that followed her words was heavy, and when Crowe spoke again, her voice was like ice, devoid of emotion.

"Who is Adam?"

Sage hesitated, her mind racing. How could she explain? How could she make Crowe understand. She had formed a bond with the man she had found in the darkest depths of the tunnels. "The man with the mask," she said, her voice barely a whisper.

"The one they've been torturing. I promised him I'd get him out."

Crowe's response came quickly, her voice trembling slightly, though she tried to hide it beneath her usual steely exterior.

"He's here. Strapped to the throne. You made sure the other cells were empty, right? Then we have no time. Sage they've taken Zander. We are a man down. The chanting has started. The ceremony is about to begin. We only have twenty minutes left. We need that diversion, Sage."

Sage's heart raced, her chest tightening with fear and indecision. Twenty minutes? How could she possibly find the others in that short time? But Crowe was right, the stakes were far too high. If they didn't stop this, if they didn't capture everyone involved in the ritual, whatever horrors the cult was trying to unleash would claim more lives than she could fathom.

"Sure, I'll let Noah and Samson know," Sage replied, her voice betraying the turmoil boiling inside her. Crowe's voice crackled back through the earpiece, harder now, as if she could sense Sage's hesitation.

"Sage, listen to me very carefully. We must consider the greater good here. If they complete this ritual, more lives will be lost, and all the deaths, all the victims won't get justice. We need that diversion, and we need it now. There is no time for anything else."

Sage's fists tightened until her knuckles turned white, her nails digging into the flesh of her palms. The weight of her promise to Adam pulled her in one direction, while the harsh reality of the mission and the potential for catastrophic loss of life pulled her in another.

"You only have twenty minutes left before the tunnels are blown."

The clock was ticking. Sage knew what needed to be done, but every fibre of her being screamed against it. She had to risk it, she had to find the others. Her thoughts raced, her mind spinning with possibilities, with ways to buy more time, to find a way to save everyone. But time was slipping through her fingers like sand.

"We're on our way," she finally said, forcing the words through clenched teeth. The weight of her decision pressed down on her, threatening to crush her beneath its enormity.

In the silence that followed, Sage could almost hear Crowe's sigh of relief, though it was brief. The captain's voice returned, colder now, more resolved.

"Okay. Only twenty minutes, no longer. You're going to have to make a run for it. Get in, get out, and hope to God, you find them."

Sage glanced at Martinez, his face was grim, but resolute. He trusted her. He believed in the mission. But Sage had to find the others, she had to try, she couldn't let them down.

"I'm making my way to the chambers now," Sage said, her voice steady despite the chaos roiling inside her. "Instruct Noah and Samson to detonate the tunnels, no matter where we are. It's going to be tight, but I'm sure we can make it."

Her team moved swiftly, their steps precise. The tunnels loomed before them like the mouth of a beast ready to swallow them whole once more. The cold air bit at their skin as they entered, but it was nothing compared to the icy fear gripping Sage's heart. Time was slipping away, the seconds ticking by with ruthless precision.

"We only have twenty minutes until the tunnels are destroyed. We have to go back to see if we can find Zander and the others," she said, her voice firm but low, the tension in her words unmistakable. Martinez moved forward, his face a mask of grim determination, his eyes blazing with resolve.

"Let's do this," he said, his voice cold and hard.

Leaving the hostages in a secure location, with Babineux keeping watch back at the chalet, Sage and a handful of operatives plunged back into the darkened maze of tunnels. Every step felt heavier, the weight of their task propelling them forward. The oppressive atmosphere of the underground complex seemed to swallow them whole, the flickering light of their torches casting grotesque, shifting shadows on the stone walls. There was no time to lose, yet every inch of progress felt slow, agonizing, as if the very earth were trying to hold them back. The tension was palpable, their every movement laced with urgency. The tunnels seemed to stretch on endlessly, the darkness deeper and more suffocating with each step. Every sound was magnified in the silence, the drip of water, the shuffle of their boots on the stone floor, the echo of their ragged breaths. The cold gnawed at their bones, seeping into their flesh like the icy fingers of death itself. The farther they went, the more oppressive the air became. It was as if the very walls were alive, watching them, waiting for them to falter. Every corner they turned felt like it could lead them straight into the mouth of something unspeakable.

But they pressed on, driven by the ticking clock and the knowledge that their window for success was closing fast. The air in the tunnels was suffocating. Each breath felt like a struggle against the weight of the darkness that clung to every surface. Sage and Martinez moved swiftly but cautiously, their footsteps barely a whisper in the oppressive silence. Every second counted. They had only minutes left before the tunnels would be blown, sealing everything beneath the earth forever, along with James, Jules, and Zander if they didn't find them in time. Sage led the way, her flashlight beam cutting through the thick blackness, illuminating the rough stone walls that seemed to close in tighter with each step.

Her heart pounded in her chest, each beat a reminder of how little time they had. The cold air stung her lungs, but she pressed on, her mind racing as she counted the minutes in her head.

"We need to split up," Martinez whispered, his voice tight with urgency. He was right behind her, his eyes scanning the dark corners as they moved. "We'll cover more ground that way."

Sage hesitated, the idea of splitting up in these tunnels setting her nerves on edge. But Martinez was right. They had no choice. They were running out of time, and if they didn't find the others soon, there wouldn't be anything left to save.

"Okay," Sage agreed, her voice barely audible.

"You take the left wing. I'll check the right. Stay in radio contact. If you find anything, anything at all, you let me know."

Martinez nodded, his face grim in the dim light. "Got it. Be careful."

"You too," Sage said, her voice steadier than she felt.

With a final glance, they parted ways, Martinez disappearing into the shadows of the left corridor while Sage turned down the right. The tunnel she entered was narrower, the air even colder, and the walls seemed to close in, tighter with each step. She moved quickly but methodically, sweeping her flashlight across every inch of the stone walls, every corner, every crevice. Her heart raced as she came upon the first chamber, a small, square room carved out of the rock. The air was damp, and the stench of decay was overwhelming. Sage's stomach churned, but she forced herself to keep moving, to keep searching.

She scanned the room, looking for any sign of life, any hint that James, Jules, or Zander had been there. But the room was empty, save for the rotting remains of what looked like old, rusted chains hanging from the walls. She moved on, her mind focused, her body tense with the knowledge that the clock was ticking. Every second that passed was one less they had to find the others. The tunnels were a maze, a twisted labyrinth of dead ends and empty chambers, each one feeling more like a tomb than the last. The walls seemed to pulse with a life of their own, the shadows shifting and flickering in the corners of her vision, as if something unseen was watching her from the darkness. Sage's hand tightened around her flashlight as she pressed forward, her breath coming in short, sharp gasps. Her radio crackled to life, Martinez's voice cutting through the silence.

"Anything on your end?" he asked, his voice strained with the same urgency she felt.

"Nothing," Sage replied, her frustration bubbling to the surface. "Just empty rooms. You?"

"Same. Keep moving. We don't have much time."

The crackling silence returned, and Sage pushed on, her mind racing. She checked room after room, each one a mirror of the last. Cold, dark, empty. The deeper she went, the more hopeless it felt. Every door she opened, every chamber she searched, brought her one step closer to failure.

CHAPTER 39: THE PROMISE

The tunnels were suffocating. Every breath felt heavy, each step a reminder of the crushing weight of failure looming over them. Sage and Martinez had been running through the labyrinthine passages for what felt like hours. They were racing against time, against fear, against the growing dread that had taken root deep in Sage's chest.

They hadn't found Zander. They hadn't found Jules or James. The tunnels had been nothing but an endless maze of dead ends and empty rooms. Now, with the clock ticking down toward their imminent destruction, they were left with no choice but to return to the basement's ritual chamber. To regroup. To face whatever awaited them.

Sage's hands shook as they hurried back, though she did her best to hide it from Martinez. The air felt colder here, the smell of damp rot and decaying flesh clinging to her nostrils. Her mind raced, flashes of Zander's face, of Jules and James, spinning in her head like a nightmare she couldn't wake from. She had promised herself she wouldn't leave without them, but with every passing second, it felt like that promise was slipping further out of reach.

"Nothing," Martinez muttered, his voice tight with frustration. "No signs of struggle, no blood, no footprints leading deeper into the tunnels. Just emptiness, it's like they have vanished into thin air."

"They have to be somewhere," Sage whispered, more to herself than to him, her voice hoarse. "They can't just disappear."

Martinez gritted his teeth, his jaw tense as they rounded another corner, their footsteps echoing off the cold stone.

"We're running out of time. You know what Crowe said. If we don't get out of here before the explosives go off..."

"I'm not leaving without them," Sage snapped, her voice harder than she intended. She could feel the panic clawing at the edges of her composure, threatening to spill over. But she had to hold it together. Martinez didn't argue, but the tension between them was palpable. He knew as well as she did that time was their enemy now, and it was running out fast. They emerged from the tunnels into the sprawling, cavernous basement, a place where nightmares lived and breathed. The air was thick with decay, with the sickeningly sweet stench of blood and rot. The walls were adorned with grotesque symbols, etched in a language older than time, pulsing with an unholy energy that made the hairs on the back of Sage's neck stand on end. In the centre of it all, Adam sat slumped on the twisted, black stone throne, his body limp and lifeless, chains and iron cuffs biting into his wrists and ankles. His head hung low, his breathing shallow, and his eyes were closed, as if he were lost in some dark, drug-induced stupor. Captain Anne Crowe stood near the far end of the room, her gaze fixed on the entrance to the chamber, her earpiece buzzing with static as she communicated with the rest of their team. She was a picture of cold control, her eyes sharp and calculating, her mind always two steps ahead. But there was something in her posture, a tension that Sage had never seen before. Something was wrong. Very wrong. Crowe glanced at them as they entered, her eyes narrowing.

"Anything?" she asked, her voice clipped, business-like.

Sage shook her head, fighting to keep the frustration and fear from seeping into her voice. "Nothing. No sign of them."

Crowe's face tightened, her lips thinning into a hard line.

"Damn it," she muttered under her breath, turning her gaze back to the tunnel entrance. "We're running out of time."

Sage's eyes flickered to Adam, slumped on the throne like a broken doll. His skin was pale, a sickly grey in the dim light of the chamber, and she could see the faint rise and fall of his chest, the slow rhythm of his breathing.

"I'm going to get him out of here," Sage said suddenly, the words spilling from her mouth before she had fully thought them through. Crowe's head snapped toward her, her eyes flashing with a sharp, icy warning.

"No. You'll blow our cover. The ritual is about to start, Sage. We need to be in position. Now."

"I promised him," Sage said, her voice low, trembling with barely contained emotion. "I promised him I'd come back for him."

"He's not your mission," Crowe snapped, her voice like the crack of a whip. "Zander, Jules, James, hell, all of us, are counting on you to keep it together. We can't afford for you to go rogue now. Not when we're this close." Sage shook her head, her fists clenching at her sides.

"I'm not leaving him here to die."

Crowe stepped forward, her voice dropping to a dangerous whisper.

"Stand down, Sage. That's an order."

But Sage couldn't hear her. All she could see was Adam, his bruised, broken body slumped in those chains, his face twisted in agony even in his unconscious state. She had failed Zander, Jules, and James. She couldn't fail Adam too. Not again. Ignoring Crowe's glare, Sage crossed the room in long, quick strides, her heart pounding in her chest. The chains rattled as she knelt beside Adam, her fingers fumbling with the rusted iron cuffs that bound his wrists and ankles.

"Sage!" Crowe hissed, her voice sharp with anger. "Get back here, now!"

But Sage didn't listen. She worked faster, her hands trembling as she unshackled Adam's bonds, the heavy iron clattering to the floor with a dull, echoing thud.

Adam stirred, his eyelids fluttering, his breathing quickening as he began to regain consciousness. His eyes flickered open, glazed, and unfocused, and for a moment, he didn't seem to recognize her.

"It's okay," Sage whispered, her voice soft, almost pleading. "It's me. I told you I'd come back for you."

Adam's lips parted, his voice weak and ragged. "S-Sage?"

She nodded, her heart aching at the sight of him. "I'm getting you out of here. Can you stand?"

He tried to move, but his body was still too weak, too broken from the vile concoction they had pumped into his veins. His limbs trembled, his muscles straining, but he couldn't muster the strength to rise.

"I... I can't..." Adam's voice cracked, his breath laboured. "Too... weak."

Sage's heart clenched with a mixture of frustration and sorrow. She glanced over her shoulder at Crowe, who stood rigid near the entrance, her face a mask of cold fury.

"You're going to blow our cover!" Crowe hissed, her voice barely above a whisper, but laced with venom. "Get back here, now!"

But Sage couldn't leave him. Not like this. She had made him a promise.

"I'll come back for you," Sage whispered to Adam, her voice thick with emotion. "I swear I will. But I need you to hang on, okay?" Adam's eyes flickered with something close to gratitude, but it was fleeting. The chanting in the chamber began to grow louder, a low, guttural sound that reverberated off the stone walls, filling the air with a sense of impending doom.

"Sage, get out of sight!" Crowe snapped, her voice rising above the eerie chant. "The ritual is starting. We're out of time." Sage cast one last glance at Adam, her heart heavy with the weight of her promise. She hated herself for leaving him like this, for failing again.

But there was no other choice.

"I'll be back," she whispered to him, her voice cracking with the intensity of her words. "I swear it." With that, she rose to her feet and hurried to join Martinez and the other agents, who had taken cover in the shadows, hidden from view. The chanting was growing louder, filling the chamber with an almost tangible sense of dread. Whatever was about to happen, it was going to be bad. Unbelievably bad. Sage crouched beside Martinez, her heart hammering in her chest. The weight of the explosives in the tunnels, the countdown to destruction, pressed down on her like a lead weight. The ritual was starting, and soon, the tunnels would be blown. They just had to survive long enough to see it happen. The shadows flickered as torches were lit around the chamber, casting long, twisted silhouettes across the stone walls. The grotesque symbols etched into the stone seemed to writhe and pulse in the flickering light, as if they were alive, feeding off the dark energy gathering in the room. Sage's breath caught in her throat as she watched, her pulse racing. This was it. The moment they had been dreading. The ritual was beginning.

CHAPTER 40: TAKE DOWN

The air was heavy with an unnatural stillness as the first figure, draped in a crimson cloak, entered the expansive chamber. Every step the figure took echoed ominously through the vast stone room, each footfall a reminder of the foreboding ceremony about to unfold. The walls, ancient and worn, seemed to absorb the malice in the air, as if they had borne witness to countless horrors throughout the ages. The chamber, dimly lit by flickering torchlight, was a place where time itself felt suspended, the oppressive atmosphere growing more suffocating by the second. One by one, more figures clad in crimson cloaks followed, their faces obscured behind grotesque, gold featureless masks. There were forty in total, each moving in perfect, eerie synchronization as they silently formed a wide circle around the room's perimeter. The torches lining the walls spluttered as if recoiling from the malevolent energy that now filled the space. The masked figures collective presence was overwhelming, their crimson robes a stark contrast to the cold, grey stone of the ceremonial chamber. There was a palpable sense of dread that thickened the air with every passing moment.

Then came the sound of dragging feet. The guards entered, their masks blank and emotionless, as they escorted the captives into the chamber. Jules, Zander, and James, stripped of their clothing, were forced forward, their nakedness rendering them vulnerable under the cold gaze of the masked assembly. Jules's face was etched with sheer terror, her skin pale under the flickering torchlight. She was being half-dragged, her legs barely able to hold her weight. Her wide eyes darted around the chamber, searching desperately for any way out, any sliver of hope, but there was none. James, a young man once admired for his bravery on the slopes, now looked broken. His lips trembled as he tried to form words, but all that came out was a whimper, his body shaking uncontrollably as he was manhandled by the guards.

"Please," he muttered, voice hoarse and barely audible. "Please don't do this..."

His pleas fell on deaf ears, the masked figures watching him with cold indifference. Zander, shackled in archaic wooden stocks that bit cruelly into his wrists and ankles, was pushed roughly to the centre of the chamber. His movements were awkward, restricted by the ancient device that held him, and the guards made no effort to hide their sadistic pleasure as they forced him to kneel. The stocks were old, their jagged edges tearing into his flesh as he struggled to maintain balance. His muscles strained against the unforgiving wood, but he was powerless, trapped like a beast waiting for slaughter. The guards wasted no time. Jules and James were each forced onto stone altars, their limbs secured with thick, leather straps. Jules gasped as the restraints bit into her skin, her breath coming in short, panicked bursts. She twisted her head to look at Zander, silently begging him to do something, but there was nothing he could do. James, the athletic, courageous young man he had once been, was now reduced to sobbing, pleading for his life, his voice cracking with each desperate word.

"Please... someone help us... don't let them do this!"

The masked figures paid no heed to their cries. They stood silently, like statues, their presence looming over the captives like spectres of death. The guards secured the final straps with an almost ritualistic precision, and then stepped back, leaving the three prisoners at the mercy of whatever dark force controlled this nightmarish gathering. At the far end of the chamber, a slow, haunting melody began to rise. It started as a low hum, barely audible at first, but it grew in volume, filling the chamber with a sense of ancient, malevolent power. The sound seemed to come from everywhere and nowhere at once, as if the walls themselves were singing a dirge for the doomed souls within. The chanting was low and guttural, the words twisted and alien, spoken in a language long forgotten by time. It resonated deep in the bones, causing an instinctive shiver to crawl up the spines of anyone who heard it.

The torches flared, their flames suddenly burning brighter, casting long, twisting shadows that danced wildly along the stone walls. The chamber was bathed in a sickly, red glow, as if the very air itself had been tainted with blood. From the circle of cloaked figures, one man stepped forward. He was taller than the others, his presence commanding, radiating authority. His crimson robes were more ornate, embroidered with intricate symbols that seemed to pulse with a life of their own. His mask, while similar to the others, had been carved with more care, its features more menacing and exaggerated, as though the face of death itself had been given form. He was the High Priest of this unholy congregation, and his movements were slow, deliberate, exuding an air of absolute control. In his hand, he carried a ceremonial knife. Its blade was long and wickedly sharp, catching the light in a way that made it seem to glow with a life of its own. The High Priest moved in a slow, deliberate circle around the prisoners, his steps measured, each one a part of the ritual's terrible rhythm.

As he passed Jules, the knife's edge lightly grazed her skin, drawing a thin line of blood. She whimpered, biting her lip to keep from screaming. The coldness of the blade felt like death itself brushing against her. The chanting grew louder, more intense. The masked figures swayed in unison, their voices rising to a fever pitch. It was as though the chamber itself was alive, a living entity feeding off the terror and despair that now filled the room. Suddenly, the chanting stopped, leaving behind a deafening silence. The abruptness of it was like a physical blow, the quiet pressing down on the captives like a weight. The High Priest turned his attention to Jules, his masked face mere inches from hers. She could feel his breath on her skin, cold and unnatural. His gaze bore into her, even though she couldn't see his eyes behind the mask, she felt them stripping her of hope, filling her with dread. Then, from the shadows, a figure emerged. Jules's eyes widened in horror as she recognized the face that had haunted her nightmares for years. Her father, now stood before her, his face twisted with malevolence. His mask had slipped, revealing the man now consumed by darkness.

"Dad... no," Jules's voice was a broken whisper, her plea hanging in the air like a final breath. "Please, don't do this."

But her father's eyes were empty of compassion. There was only a cold, ruthless resolve. He raised the knife high above her, his hand steady, his intentions clear. The blade glinted in the red light, poised to descend, and end her life. Just as the knife began its deadly arc downward, a sudden, deafening explosion rocked the chamber. The earth shook with violent force, dust and debris raining from the ceiling as a tremendous roar filled the room. The cultists staggered, some losing their footing as panic spread through the assembly. The air was thick with chaos, the sinister order of the ritual now shattered by the sheer force of the blast. Screams filled the chamber as the cloaked figures scattered, abandoning their solemn positions, and running for the exits in blind panic. The doors, however, were blocked. Armed intruders poured into the chamber, their guns raised, their faces masked with grim determination. Captain Anne Crowe led the charge, her voice sharp and commanding as she ordered her team into position.

"Secure the perimeter! Take them down!"

Bullets tore through the air, the sharp cracks of gunfire cutting through the smoke and chaos. The cultists scrambled to escape, but there was no mercy in Crowe's team. They were relentless, cutting down anyone who stood in their way. The ritual chamber, once a place of dread and silence, was now a battlefield, blood splattering the stone floors as bodies fell one by one. Sage moved like a shadow through the chaos, her twin revolvers blazing. She moved with deadly precision, her eyes locked on one target, the stocks that held Zander captive. She reached him in seconds, her revolvers spitting death as she shot the lock holding the stocks in place. Zander collapsed forward, gasping as the wooden stocks fell apart, freeing his battered wrists and ankles. Sage quickly knelt beside him, her eyes scanning his bloodied form.

"You, okay?" she asked, her voice cool but tinged with urgency.

Zander nodded weakly, his muscles trembling from the strain.

"Jules... James... we have to get them out."

Sage's gaze flickered toward the stone altars where Jules and James were still bound. Jules's face was frozen in shock, her father lying motionless beside her, the knife still clutched in his hand. James was barely conscious, his body limp against the straps. The High Priest was nowhere to be seen, having vanished into the chaos.

"Go," Sage commanded. "I'll cover you."

Zander, despite the pain, found his feet. He stumbled toward Jules; his legs unsteady but driven by the need to free her. The gunfire around them was deafening, the cultists fighting back in small pockets of resistance as Captain Crowe's team advanced with brutal efficiency.

Zander reached Jules, his hands shaking as he fumbled with the leather straps that bound her. Her eyes were still wide, fixed on her father's lifeless form, her breath coming in shallow gasps.

"Jules," Zander whispered urgently, "we have to move."

She blinked, as if snapping out of a trance, and nodded slowly. Together, they freed the final restraint. Zander pulled her off the altar, and as soon as her feet touched the ground, she collapsed into his arms, her body trembling with fear and exhaustion.

"James..." she murmured.

Zander turned to see Sage already at the other altar, her revolvers still smoking from the last few cultists she'd dispatched. With a quick, fluid motion, she cut the straps binding James and slung him over her shoulder like he weighed nothing.

"Let's go!" Sage barked over the noise, her voice sharp as a blade. "We don't have much time. This place is going to fall."

The roar of the gunfire was subsiding, replaced by the low groans of the wounded, and dying. Captain Crowe's team had almost cleared the room. Some of the crimson-cloaked cultists lay scattered across the stone floor, their blood mingling with the remnants of their ritual. But even in victory, the air felt charged, wrong, as if the dark energy they had summoned hadn't been fully vanquished. Zander glanced around, his instincts screaming that something wasn't right. The High Priest's sudden disappearance gnawed at him. He should have been there, leading the resistance, fighting for whatever dark purpose they had started this ritual for. But he was gone, along with half the masked figures that had encircled them moments before.

"We need to find a way out before reinforcements come," Zander muttered, pulling Jules closer to him. She was pale, still dazed, but she kept moving.

Before they could make it to the entrance, the torches lining the walls flickered, spluttering with an unnatural force. A low rumble reverberated through the chamber. Sage spun, her revolvers raised as the shadows seemed to twist and darken. The very stone under their feet felt alive, pulsing with some ancient, malevolent force.

"What the hell is that?" Crowe shouted, her voice cutting through the tension. Her team had gathered near the doors, their weapons trained on the far end of the chamber.

A deep, guttural growl echoed through the room. From the corner where the High Priest had stood, the shadows seemed to coalesce, growing denser, darker. Out of the blackness stepped a figure. But it wasn't human. Its form was hulking, twisted, its skin slick and leathery, like something pulled from the deepest nightmares. Its face was a grotesque parody of a man's, twisted and stretched, its eyes burning with an unnatural, crimson light. The ceremonial knife still gleamed in its clawed hand, though now it seemed to pulse with the same dark energy that filled the room.

"Fall back!" Captain Crowe ordered, but before her team could react, the creature lunged. It moved with terrifying speed, crossing the chamber in a blur. One of Crowe's men fired, but the bullets seemed to bounce off the creature's thick hide. It let out a deafening roar, and with one swipe of its massive arm, it sent two of Crowe's men, crashing into the stone walls, their bodies crumpling like rag dolls. Sage took aim, her revolvers blazing, but even her deadly accuracy had no effect. The creature kept advancing, unstoppable, its eyes locked on Zander, Jules, and James.

"We have to go!" Zander shouted, pulling Jules toward the exit, but the doors were blocked by more of Crowe's team, all struggling to contain the monster.

CHAPTER 41: BATTLE OF THE TITANS

The chamber erupted into chaos as the monster attacked. Interpol agents and Zander's team were firing rapidly, trying to bring the beast down, but their bullets did little more than irritate it. The hulking creature, a twisted abomination with leathery skin and eyes that burned with malice, swung its massive arms, crushing anything in its path. A sickening crunch echoed through the stone room as it tore through one of the pillars, debris crashed to the ground. Zander struggled to shield Jules; his body already battered from the stocks that had held him. His eyes flicked toward Sage, whose guns blazed in the smoke-filled room. She was cutting down cultists left and right, but even she was starting to feel the weight of the creature's monstrous presence. Then, in an instant, something changed.

A thunderous roar filled the chamber, shaking the very stones beneath their feet. It came from the throne at the far end of the room, a sound so deep and primal that it froze everyone in place for a split second. From the shadows behind the altar, a new figure emerged, Adam. His eyes glowed with rage, his chest heaving as he strode toward the monster with terrifying purpose. The monster turned toward the sound, but before anyone could react, Adam launched himself at it, his speed and power unmatched. The two titanic beings collided with a force that made the ground tremble. The air was filled with the sounds of ripping flesh and bone as Adam's claws tore into the creature's hide. The beast let out an ear-splitting roar of pain, swinging its enormous arm in an attempt to knock Adam away, but Adam was relentless. The fight between them was brutal, each blow a testament to the raw strength and fury they possessed. The monster's claws raked across Adam's chest, sending sparks of blood flying, but Adam didn't even flinch. He responded with a savage uppercut, his fist connecting with the monster's jaw in a sickening crunch. The creature staggered back, crashing into one of the altars where several prisoners were held. Screams filled the room as Diouf, Scooby, and Martinez struggled to control the panicked captives. But there was no escape.

The prisoners, bound and terrified, were helpless as the two monsters fought their deadly battle in the confined space. A group of prisoners, huddled together near the walls, were caught in the path of the monster as it stumbled. One swing of its massive arm sent three of them flying, their bodies smashing into the stone walls with bone-shattering force. Blood spattered across the room as more prisoners screamed in horror, desperately trying to get away from the deadly struggle.

"Get them out of here!" Martinez shouted, grabbing one of the prisoners and pulling them to safety as debris rained down from above. Diouf wasn't so lucky. She tried to help a group of prisoners near the altar, but the monster crashed into her, sending her sprawling. One of the prisoners she was helping was crushed under the beast's enormous bulk, their scream cut off as their body was flattened into the stone floor. Adam, fuelled by rage, pressed his advantage. He lunged at the creature again, this time grabbing it by the throat. His fingers dug into its flesh, black blood oozing from the wound as the monster let out a choking howl. With a brutal twist, Adam hurled the creature across the room. It slammed into the far wall with a deafening crash, cracking the stone and sending chunks of rock tumbling to the ground.

But the monster wasn't done. It scrambled back to its feet, its eyes burning with renewed fury. It roared, charging at Adam like a juggernaut. The two collided again, the impact sending shockwaves through the room. They tumbled across the chamber floor, crushing everything in their path. More prisoners screamed as they were caught in the carnage, their bodies broken by the weight of the battling titans.

Scooby barely avoided being trampled as he pulled one of the injured prisoners to safety. "This is madness!" he shouted to Martinez, who was desperately trying to hold back another wave of panicked prisoners. "We can't control this!"

"Just get them out!" Martinez yelled back, dragging another prisoner out of the chaos. But even as they moved to save the remaining prisoners, the battle between Adam and the monster raged on, each blow causing more destruction, more bloodshed.

Adam's eyes were wild with fury as he slammed the creature into the floor, his fists pounding into its skull with brutal precision. The monster's roars became weaker, its massive body struggling to keep up with the relentless onslaught. Adam's strength was terrifying, each punch reverberating through the stone chamber like thunder. He gripped the monster's throat once more, his hands tightening like a vice. The creature thrashed wildly, its claws scraping against the ground, but it was no match for Adam's raw power. With one final, savage twist, Adam snapped the creature's neck. The room fell into an eerie silence, the only sound the crackling of the torches and the groans of the injured. Adam stood over the monster's corpse, his chest heaving, blood dripping from his fists. But his rage wasn't satisfied. His eyes, glowing with barely contained fury, turned toward Phillip and Vanessa, who had been watching from the far side of the room, their faces twisted with terror.

Vanessa, trembling, tried to back away, but Adam was already moving. He crossed the chamber in an instant, his hands outstretched, and before she could scream, he grabbed her by the throat. She choked, her eyes wide with fear as Adam lifted her effortlessly off the ground. For a brief moment, she struggled, her hands clawing at his arm, but it was useless. With a growl of pure hatred, Adam hurled her across the room.

Her body slammed into the stone wall with a sickening crunch, her skull cracking open on impact. She fell lifeless to the floor, a pool of blood spreading beneath her.

Phillip screamed, backing away in horror.

"No! Please! Please son don't do this!" he shouted, but Adam's eyes burned with fury. There would be no mercy. Phillip stumbled, falling to his knees, his hands raised in a desperate plea for his life. But Adam didn't care. He grabbed Phillip by the arm, yanking him to his feet before slamming him against the wall with bone-shattering force. Phillip's body crumpled under the impact, his spine snapping audibly before he slumped to the ground, lifeless.

The carnage was complete. The chamber was filled with the bodies of the dead and dying, the smell of blood and dust heavy in the air. Adam stood amidst the destruction, his body tense, his chest heaving with rage. His eyes, still glowing with that unnatural fury, flickered around the room, as if searching for more enemies to destroy.

It was then that Sage stepped forward.

"Adam," she called softly, her voice cutting through the silence. She approached him cautiously, her hands raised slightly, her expression calm. "It's over."

Adam's head snapped toward her, his body tensing as if ready to strike. But something in Sage's voice, something in her presence, seemed to reach him. His breathing slowed, the glow in his eyes dimming slightly as he looked at her.

"Sage..." His voice was a low growl, full of confusion and anger. But he didn't move toward her. He stood frozen, his fists still clenched, but the fury was slowly ebbing from him.

Sage took another step closer, her eyes never leaving his.

"It's okay," she said softly. "You did what you had to do. It's over now."

Adam's chest heaved, his breathing heavy, but his eyes were locked on hers. She was the only one who could reach him, the only person who could calm the beast that raged inside him. Slowly, his fists unclenched, his shoulders relaxing as the tension drained from his body. Sage moved closer, placing a hand gently on his arm.

"You're okay," she whispered. "You're safe. I'm here, you're with me."

Adam looked at her, his eyes losing their unnatural glow, and for a moment, there was a flicker of something human in them. He nodded slowly, his body finally relaxing. Sage smiled softly, her hand still on his arm.

"Come on," she said. "Let's get out of here."

Adam nodded again; the rage gone from his eyes now. He followed her, leaving the destruction behind as they walked through the ruined chamber, the bodies of Phillip and Vanessa lying forgotten in the blood-soaked room. The battle was over, but the darkness lingered, heavy in the air, a reminder of the violence that had unfolded.

As they made their way out of the chamber, Sage glanced back one last time at the carnage, her mind heavy with what had transpired. But she didn't look for long. She knew the battle wasn't over. Not truly. There were always more monsters to fight.

CHAPTER 42: AFTERMATH

The press conference room was packed, the weight of recent events palpable as journalists, news crews, and law enforcement officials filled every available space. Cameras flashed, microphones jostled for position, and murmurs of anticipation rippled through the crowd.

At the front of the room, Captain Anne Crowe stood at the podium, her face a mask of professionalism, but her eyes were heavy with the grim knowledge of what had transpired. This wasn't just another operation. It was something far darker, and the world was waiting for answers. She took a breath, adjusting the microphone, and began to speak.

"Good evening," she started, her voice clear but tinged with the fatigue of a woman who had just overseen one of the most intense operations of her career.

"I stand before you today after the successful take down of the notorious cult known as 'The House of Asmodeus.' This operation, carried out at the Burlington Mountain Resort, has uncovered a horrifying network of human trafficking, black-market organ trading, and ritualistic killings that spanned across multiple countries."

The room fell into a stunned silence. Even though many had speculated about the scope of the cult's activities, hearing it laid bare like this was chilling.

"We have arrested 29 cult members at the resort, and arrests are currently being made worldwide for their involvement in this criminal organization," Crowe continued.

"The victims of this cult were treated as mere commodities, bought, and sold, their organs harvested, their bodies used for unspeakable rituals. Thanks to our team and the swift action of local and international law enforcement, we have been able to dismantle their network."

She paused, letting the weight of her words settle.

"Unfortunately, not everyone survived the raid. Elijah Burlington and his son, EJ Burlington, perished in an explosion during the operation. They were both key figures in orchestrating this human trafficking ring and were involved in countless atrocities."

Crowe's gaze moved briefly to the floor before returning to the room. "Olivia Burlington, Elijah's wife, and their daughter survived the raid and have been arrested. Both face multiple charges for their roles in this conspiracy. Mamosita Morales was also arrested at the scene, for her involvement in the cult's heinous activities."

A ripple of gasps and murmurs spread through the crowd. Olivia Burlington had once been seen as the matriarch of a prestigious family, a public figure that no one would have suspected. Now, she was exposed for her complicity in the nightmare her family had orchestrated.

"We've also uncovered evidence that the cult was being protected by powerful people worldwide," Crowe went on, her voice hardening. "We're working with international agencies to track down every last one of them. This is just the beginning."

She took another breath, preparing for the next revelation. "One of the most disturbing findings during this operation was the discovery of the true nature of Henry Lund, a long-time associate of the Burlington family. Our forensic analysis of computer systems at the resort has revealed that Lund was responsible for the murders of multiple boys across Europe over the last decade. His victims, often orphans or boys from disadvantaged backgrounds, were taken under the guise of charity, only to disappear."

The audience was visibly shocked by this revelation. Lund had been seen as a trusted figure, working with powerful elites, his reputation spotless. The fact that he had used his position to prey on the most vulnerable was beyond horrifying.

"Henry Lund was killed during the raid," Crowe continued. "As were Mike Rowlands, and Drake Morrison, two famous actors who, as it turns out, had deep connections to the cult. These men were active participants in the cult's activities, and they fought back when law enforcement attempted to arrest them."

Crowe's voice grew grim as she recounted the final deaths. "The Ivano family, another powerful family linked to this operation, also perished in the raid. In addition, we lost one of our own, Agent Dimitri Popov, who was a hero throughout this mission. He was killed in action while trying to protect one of the victims."

The air in the room became heavier, the tragic toll of the operation weighing on everyone present.

"As for Adam, one of the most unique individuals involved in this case, he was taken to the hospital under the watch of Sage, a member of our team." Crowe hesitated for a moment, as though unsure how to explain Adam's story. "Adam was created as part of the cult's grotesque experiments, genetic manipulation meant to turn him into something inhuman, something monstrous. His parents, Phillip, and Vanessa, were leading figures in the cult, and they subjected him to unspeakable horrors as part of their twisted quest for power."

A ripple of discomfort passed through the room as the details began to sink in.

"Adam's brother was their first experiment, a creature completely consumed by their evil, turned into nothing more than a killing machine. Adam knew that his brother couldn't be saved, and he fought and killed him during the raid. His brother was used as a tool by the cult, a weapon, but Adam fought back. He resisted, and in the end, he made the decision to end his brother's suffering. This was not an easy fight for him, but it was necessary."

There was silence in the room as Crowe moved on, shifting the focus to the ones who had made it out alive.

"James, one of the survivors, was severely injured during the operation. He is currently being taken to the hospital but is expected to survive. His bravery throughout this ordeal cannot be understated. He will recover, but his journey will be difficult."

As Crowe spoke, outside ambulances lined the area, medics were rushing to tend to the injured. Inside one of the ambulances, Zander lay on a stretcher, his body bruised and beaten, but his thoughts were not on his own pain. He glanced over at the ambulance beside his, where Jules was lying, still in shock from the horrors she had witnessed. She had been strapped down, her eyes staring up at the ceiling, distant, lost.

Zander struggled to sit up, wincing from the pain in his ribs.

"I'm not going to the hospital," he growled, pushing against the medic who tried to hold him down.

"Sir, you need medical attention..."

"I need to be with her," Zander interrupted, his voice sharp. "Jules. I'm not leaving her."

The medic hesitated, glancing toward the ambulance where Jules lay, before finally relenting. "Fine. We'll take you with her, but you're still going to the hospital."

Zander nodded, breathing heavily as he was helped into the ambulance next to Jules. He reached out, gently taking her hand in his.

"Hey," he whispered softly. Jules blinked, her gaze slowly focusing on him.

"Zander..." Her voice was weak, barely audible.

"We're going to be okay," he said, squeezing her hand. "I'm not leaving your side."

Tears welled in her eyes, but she nodded.

"I thought I lost you," she whispered, her voice cracking. "I thought we'd never get out of there." Zander leaned closer; his voice filled with emotion.

"You're not losing me, Jules. Not ever. I need you in my life. I can't do this without you."

Jules swallowed, her tears spilling over as she squeezed his hand back.

"I don't want to lose you either. I love you, Zander."

Zander smiled, his heart pounding as he leaned down and kissed her gently on the forehead. "I love you too," he whispered. "We're going to get through this. Together."

Meanwhile, outside the ambulances, Sage stood by Adam, her hand resting gently on his arm. Adam was sitting on the back of the ambulance, his bulky frame barely fitting inside. His face was bruised, his knuckles bloodied, but there was something more than physical pain in his eyes. There was grief, anger, and confusion.

"They were my parents," he muttered, his voice barely more than a growl. "Phillip and Vanessa...they did this to me." Sage nodded, her eyes soft with understanding.

"I know," she said quietly. "I know it's hard to believe, but they were monsters, Adam. They turned you into something you never wanted to be. And your brother... he was their first victim." Adam clenched his fists, his muscles tensing as he fought back the flood of emotions.

"I had to kill him. I didn't have a choice. He wasn't... he wasn't my brother anymore. He was just... a weapon." Sage stepped closer, her voice soft but firm.

"You did what you had to do. You saved lives today, Adam. You fought back. You broke free from them."

Adam looked at her, his glowing eyes dimmed with sadness.

"I'm not a hero, Sage. I'm a monster. They made me this way."

Sage shook her head.

"You're not a monster, Adam. You're a survivor. And you're not alone." The two shared a quiet moment, the horrors of the day weighing on them both, but at least they had each other.

Back at the scene of the raid, the rest of the team were saying their goodbyes. Diouf, bruised and bloodied, was being helped into an ambulance by Scooby and Martinez, who were both bandaged but still standing.

"You're a tough lady," Martinez said with a grin, clapping Diouf on the shoulder. "You'll be back on your feet in no time."

Diouf chuckled, wincing from the pain in her ribs.

"Yeah, yeah. Just make sure you don't screw anything up while I'm gone."

The team shared a laugh, the tension of the day starting to lift as they realized they had made it out alive. As the ambulances pulled away, the mountain resort now just a smouldering ruin in the background, there was a sense of bittersweet victory. The cult had been dismantled, the monsters defeated, but the scars left behind would take time to heal.

To be continued.

Did you love *Tainted*? Then you should read *Afflicted* by Roxy Rich!

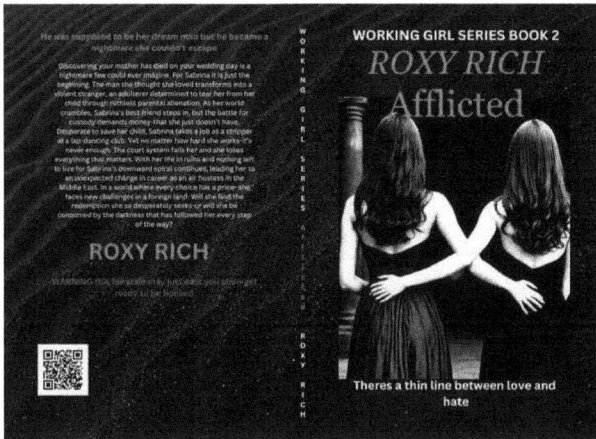

He was supposed to be her dream man but he became a nightmare she couldn't escape.

Discovering your mother has died on your wedding day is a nightmare few could imagine. For Sabrina this is just the beginning. The man she thought she loved transforms into a violent stranger, an adulterer determined to tear her from her child through ruthless parental alienation. As her world crumbles, Sabrina's best friend steps in, but the battle for custody demands money-that she just doesnt have. Desperate to save her child, Sabrina takes a job as a stripper at a lap-dancing club. Yet no matter how hard she works-it's never enough. The court system fails her and she loses everything that matters. With her life in ruin and nothing to left to live for Sabrina's downward spiral continues, leading her to an unexpected change in career as an air hostess in the Middle East. In a world where every choice has a price-she faces new challenges in a foreign land. Will she find the redemption she so desperately seeks- or will she be consumed by the darkness that has followed her every step of the way?

WARNING This fairytale may just eat you alive- get ready to be hooked.

About the Author

ABOUT THE AUTHOR.

ROXY RICH

I am an author with a disability who lives in Somerset with my two children and my husband. My unusual experience, which includes having worked in the sex industry over 17 years ago, serves as a source of inspiration for my writing. I feel it is my duty to bring light on the tales of working girls, the social injustices they suffer. This experience has provided me with unique insights into the life of working girls. I am currently working on my second novel, as I intend to write a whole series that will be devoted to investigating the lives of women who work in the sex industry. Each new installment will focus on a different aspect of their life, thereby delivering a holistic and compassionate perspective of the world in which they live. By combining my years of lived experience with a more mature view on the complexities of the human condition, I believe that now is the ideal time in my life to offer these stories to a broader audience.

jeopardize the mission. Reluctantly, she had to concede, acknowledging that she had never even held a gun, let alone fired one.

So, she would wait anxiously in the safety of Zander's room, providing a much-needed alibi. With each girl that vanished, a crucial piece of the puzzle fell into place, heightening the stakes and intensifying the peril. As the winner of the competition was announced, Zander led Jules back to his room. In a matter of seconds, a sharp rap echoed through the door, prompting a frantic discarding of garments between the pair. They hurried beneath the covers, heartbeats pounding in synchrony. Vanessa and Phillip had been acting strangely lately, watching them closely, as if ready to pounce on their prey.

"Doors open, come in," Zander called, his voice steady as Vanessa's puzzled expression materialized through the slightly ajar door.

"I just wanted to check on you two. You left the party in such a hurry," she interjected, her eyes darting suspiciously between them. "Excuse me for the interruption, but I didn't see you leave, and I wanted to make sure everything was alright."

"Well, you know, I just couldn't wait any longer. A man has needs, you know?" Zander flashed her a disarming smile, his charm oozing like poison. "We're making the most of our time together, that's all. Thank you for checking on us, though we're all good here. That is, of course, unless you'd like to join us?"

Zander arched his eyebrow suggestively, while Jules felt heat flood her cheeks, mortified.

"I would love to, but sadly, I have the other guests to attend to this evening. How about a rain check?" Vanessa remarked before slipping away, leaving Jules and Zander perched on the bed. Jules slapped Zander across the arm.

"Ouch! What was that for?" he quipped, feigning innocence.

"You know full well! What were you thinking, asking Vanessa to join us?" she seethed.

"Listen, I knew she would refuse. It will help with my alibi," Zander replied, trying to placate her.

"It was stupid! What if she thinks she can join us later?" Jules shot back, her voice a hiss as she bit her lower lip.

"Just keep the door locked, and she'll think we're asleep," Zander insisted, his tone firm.

"That was too close for comfort," Jules whispered, shattering the silence that enveloped them.

"But now she'll believe we're here having the time of our lives. This part of the plan went off without a hitch," Zander remarked, his gaze lingering on her bare shoulders, the flickering candlelight dancing in his dark eyes. He wanted her, desperately. But today wasn't about them. It was about the mission. One day, he promised himself, one day he would have her, but not tonight. Tonight, he had to focus, his sole aim on rescuing the girls.

"Are you certain you can do this?" Jules inquired, her voice trembling with concern.

Zander locked eyes with her, a mischievous grin dancing across his lips.

"I've faced far more challenging situations than this. The most important thing is to rescue those girls." Jules's words slipped out involuntarily.

"It's as if your indifference towards me knows no bounds." The statement caught Zander off guard, and he glanced at her with newfound intensity. There was a vulnerability in her eyes he hadn't noticed before.

"Trust me, Jules. I'm doing this for you, too." He said softly, sincerity threading through his voice before he smoothly slipped through the patio doors, leaving Jules alone to wrestle with her swirling thoughts. The room was cloaked in moonlight, shadows creeping ominously as she secured the door, her mind clouded with anxiety. Meanwhile, Zander rejoined Andy and their squad, equipped, and prepared to plunge into the abyss of their mission. Clad in dark attire, heavily armed, they steeled themselves for the confrontation awaiting them.

As they shadowed the truck transporting the abducted girls, an atmosphere of palpable tension enveloped them. Each member of the team braced for the perilous endeavour ahead, the weight of their mission pressing heavily on their shoulders.

CHAPTER 21: STEALTH

The biting wind howled through the mountain pass, carrying with it the whispers of impending danger. As the team trailed the truck transporting the captive girls, the surrounding world unfolded in a way that would be breathtaking, were it not for the sinister weight of their mission. Every flake of snow that drifted from the heavens, delicate as a lace veil, transformed the brutal landscape into something deceptively serene. Majestic peaks loomed in the distance, their towering forms adorned with the untouched purity of fresh snowfall. Dense pine forests bordered the winding roads, their heavy branches bending under the weight of white blankets, masking the horror that lay ahead. The air was sharp with the scent of pine, each breath a reminder of the alpine cold that gnawed through even the thickest layers of clothing. Andy's van, a hulking metal beast, growled low and constant as it navigated the treacherous terrain. The twisting mountain path slithered through the landscape, climbing steep slopes, and hugging tight curves, a lethal combination in this icy environment. One wrong move, one moment of hesitation, and they could plummet into the abyss below. Zander sat in the passenger seat, watching the truck ahead with a burning intensity.

The truck's taillights glowed red in the gloom, twin beacons piercing the swirling storm, leading them toward whatever nightmare awaited in the shadows of Lake Geneva.

His heart pounded in time with the van's engine, each thrum a reminder of the thin line between success and disaster. He glanced at Andy, whose hands were steady on the wheel, the only indication of his nerves a tightness in his jaw. Andy was a master of this, a man